To: Pinki.

LIVING
RAUNCHY

Mary L. Wilson

Thank you for your support. Hope you enjoy

M. L. W

P.O. Box 2535
Florissant, Mo 63033

Edited by Kendra Koger

Cover Designed by Majaluk

ISBN: 9780989650250

Library of Congress Control Number: 2013921302

Manufactured in the United States of America

For information regarding discounts for bulk purchases, please contact Prioritybooks Publications at 1-314-306-2972 or rosbeav03@yahoo.com. You can contact the author at: marylwilson2003@ymail.com or Marylwilson2003@yahoo.com.

Acknowledgements for Living Raunchy

Wow, what can I say, another novel? Lord, I thank You, first and foremost, for blessing me with the ability to display my thoughts on paper. What began as a stress reliever formed into something I love beyond words. Without You I'm nothing, and with You I'm everything. I give You all the glory.

I thank my mother, Patricia Hatton, for all that you have done for me over the years and to date. You built a strong, beautiful woman.

Here's to the people I love the most without any questions, my children: Anitra. Tony and Manuel. I may fuss, and curse sometimes but that doesn't make me love you guys any less. Parents make mistakes, but you guys helped me grow. We have been through some extremely rough times, but as always we pulled through. We are all we got! We gon' be all right, this I know.

I'm most thankful for the small blessings that have been dropped upon me, Jayden and Tonio, my grand boys. However, Jayden is no longer here on earth with us, but he forever lives in my heart. God bless his soul. Tonio aka Mena, you bring me joy, and I love your smile. Mema loves you both.

My old man Russell, I love and adore the relationship we have established the last few years. It can only get better with time as I stated before.

Tammie, Shanquita, Adrienne, Lil Russell, Tia and Jermon, my siblings, nieces and nephews, I love and appreciate you all.

Sha and Vershell, my road divas, yes we travel these states. Love you ladies beyond. Coco and my entire family, y'all know what it is, nothing but love for you, baby! Shorty (Curt), no one can ever define our friendship, no matter what the situation is. Besties for life! No matter what my Fatty Baby aka Setha Mae!

I have many talented divas in my life, and they all have served a purpose, and it's call LOYALTY! Something they have demonstrated at some point in time. I love y'all to pieces, true talk, Tonya Crossland, I have so many reasons to love you, just know that I do without a doubt. You're my dirty for life. You gutta, baby! Lisa (Lola) Roberson, see you the type of friend that goes up and beyond to help a person in need. I thank God for putting a friend like you in my life, funny and real, tell it like it is. No more words needed. Tierra Greenlea, I'ma need you to put up another bathroom door, that you can't see through, but I love your unique style. Monica S, Kelly R, Katina D, Sissy, Tiffany Ross and Jeaneen McClendon thanks for listening when I needed to vent. You are my Ghetto Luv queen. Denise Perkins, I wouldn't trade our time as friends for nothing. I will always be here for you as you always have been there for me. No judging zone, that's how we roll. B.A.P.S for life, friend, BOOYAH! Theresa Myers, girl, you keeps me laughing. Your spirit is beautiful. Thanks for the wonderful trips. You ladies are truly embedded in my heart for life. Real divas, baby! I love y'all whole family. Rhonda Crossaland, Micca Loc and Leslie I so love the girls days we share.

To my literary family, Rose Jackson-Beavers, Teresa Seals (my crony), Kwan, Endy, Jason Poole, Allysha Hamber, Johnna B., and my fellow authors, I wish you guys nothing but success.

Tanesha (BuBu) Baker, thank you for the hard work of helping me edit my novels and being my hype team. You are truly my # 1 reader and fan. Bree Jones thank you as well, Hunny. You guys are the best.

My extended families, Brights, McKinneys, McClendons, Browns, Madisons, Crosslands and Boykins, thumbs up, baby.

Know that I didn't forget about my hood, Lawanda (Bay) Starr. I didn't want you cursing me out, so this is for you, baby, and know that God will be with you in your time of need, and I will be there for you as well. The rest of you west side niggas, divas and dons, SHOE SHINE, NIGGA! Y'all know what it is! Keke!

A special shout out to the Williams Family, my Boo Boo's, I'm so sorry for your loss. We all lost a remarkable person Joseph (Magic Man) Williams. He forever lives in our hearts. (TEARS)

Another special shout out, Tamia Ware-Williams, this girl can get a prayer through. I so thank God for you. You have lifted me up so many times. Know that! I'm so blessed, and I know Jesus Will Work it Out. Lee Spears, my work brother, you have nothing but jokes and you have made a place in my heart for you. You are truly something else, Brutha', Damika, my spoiled work daughter. Yes, you have many names, and you answer to all of them. I love and adore your little spoiled, pretty tail.

Annkesha, my sissy, I'm so grateful for your friendship under the strange circumstances. LHH. Go 'head baby! Also, my new son-in-law Montey, welcome to the family.

To my readers across Facebook, Twitter, Instagram, and all the social networks, I thank you all for your support, regardless if it's positive, negative, constructive criticism or negative criticism, it keeps me wanting to give you more and the best of me. I will forever be grateful to you.

Haters, I honestly don't know why I'm taking my time and energy to acknowledge you, but you all motivate me to the max. While you're running around being judgmental, running your mouth, get the sleep out of your own eyes. Know that you're only talking to nothings that will listen. I rap nationwide, with people that hear everything I'm speaking on. When you're dusty, ugly, do too much when the least is required, attention seeker and don't have anything going for you, people tend to venture out on others. Find something to do. How 'bout that?! See, why did I go there? Just know that God is still working on me. Don't judge me. I am a work in progress.

On a more positive note: When you do positive things, you get positive results. Now wrap it up. Safe sex please, and put God first in everything you do.

1. Night Life

The present:

Sya comfortably sat at her black and white marble vanity set organizing for the night ahead of her. Her body efficiently occupied the pink Victoria Secret lace bodysuit and black fishnet stocking, along with a pair of pink and black Michael Kors Mary Jane heels to complete and compliment her look. She outlined her lips with the Queen Collection by Cover Girl chestnut lip liner, and then she applied the lip gloss. She was equipped for her mission of the night, and that was to make that money, baby.

Living in a two bedroom, duplex had several advantages for her lifestyle. She utilized the upstairs of her living quarters to entertain her prosperous clientele. Making an exit through the side door, she activated the ADT alarm system, making sure everything was secured as she stabbed the hard wooden floors with her heels entering the place she calls The Pleasure Pleazers.

Sya altered the surround sound as Trey Songz's charming voice began grooving through the speakers. *"Don't it feel good when I touch on it, would it be nice if all night I was in you? Come kiss me, come with me, down the hall to my bedroom. Tonight we'll be making love faces."*

The room was flooded with a hint of red light exposing the oval shaped king size bed. The black and red leopard comforter ensemble wrapped around the bed perfectly. In addition to that, she made sure the Glade oils were in sync with the mood she was about to exude: erotic and sexual. She observed the red lights on the phone blinking uncontrollably.

"Damn, I'm going to have to hire some help soon." She spoke out loud talking to no one in particular. "I have twenty more minutes before I entertain these thirsty muthafuckas, they can wait." She continued talking to herself as she flounced to the bar area, pouring herself a glass of red wine and rolling herself a nice size blunt. "I'm ready to get it in now," she grinned, sipping her drink while strutting to the red chaise, singing along with Trey Songz, *"Making love faces, making love faces, my hands rubbing on your skin, let's go hard, don't hold it in. That's my shit."* She professed before licking her lips and conducting the business at hand. She picked up the phone with the red light blinking. "Tell China what you want her to do for you, daddy." Her tone was sexy and inviting. The baritone voice on the opposite line was seductive and fully ignited Sya's fire. She was willing to give him the best performance of her career.

"I want you to make me cum all over myself as if I was inside of you, China." The guy on the other end of the phone announced breathing hard.

"That's what you want me to do, daddy?" She inquired seductively.

"Yes, baby, that's what I want you to do." He replied. Sya imagined the man rubbing his penis.

"You ready?"

"Yes, I'm ready." He whispered softly.

"First, I want you to take off your clothes down to your birthday suit." She ordered.

"It's done already." He replied before she could say anything else.

"Now, sit down and open your legs and say nothing else unless I ask you to. I'm giving the orders," she expressed demandingly. "So receive them and benefit from them, daddy. Do you understand?" She paused to make sure he understood her commands. "I'm about to take you on a breathtaking journey. Are you prepared?"

"Like never before," he uttered breathlessly.

Sya took a massive pull from the blunt and sipped her drink as she opened her thick legs and extended them, breathing slowly. "I want you to suck my pussy well and don't stop until I tell you to." She could hear him flicking his tongue in and out of his mouth. That made her cat super moist. "Don't my hands feel good on your penis, stroking it as it should be?" She queried, inserting her finger in and out of her at a stimulating pace.

"Yes, baby, that feels excellent. Stroke it harder." He ordered, letting out a loud moan.

"Daddy, your wish is my every command." She murmured in a sexy low voice.

Sya wondered if this man on the other end of the phone looked as good as he sounded. His voice alone made her release more times than she could explain. "Yes, baby, don't take your good pussy away from me." His voice became more tantalizing. He said he was stroking his manhood faster and harder. She has never had a client to make her feel this way.

"It feels wonderful." Sya felt the indescribable feeling creep through her body. "This shit feels good." Not realizing the words had escaped her mouth, with her being so into the moment. Her duties were to please her client, and she didn't want him to think that he had control over the situation, nor her. "Are you where you need to be, daddy?" She asked, hearing him release an earsplitting groan of satisfaction.

"Yes, I'm very pleased, mami." He answered extra thrilled. She never mixed business with pleasure. It was all about the Benjamin's in her eyes. But a miniature part of her wanted to get to know him in some other way. As the night continued Sya had more calls than she'd anticipated that night. Once the weed and wine kicked in, she was ready to get it in and make her cash for the night.

2. A Different Façade

"Good morning and happy Monday, class." Ms. Fields greeted her fourth grade students.

"Good morning, Ms. Fields," the children replied in unison.

"Did everyone have a good weekend?" Sya asked, preparing to take attendance.

"Yes," the children replied.

"When I call your name, everyone knows what to do." She began to call the children's names in alphabetical order. As she went down the list, the children replied with either 'here' or 'present,' as well as raising their hands. After that was done she launched into her lesson.

The day seemed to move by swiftly, and Sya was ready to get it over with. She was sorting out her weekly lesson when one of her students became sick and disgorged all over himself, as well as his desk and the floor. " Nuuuun, he nasty," one of the children shouted, and the entire class became loud and noisy.

"Calm down, class. Tory just made a boo boo. I'm going to the office to call his parents, and I need you all on your best behavior until I take care of this. Does everyone understand?"

"Yes, Ms. Fields." Everyone recited together.

"Now open your English books and read chapters one through four. I'll be right back." She placed paper towels over the contents Tory discharged until the janitor came to clean it up. She then exited the room, strolling to the office, murdering the marble floor with her Valentino platform heels.

****

Sya was wrapping up her lesson when Tory came back to the classroom to get his things, followed by a man. Sya was caught entirely off guard at this man's beauty. Standing at 6'4, broad shoulders and dark milky skin and a gorgeous face brought a smile to her pretty face. "Hi, I'm Jabari, Tory's uncle. Nice to meet you." He extended his huge manicured hand for a shake.

"I'm Ms. Fields and the pleasure is all mine." She flirtatiously replied, checking for a wedding band before they both locked eyes.

"Uncle Bari," Tory whined pulling at his brown uniform shorts. "I'm ready to go. I don't feel well." He pouted, holding his stomach.

"My bad, lil' man, let's roll out. Do you have all of your things?" He asked, breaking eye contact with Sya.

"Yes." He wept.

"Ms. Fields, does he have any homework?" Jabari inquired, licking his full round lips. Loving the way his tongue assaulted his lips Sya took a second to answer back.

"Yes he does. He needs to read chapters 1-4 in his English book and write a one page report. It's due a week from today." She rubbed Tory's cheeks and he smiled.

"He'll have it done." Jabari assured her. "It was nice meeting you, and thank you very much."

"Likewise, and Tory, I hope you feel better." Sya patted him on the head. She had a special liking for Tory. It was something about this kid that warmed her heart. "Class, tell Tory bye."

"Bye." The children said in unison and Tory waved bye as he and Jabari exited the room.

Nice ass, Sya thought, her eyes glued to his entire backside. Her intimate section became overly moistened, and she had to refocus quickly.

3. Cruel

Sya's childhood: The Past

"Sya, you smell like pee." *One girl teased, turning up her nose, frowning. "Your clothes are dirty, old and funky. Look at your dusty shoes. Don't nobody wear buddies anymore! They don't even have a name on them." The girl continued to make fun of her, as well as the other kids. Sya's feelings were hurt beyond belief, but she stood her ground, knowing that she didn't smell. One thing about Frances, her mother, she never let Sya leave the house hungry, funky or with uncombed hair. She just didn't play those types of games. She felt that a girl should always be well groomed, no matter what, and trust and believe, Sya was well put together always, even though she didn't have the latest fashion.*

"No, never that, hater." *Sya retaliated.* "I'm cute, and your fat ugly ass needs a facelift." *She came back hard with the onlookers laughing. The girl then got in Sya's face and slapped her with an open hand. The other kids were egging the fight on as Sya wrestled the girl down to the ground and begin stomping her. The teacher that was on duty used his large hands to break up the fight. hen the girls were apart Sya had a big patch of the girl's hair in her hand.*

"Break this nonsense up! The both of you, go to the principal's office right now. And the rest of you all go somewhere and play before you all are suspended, now get gone!" *He said, clearly upset.*

Sya remembered the incident as if it was yesterday. She went home many days crying and wishing that she could have what the other kids had. She wanted new clothes and shoes, but her mother just couldn't afford to give her those things. Her mother lived off the government and received a check once a month, as well as food stamps. She had to make sure the rent and utilities were paid. Things were hard for Sya and Frances after her father lost his job and left them to fend for themselves. Sya had come home on more than one occasion to find the lights and gas shut off for nonpayment. There was barely food in the refrigerator at times, but Frances would make a meal out of nothing. Sya hated when she had to go with her mother to food pantries or other agencies that assisted with the utilities bills. They would be in line for hours. She also recalled how nasty the workers' attitudes were, as if the funds were coming directly out of their pockets. She felt ashamed but knew that her mother did the best she could at that time. Sya knew that her mother hated to see the dejected look on her face.

"Mama, why do we have to live this way?" Sya asked on many occurrences. "I get tired of those hateful kids making fun of my clothes and shoes. I don't even care about having designer's clothes. I just want some new clothes, not those hand-me-downs from the churches and Goodwill's stores." She said on the brink of tears.

"Baby, don't worry about what people say. Things will get better and you'll be able to wear new clothes and shoes. But right now it's hard, I don't get many hours at the store and your dad gave up on us. He left me with all the bills, to be out there in the streets doing nothing with his life. He doesn't even think about his family and what we need, so I have to do the best that I can, with what I have at this moment." Frances hugged her daughter to comfort her. "I'm going to get more hours at the store soon. We're going to be fine." Frances assured her.

"Ma, when I grow up I'm going to have everything I want and more, and I promise that you will too. But Joseph, he has nothing coming. As far as I'm concerned, he's dead to me. It seems like everyone is cruel to us." Sya finished with tears in her eyes.

Frances hugged her daughter, kissing her on the forehead. Frances hated the way things ended between Joseph and her, but shit happens and life carries on.

"No matter what happens, know that we'll always have each other." Frances held Sya in a tight embrace while reminiscing on her past with her missing husband.

✸✸✸✸✸✸✸✸✸✸✸✸✸✸✸✸

Joseph was such a proud father based on what her mom said. When Sya was born. He worked as a construction worker at a prominent company for ten years. On one particular day, he went in as usual, fifteen minutes before starting time. There was a memo on the front door explaining that all checks would be mailed and the company had been shut down until further notice. This came as a total shock to Joseph. Joseph was devastated as he searched for work every day. He never informed his wife or daughter that he wasn't working. He continued his daily routine until one day Frances decided to surprise him for lunch and found the same exact memo on the door. When her husband came in that evening she went along as if she knew nothing. "How was your day, Suga'?" She inquired, kissing him and helping him free his hands of the lunch box he carried each day.

"Just another day." He answered back walking to the bathroom.

"I bet it was." Frances whispered under her breath.

Half of the evening had passed before Frances revealed her husband's secret. They were eating dinner as usual and he helped Sya with her homework. After completing homework, they took in a movie.

He noticed that Frances had been giving him side glances that night, and he prayed that she wasn't on to him. He'd been staying up later than normal on work nights, but she never mentioned anything about it. She still seemed clueless, and he just hoped that she could stay that way.

They were retiring for the night when Frances exposed what Joseph didn't want her to know.

"Baby, how long have you been out of work?" Frances confronted him, "and don't lie." She told him, throwing his check on the bed. "Since when did they start mailing your checks, Joseph?" She looked at him with flaring nostrils. "And don't lie to me either." She reiterated strongly.

Knowing that he couldn't lie any longer, he disclosed the truth. "Frances, before you create your own theory, hear me out."

"That's what I plan to do, now continue." She folded her arms across her chest giving him direct eye contact.

"I went to the office almost a month ago to find out what site I was assigned to, being that the guys and I finished our last contract a month ahead of schedule. I needed to know my next destination. Well, there was a note on the door, informing me that the company was shut down and all checks would be mailed. I didn't want to come home and tell you that I didn't have a job, so I figured that I would follow my everyday routine and pretend that I was going to work, but I was searching for another job." He explained sincerely. "I was hoping I could find something, that way I could still have income flowing through here.

And that's the truth, Frances. This is a cruel world, baby, but I'm doing everything I can to make something happen. I'm going to find a job and we're going to be fine." He stood and reached for Frances and held her in his arms. "But do me this one favor?" He glanced into her eyes, holding his index finger in the air.

"Anything, baby. Anything." She responded, enclosed in his arms tightly.

"Don't mention this to Sya." He said. "Things are stressful as it is. I just want her to go to school and make something of herself, not worrying about where her next meal will come from." He hugged his wife extra tight, hoping that he would find work soon.

"Sure, baby, but you have to promise me that you will keep me informed on what's going on and allow me to find a job. I can help out. We married for better or worse." She kissed him passionately.

"Frances," Joseph clarified. "You can only work part-time. I'm the man of this house and I will handle things around here. You can work only until I find a job. My queen doesn't need to work." He ended the conversation making sweet love to his wife, and she allowed him to explore every inch of her toned body.

4. So Long, Bye, Bye, Bye

Things appeared to get just a tad bit better for Sya and Frances. Frances was hired at Salama's, a corner store, as a cashier. The owner had been informed by one of his workers that Frances had inquired about a job. She'd asked numerous times to speak with the title-holder. Witnessing her continuous persistence, he decided to give her a shot. At the beginning, she was getting paid under the table to maintain her government assistances. She needed all the aid she could obtain, but once Frances proved her loyalty, her position increased as well as her duties and pay. She was then able to retire her government assistance and Sya received new clothes and shoes and the bills were paid on time, along with her federal taxes return at the beginning of the year. God had truly answered their prayers.

Joseph's manhood felt like it had been robbed from under him after he sought work for well over a year, and still couldn't muster up anything. Frances was working twelve-hour shifts, still coming home, preparing dinner, keeping the bills afloat and making sure their laundry was done, as well as making sure the house was in order. When Joseph wanted sex she was available to him to supply his needs without as much as a word. He knew that Frances valued their marriage vows; for good or worse, sickness and health, she had his back. However, Joseph let his pride get the best of him and took the cowardly way out and left his family without so much as a goodbye.

Frances came home one night from working at the store from 7am to 10pm, to find that her husband wasn't home. She didn't put much thought into it, but it was rather strange for Joseph to be out past 9:00 p.m. Joseph never stayed away from home or out all night for that matter. Two days had passed and still no

Joseph. Frances was worried, but she felt in her heart that things were ending between the two of them. When Joseph was home, he refused to do the small things, such as taking out the trash, making the bed or cleaning up behind himself during the day. He'd become extremely inconsiderate.

Frances reported her husband missing after a week. She bugged the police department day in and day out until she later heard through the grapevine that her husband was seen downtown at St. Louis City Hall, dressed nicely and professional. He looked to be doing well for himself. The fact that he didn't contact her to at least schedule some child support payments was beyond her. She couldn't believe this type of behavior was coming from a man she was once madly in love with. She wanted to lose all respect for him, but first she needed to make sure that this information was on point.

Frances wasn't big on taking others' words. Her knowing the truth about her husband leaving was on her mind often. She told herself that if she ever saw him again, she would curse him out bad for Sya, and then for herself. She trusted no one and she instilled that trait in her baby girl. Frances would find out, one way or the other, a promise she made to herself. She hoped like hell that Joseph wasn't living raunchy.

5. Getting Older

Sya was getting older and forming into a young woman, admiring the good life. She enjoyed reading fashion magazines, such as Essence and Jet. Frances made certain she had the magazines faithfully. Looking at music videos, Sya began noticing the way women were exposing themselves in them. She saw that sex sells and the videos were major proof, so she had to formulate a plan. She needed some of that paper, with no physical contact. She began to research Goggle, a search engine, for profitable ventures. She needed to keep this one on the down low, away from Frances. Looking through a magazine, Sya discovered a job listing and read through it carefully. Following the article was an 800 number. She wanted to inquire more about the position noted, to see if it accommodated her schedule, in between school and homework. Sya was an inquisitive teen with a good head on her shoulder. She proceeded to dial the number.

"Thank you for calling, how may I help you?" The sexy voice answered.

"Hi, I was reading your listing in a magazine. Please explain the duties." Sya demanded in a more fascinating tone, trying to ensure the person on the other end was aware of her abilities; letting them know she was built for this job.

"You have passed the test. You have the precise voice for the position, and judging correctly, you can get paid." The voice complemented her.

"Why, thank you." She was flattered knowing what she was doing. "I also read where you can set your own schedule. How true is that?" The questions flowed as she became more intrigued.

"So very true." The lady answered sincerely. "Tell me something, Ms. Lady-"

"Danger, it's Danger, in a good way." Sya interrupted the lady, but hoping that she could be admired for her forwardness.

"Okay, Danger. How old are you, sweetie, and can you provide proof of your age?"

"I'm eighteen," she lied. "Yes I can get a hold of the correct documentation." She threw back at her confidently. "What do you require and how do I apply?" She wanted to know more.

"Here, take down this information and come see me tomorrow, with a state ID or birth certificate." The lady gave her the details. Sya took down the information and thanked the lady before disconnecting the call. On a mission, Sya began walking to catch the next 70 Grand Bi-State bus to the North side to retrieve a fake birth certificate and state ID from The Spot. This is where the underage kids go to get fake ID's to get into clubs. She was determined to get the phone sex operator position.

Frances came home from work happier than a fat kid that loves cake. She was doing speculator at the store and the owner promoted her to floor manager, and of course that brought in more money. Now that Frances was making more money, she could begin the search for Joseph by hiring a P.I.

She searched the house for Sya but came up empty. However, she did find a note informing her that Sya would be home later, and she was out with her home girl. Frances was glad her daughter applied her social skills a bit. Sya didn't befriend many, and due to their living situation, she'd refused to invite or bring anyone home. Frances couldn't blame her, because she was embarrassed of their home at one point. But now, since she had *a job, and money was flowing better than ever, Frances was glad that Sya wasn't as closed off to people anymore. Joseph had been gone for close to eight years now, and Frances felt comfortable allowing Sya to start inviting her home girl Kendra over.*

Frances kicked back on the couch, sweeping through the mail. She fell deep into thought about her life and how it had changed. "Lord, I remember when I hated to see bills. I want You to know that I'm most grateful and thankful. I'm blessed for the golden faith and platinum direction." Frances stated, reaching for her Dooney and Burke bag. She began to write three checks, all under a hundred bucks to cover the household expenses. There was a time in her past when she couldn't afford to pay at all. She was beyond appreciative. She reached over and turned on the radio. The gospel song "Nobody Greater," by VaShawn Mitchell was pouring through the speakers and she closed her eyes and sang along with the artist.

✳✳✳✳✳✳✳✳✳✳✳✳✳✳✳✳

The Interview:

Sya sauntered into the interview, looking fabulous. She was smashing a red, low cut, Donna Karan dress that flared out at the end with black pumps rounding out her outfit, which complimented her full figured frame and well defined legs. Her lengthy hair swept around her wide face that was lightly coated with makeup.

"Hi, I'm Danger and I have a 4:30 appointment today." She politely told the female that buzzed her in the nice sized condo that was used as an office. As she waited, she looked around. It was decorated perfectly with high ceilings, state of the art kitchen, with a large island with stone counter top. There were French doors that lead to the master bedroom, occupied as a

conference room, to a private balcony. The other three bedrooms displayed arched doorways and fireplaces. The expensive furniture donned the office exquisitely. This could've very well been someone's home.

"Why yes, we've been expecting you." The lady rose from her seat and extended her hand to Sya. "I'm Glitter. Right this way." She led the way down a short corridor, strutting like she was on a catwalk. Her long legs were enhanced by a pair of Michael Kors heels that assaulted the shiny wooden floors, sashaying to a large door. Glitter knocked lightly on the half opened door. When entering the room, there sat two guys and a woman.

"Excuse me, your 4:30 appointment has arrived," Glitter had entered with Sya in tow. "This is Danger." She finished and left the room, closing the door behind her.

"Hi, I'm Danger." Repeating her name as she walked over and shook the men's hand.

"I'm Bunnee," she continued to sit, while both men stood up.

"I'm T-Money, and this is Damon." T-Money gestured toward Damon with one hand while he held Sya's hand a second too long. Sya could tell by the smiles and the glow that seemed to twinkle in their eyes they were pleased. There was a gaze-like look on T-Money's face. He appeared to enjoy what he was looking at. Ray Charles could have observed that and he was blind. Damon took pleasure in the sexiness of her tone, always thinking about the business.

"Have a seat." Damon gestured with his hand as he and T-Money lowered themselves back into their seats.

Sya observed Bunnee's direct eye contact. I don't do pussy, honey. Sya thought silently. I don't even know what penis feels *like yet. She gleamed on the inside. Let me get my Marilyn Monroe voice together. She chuckled internally.*

"Can you tell us a little about yourself, Danger?" *Bunnee broke the pregnant pause, speaking for the three of them. She began fondling with the expensive ring on her finger, as if to let Sya know she makes paper, and there's plenty to be made.*

"What is it that you want to know?" *Her tone remained calm, but sexy was written all over Sya's face.*

"Where did the name Danger come from?" *T-Money inquired boldly.*

"It's for me to know and you to find out." *She replied more fearlessly.*

"She's swift; I like that in you." *T-Money nodded his head in approval.*

Bunnee finally stood up and walked over to Sya and shook her hand. "It was a pleasure meeting you, Danger. I hope to see you soon." *She exited the room, rocking her Miss Me jeans and tank top.*

"You are extremely beautiful." *T-Money spoke breaking the silence once again.*

"Thank you, but can we get down to business?" *She looked at both men.*

"Sure," *T-Money nudged Damon, making sure he was paying attention. Damon was always sidetracked by beauty. He continued.* "First off, you do know that this is adult entertainment?" *Sya noticed him searching her face for any uncertain vibes from her, and then he continued.* "Generally, anything is permitted."

"You have to be willing to accommodate your clients at any cost. They are your main priority when in this type of industry." Damon followed up.

"We are talking about the Phone Sex Operator position, correct?" Sya looked baffled with an arched eyebrow. This time both men were checking for Sya's insecurities. She maintained her cool.

Bunnee re-entered the room with a fruit and wine basket. *"Excuse me, Danger, this is a gift for your time."* She passed Sya the basket.

"Thanks you guys." She accepted the basket and adored the erotic fruit and expensive bottle of wine.

"You're more than welcome." Bunnee replied, exiting once again.

"We would like for you to take a small personality and social skills test." Damon finished.

"What does that consist of?" She wanted to clarify the matter, so she would know exactly what she's up against.

Damon dimmed the lights. *"Watch this five minute tutorial."* He told Sya, pushing a button on the oversized remote control that was on the table in front of him. The soft whispers and sensual voices came to life from the projector on all four walls, and a scene began to play on the screen in front of them.

"What's your pleasure, daddy?" The female asked rubbing her grapefruit shape breast.

"Everything, I've had a long week at work and I need to relax. I was hoping you could stimulate my mind and body. I'll worry about my soul later." The smooth baritone voice quipped, hold-

ing his soft penis muscle in his hand stroking it to life.

Sya really didn't desire to watch, but she knew it was mandatory that she do so. *I would've had his penis hard in a millisecond at the sound of my voice.* Sya thought to herself. As the film continued to play, Sya's mind roamed on her past. She knew her new gig would bring about a major change, something she was more than ready for. Knowing that all she had to do was utilize her seductive voice. That was going to be a smooth walk through the park, but having sex with men wasn't in her plans and she would not do that. No living raunchy for her.

6. Hate On Me Haters!

Three and half years later:

Here it was, Sya's last year of high school and things were going great. She stuck to her guns and didn't have sex with her clients or anyone the entire three years she had been in the business. Sya saved her money and purchased herself a car while Frances continued to support her while in school. Frances questioned where'd she got the money from but Sya would lie and say that she braided hair. Frances knew Sya was tough with braiding hair. She could easily make two hundred dollars a day doing one head. Braiding hair is time consuming and could most times take up to eight hours to finish. With that being said Frances didn't pry.

Sya cherished her 1999 Honda Accord. She treated it as if it was a BMW. Sya only kicked it with one female, and that was Kendra. Kendra and Sya went to school together most of their lives. They would always see each other in passing but never took the time to introduce themselves until one day the same girl that use to try to bully Sya had Kendra hemmed up in a corner bullying her. Sya wasn't afraid of the girl and they had had many altercations in grade school. This girl had intimidated many kids for the reason that she was tall and big for her age, like the talk show hostess. She was a Wendy Williams' look-alike. Back in grade school, Sya had come to Kendra's rescue and fought this girl all by herself. But she and Kendra never talked, just spoke to one another and continued about their day.

Entering high school, the girls shared a few classes together. They embarked upon a project that allowed them to work together, in which they grew very close and that's how they became home girls. They would hang out at each other's houses and go shopping together. Nevertheless, Kendra never shared her money making tips with Sya. She stumbled upon this job all on her own. Sya didn't appear to Kendra as a get-money-chick.

Sya didn't fool with females; they were to extra for her taste. Kendra got down like Sya. Up until her interview, Sya didn't know that Kendra was in the same line of business. She saw Kendra the day she was leaving her interview.

"Why didn't you tell me this was how you made your money?" Sya inquired, looking at Kendra sideways.

"Why didn't you tell me you were coming here for an interview?" Kendra retorted back, with the same look.

"Girl," Sya snapped. "I needed clarity on this first before I could tell you about it." She said. "By the way, how long how you've known about this spot?"

"I've been working here about six months, and it's cool. It depends on you how far you want to expand. This is a demanding business and anything goes, so you have to be ready to get down like you live." Kendra cautiously enlightened Sya. "I got tired of those hateful kids teasing me so I had to do something to enhance my pockets, to uplift my appearance, and this was an easy way to make some quick money."

"Really," Sya responded.

"Yes, honey." Kendra said, bouncing around making her ass cheeks clap. Kendra refused to enter high school not having the latest fashions. She took this opportunity and did well for herself.

They were leaving school when Sya noticed her car was scratched up. She had an idea who was responsible for this. Glenda, the girl that always bullied her. She had whipped her ass on several occasions. As they became older Glenda kept slick shit coming outta her mouth on a regular. The only difference from then and now is that Sya drew blood, something she didn't do in the past. She was sick of tripping with Glenda. She had to let her know that she wasn't playing games with her anymore. But when she saw her car scratched, this shit just became real.

Sya and Kendra were walking to their lockers when Glenda stood next to Sya's locker without moving, not acknowledging that Sya had said "excuse me" more than once. Glenda got in Sya's face. *"I see you not that dirty, dusty ass lil' girl from back in the day anymore."* She smirked at the forming crowd.

"I see you're not that fat ass lil' girl from back in the day, bitch." Sya returned the sarcasm.

"Bitch, don't get cute." Glenda grew mad that Sya cracked back on her.

"Bitch, I'm past cute, that's for lil' girls. I'm beautiful, can't you see that? Don't hate me 'cause I'm beautiful." She chuckled in her face. "That's why you always hatin' cause your ass is fat and still ugly." She laughed out loud this time. "Now I don't know what it's gonna take for you to become cute, or maybe halfway decent, but at this present time, you are not remotely close, sweetie."

She laughed even louder, walking away from the crowd, with the background yelling, "Ooooh, that was wrong," some giving others hi-fives. Sya humiliated Glenda horribly and she retaliated, taking her anger out on Sya's car. She wasn't a match for Sya throwing those hands.

Sya could've done the same damage to Glenda's car but she didn't play that game. *If I don't fuck with your shit, most definitely don't fuck with mine,* was how Sya felt. Secondly, Glenda's car wasn't worth her attention. Her car was already beat down. Sya would speak on it when the time was right. She would see Glenda soon. She wasn't tolerating hatin' ass bitches damaging her belongings. Now that they were older, Sya wanted to know why Glenda had a beef with her. They could talk about it like young women, or they could go out hood-style, putting her paws on Glenda. Sya was prepared for whateva' and she wasn't fucked up about it. Hate on me all you want to, bitches!

7. Money-Gettas Get Money!

Sya and Kendra worked from Kendra's house most nights, being that they only talked on the phone, providing pleasure to men and women who desired to reach their orgasms. Kendra had her own crib and she didn't have to worry about anyone all up in her business. Sya used the spare bedroom and earned her paycheck. Her voice was so seductive and soothing that her words slid off her tongue easily. Sya had been entertaining for three and a half years now and she was good at it. Kendra's word play was profitable as well. They both had lucrative sponsors and they were treated accordingly.

Sya went into character at the sound of her clients' voices. This was her job and she treated it as that. She never mixed business with pleasure. She had clients that wanted to build a personal relationship with her outside of work, but that's something she just didn't indulge in. However, Kendra got her money at all costs and Sya didn't knock her for that. It's just something she didn't do, although it was sometimes alluring. She carried a certain level of respect for herself, something she was taught.

"Hey Sweet Penis," Sya whispered loud enough to be heard. "What do you want Suga' to do for you?"

"I want to bust all over your plump juicy ass." His voice was deep and meaningful.

"I want you to bust all over my plump juicy ass, Sweet Penis." She repeated, determined to make her tone the sexiest this man had ever heard.

"Damn, baby, give me that ass." The voice became more aroused.

"Here, take it, Sweet Penis. Do what you wanna do to it." She encouraged him. She knew that her talents would help him develop an intense nut build-up.

"Tell daddy you like his sweet penis. Tell daddy how good his sweet penis feels in that ass, moving around and around, in and out." His low tone was barely audible. "Oooooh, Suga', work that ass for daddy, baby." He took a deep breath.

"Oooh daddy, this sweet penis feels soooo good," She hyped the situation more, aroused while stimulating her clit with her middle finger. "Daddy, I don't know where you at but I'm about to bust hard and good. I want you to come with me, oooh." Sya eyes were closed as she went to ecstasy land. "That penis is sliding in and outta my wet warm ass. Please don't stop, Sweet Penis Daddy."

"Baby!" He yelled. "My nut is on the edge, I can't hold it any longer." He cried into the phone loudly. "Damn Suga', that ass is wonderful."

"I know Daddy, that's why I only give it to you." She stroked his ego.

"I know, baby, that's why I left you a two hundred dollar tip," he boasted.

"Thanks Daddy. I'll talk to you in a few days. I have a special treat for you next time," and she ended the call.

After Sya disconnected the call she went to the bathroom to clean up before she fulfilled another man's fantasy. She was good at what she did, but sometimes she amazed herself. Walking to the bathroom, she heard Kendra putting her mouth piece down. The slow sexy melodies of Ledisi danced through the air. After cleaning up, Sya went to her next client and made him release in a matter of minutes.

She talked dirty to them just the way they liked it. If they wanted their penises sucked, she did it. If they wanted to hit it from the back, she did that too. However they wanted it, she gave it to them. It was all about her word play and making her paper, nothing more or less.

After her shift was over she calculated her money. Most of her clients made credit card payments and it went straight into the work account she established when she first accepted the position. For those that didn't do credit cards payments, they were prepaid clients, which meant they made payments to the PO Box that was provided, along with a number. The prepaid clients would use the number provided to call in and Sya's phone was equipped with their information, so they received their money's worth.

After proving that she could bring in the money, she only had to pay for the company's equipment after awhile. It ran her one hundred dollars a week and she paid it on a monthly schedule.

Damon was so pleased with her abilities that he would try to encourage Sya to branch out and explore more of the adult entertainment industry, reassuring her that she would be a money getta'. But he had to wait until she graduated high school, before she would think about expanding her business. But if the truth is told, Sya assumed that Damon wanted her for himself; so she made sure that she kept it professional at all times. No matter how many times he expressed that he wanted to get with her, she never took the bait.

But while trying to ignore Damon's advances, Sya didn't realize T-Money knew she was underage. He knew about everyone that worked for him. If Sya wasn't raking in the cash he would have gotten rid of her years ago, as well as Kendra.

Kendra and Sya were in their senior year of high school and everything was paid for before the due date. While Sya took it upon herself to pay for these things, Frances still fished out the dough, not knowing that Sya had taken care of it already.

Sya took her mom's money and saved it. She knew that she could use it later. After graduation she planned on moving into her own little spot. She felt she needed her space. She didn't want Frances to know the line of business she was conducting, so at this rate she had no other choice.

Frances wasn't in her business; it was just time to leave the nest. After graduation, Sya had major moves to make, so she had to prepare herself and hit Frances with news that she was moving out, but first she had to find a place. It had to be the perfect spot for the major plans she'd envision for herself.

8. Where You Been?

Frances was chilling on the couch looking at the sitcom *The Game* when Sya walked in.

"What's up, Ma?" She kissed her on the forehead.

"Hey, Hunny Bun, I didn't expect you to be home so soon." She removed her feet from the couch so that Sya could sit down.

"I'm kind of tired. High school is tiring me out. But, graduation is coming soon and it will all be over and I'll be officially grown." Sya cheesed from ear to ear.

"For real," Frances paused. "I don't think so. That's where you're wrong young lady." Frances had a serious expression on her face. "You're grown when you can pay *your own* bills and take care of *yourself.* Not to mention your college tuition." Sya wanted to tell her mom that she had this all covered and in the bag but she didn't want or need the twenty-one questions that Frances would swamp her with.

While Frances and Sya watched television together Sya's thoughts went into overdrive. The truth be told, Sya had enough money to pay for her first year of college and if things went as she'd planned, she would be able to pay for all four years. She had made up in her mind that she would attend college in St. Louis instead of going out of state like she'd planned on doing. Unbeknownst to Sya, Frances also saved for the occasion. She wanted her baby to enjoy life and not worry about unimportant issues as she had in the past, after Joseph left.

"Ma, I've decided to go to Harris Stowe State University. That's the best university for what I'm majoring in."

"So you gonna be teaching people's kids, huh?" Frances asked jokingly, knowing that her daughter would be one of the best damn teachers St. Louis has ever had.

"Yeah, that's what I'm gonna do. You know I'm gonna work at the daycare this summer on campus so I can get hands-on experience with the little people." Sya said proudly.

"Sya, if I haven't told you, baby, I'm so proud of you. We've been through tough times and we got through them. I know it has been hard the last eight years, but we made it. Nothing can stop us now." Frances was excited and hugged her daughter tightly.

"Ma."

"Yes, baby?"

"I can't breathe." Sya playfully told her. They both laughed.

Sya was proud of her mother as well. Frances was doing well, and the thought of Joseph never crossed her mind after the first year he left. She had done everything in her power to make their marriage survive after he'd lost his job. After displaying his unconcern for their union she took on the same attitude. Her only worries were Sya and how she could make a better life for the two of them. Realizing that Joseph was gone for good, Frances allowed Henry to step into her life and pamper her, as a man should.

****

Henry used to come into the store where she worked on the daily and offered to take her to dinner. She had turned him down more times than she could remember.

Henry was casket sharp. He constantly sported tailor made

suits with expensive alligator, lizard or snake skinned shoes. His neck, wrist and fingers were draped in the finest jewelry, as his head was donned with several hats cocked to the side. He always had a toothpick dangling from the side of his month. His pimp-like demeanor was fascinating to some women, but not to Frances. He was treated as the other customers were. Frances never disrespected him, but she assured him that she wasn't interested. Her first perception of him was that he was a pimp and he was trying to lure her into being one of his whores. He had the right idea, but the wrong bitch. She absolutely wasn't having it.

Henry came into the store one day while Frances was in the back getting change for the other workers, when she felt someone walk up from behind.

"What the fuck?!" She screamed ready to assault her attacker.

"Calm down, love." Henry gently grabbed her by the waist.

"You scared the shit outta me, man. Don't ever do that again." She pushed her way passed him and quickly walked toward the front.

"Hold up, wait a minute, Love." Henry jogged slightly to catch her. "I don't want you to be frightened by me, baby. All I'm tryna do is take you out for lunch, or dinner, and show you a good time. That's all, nothing more or nothing less." He genuinely told her. Frances paused with her hands on her hips and looked him dead square in the eyes.

"I'm not scared of you." She declared. "But what do you want from me?"

"A few hours of your time. I want to get to know you better. What can that hurt? That's all I'm asking and if you don't enjoy yourself," he paused, "I promise to never ever bother you again. Now, what time can I pick you up, my Love?" He articulated his words with much confidence.

"Do you have a phone number?" She inquired, never breaking eye contact with him.

"Yes," he said, walking over to the desk, retrieving a pen and piece of paper to write down the information. "When can I expect your call?" He gave her the small piece of paper.

"When I call." She said before she exited, leaving Henry standing there watching her from behind. Frances felt like Loretta Divine from Waiting to Exhale when she walked away from Gregory Hines. I'm going to give him something to watch. She thought, swaying side to side with a mean strut. Eat your heart out, Boo.

Henry's mind was on the same wavelength as he was thinking about how he was going to eat her kitty cat.

After weeks of not hearing from her, Henry discontinued his approach. Women threw themselves at him nonstop, but he wanted Frances; proving that people always want what seems to be out of their reach often times. That's life, huh? Henry thought to himself, taking inventory over the situation.

Going home to an empty house most times an empty bed all the time, Frances decided to give Henry a call after a month.

"Hello?" The deep voice echoed through the phone.

"May I speak with Henry?" She nervously uttered.

"This Henry, who this be?"

"Frances."

"Frances who?" He joked.

"Frances that's about to hang up this phone," she spat with much attitude.

"Hold up, wait a minute, Love." He chuckled slightly. "I was just teasing. I know who you are. I've been waiting on you to call me for a month now. What took you so long?" He hoped she could hear the excitement in his tone.

"I've been busy," she answered.

"How you doing, besides being busy?" He suppressed a smile.

"I'm well," she clarified. "Is that offer still on the table for dinner?" Frances got right to the point.

"Yes it is." He said. "When shall I pick you up?"

"I can meet you somewhere. I don't let strangers know where I lay my head." She playfully replied, but was serious as hell.

"I can respect that." He answered, knowing that eventually she would inform him. They continued to talk a while longer and before long it was two in the morning.

After Frances and Henry's conversation, she realized she enjoyed talking to him and became eager to have dinner with him. She yearned for companionship and Henry seemed to give her as much of it as she needed in trying to pursue her.

Henry kept their first date undemanding and sweet. He took her to his place where dinner was prepared. Frances was more impressed with the baked tilapia fish, smothered in real lemon juice, with steamed vegetables, sautéed onions and mushrooms. Henry was astounded by Frances's fashion. Her black, low cut dress accommodated her figure nicely. The black heels, gold bracelets and long gold necklace adorned her neckline perfectly, with the perfect bun topping off her hairdo. She knew that she had to come correct. Henry was a dresser and he was always on point.

After dinner they moved to the living room where they talked while sipping wine, listening to Frankie Beverly and Maze. She later found out that Henry was a silent partner of the store and he owned other properties as well. "I'm really enjoying this time with you." Henry whispered. Frances felt like a teenager again.

"I'm having a nice time with you also." She concurred, moving in to kiss him on the lips. As their lips danced, Frances could sense hesitation in Henry's body language. He seemed as though he wanted more than to bang her, but she was allowing her body language to exude her carnal desires. Frances traveled closer to Henry and put her tongue down his throat. The wine was taking control over her. She wasn't a drinker and the sips quickly took over her mind. She hadn't been touched by a man in so long that her pussy was throbbing for some male attention.

"You sure this is what you wanna do, Love?" He questioned to make sure.

"I'm absolutely positive." She announced assuredly.

Henry escorted her to the huge bedroom, confiscated the remote from the nightstand and Teddy Pendergrass's voice roared through the speakers softly. "Looks like another love

TKO." He removed each piece of clothing from her body unhurriedly. He then pulled the silky sheets back and laid Frances's body down slowly. He embraced every inch of her body, taking in the beauty of this woman. He instantly became over flooded with feelings for Frances. Although he knew he liked her, he didn't realize his feelings ran deeper for her. Gently kissing each breast, he circled them with his tongue; blowing on each of them to see the nipples expand and harden. He then worked his tongue gradually down the middle of her stomach. She arched her back, allowing her body to express how much she loved it. After his mouth found her shaved pussy lips, he began biting and licking her clit, sending her in a world that she had never been to.

The wine was really doing a number on her. "Ahhh, please, please don't stop." She cried out in unabashed bliss. Frances threw her hips in the rotation of Henry's tongue. She had his face glistening with her juices, using his finger to dip in and out of her soaked ocean, making her pussy drip with sweet fluids. "Ahhhh," she yelled again, unable to contain herself.

"You like that?" Henry asked getting familiar with Frances's body.

"I love it." Her paced increased.

Henry moved up her body and kissed her neck tenderly, rubbing his penis up and down the center of her clit. "Stop teasing me and give me what we both know I came here for. Are you scared?" She purred loudly, questioning his abilities.

"Absolutely not," Henry summed up and gently forced his penis in her tight, wet and tasty pussy.

After indulging in what seemed as a multitude of pleasure,

Frances couldn't hold it in any longer, as she shut her eyes and allowed the waves of ecstasy to engulf her. "Oh my God, I didn't know this could feel so good!" Frances declared in the mist of her climax, gripping his muscular arms.

As Frances opened her eyes, she could see him smiling while witnessing Frances's exhilaration. His strokes and the way his member throbbed in her pussy let her know he was on the brink of ecstasy and couldn't last much longer inside of her. Their bodies were harmonizing and singing the same notes. He grunted about how he hadn't felt a pussy this tight since his high school days. As she freed her juices, he followed right behind her and laid his body on top of her until he regained a normal breathing rate.

The following morning Frances woke up in Henry's arms. Her intentions were to go home but she didn't want to go to an empty house, with Sya staying the night at Kendra's. It felt so good to be in the company of a man that she didn't want it to end, but unfortunately she had to be at work. They both got up to shower, but had to get it in once more before they departed.

"Damn, Love, where have you been all my life?" He inquired while ramming his penis in her.

"The question is where have you been all my life?" Frances uttered, totally emotional. "Don't worry about where I've been; just know where I'll be." Her words resonated between the two.

9. The Time Has Come!

Frances was proud to see her baby girl walk down the aisle, displaying her accomplishment. She patted herself on the back for raising such an amazing and intelligent young lady. When Sya's name was called, Frances stood in the middle of the walkway taking pictures, making sure not to miss this once in a lifetime moment. Frances occupied the front row with Henry sitting beside her. He was smiling like a proud father. Frances shared with him how much she loved Sya and he was glad that he could be the ingredient to make Frances's life complete. Even though they hadn't been courting long, Sya had really grown to like Henry. She adored the smile he plastered across Frances's face. When she was in their presence, he displayed so much affection toward her mother. Sya was happy to know that when she moved out, her mom wouldn't be alone.

Frances and Henry wanted to take Sya and Kendra out after the ceremony, but the graduates had other plans and their wishes were respected.

Sya walked Frances and Henry to his car where they took more pictures. "Come on Sya, let me get a picture of you holding your diploma!" Frances shrieked eagerly. While Frances was trying to focus the camera, not knowing how to use today's technology, the camera focused on someone she had no desire to see.

"Come on, Ma, I have to go." Sya's words slowed down before coming to a complete halt. "You gotta be fucking kidding me! Really?!" Sya said spitefully.

"You're right, Sya. This is a fucking joke." Frances protectively grabbed Sya's hand and walked in the opposite direction, clearly irritated.

"Naw, Ma," She released her grip. "Why are we leaving? He needs to leave. He wasn't invited." Sya stated looking directly in the eyes of the man who abandoned her and her mother years ago, for what reason, she didn't know and she wasn't sure if it mattered or not at this point.

"Congratulations, Sya, baby." Joseph reached his hand out to give her the flowers he'd bought for her.

"I don't want that bullshit," she left his hand hanging. "Ma, I'm about to leave. I'll call you later." She kissed her mother on the cheek. "Mr. Henry, thank you for coming." She hugged him.

"Thank you for inviting me." He replied, not fazed by Joseph's appearance. Joseph knew about Henry and how he got down.

"Sya, baby, let me talk to you for a minute." Joseph had a pleading tone with a sad expression plastered across his face.

"Talk to me?" Sya pointed to herself removing the robe displaying the white Sista' Sista' original dress. Around her neck, hung a silver stud necklace with the matching earrings and rings adorning her fingers. She also rocked a pair of Michael Kors, peep toe platform silver heels with studs. She had on her toe ring, and perfectly pedicured toes. "We don't have a mutha'freakin' thing to talk about. And to keep it one hundred with you, you can leave. I don't want to hear shit you have to say." Sya looked her dad in the eyes. The water formed in the corner of her eyes, but she refused to let a single tear drop. She had cried enough growing up.

"Honey, I know you're upset and all, but you will respect me. I'm still your father." He moved in closer to her looking directly into her face. Frances looked from Joseph to Sya. She wanted to see how this would play out. Now being able to witness the hurt her baby was feeling she quickly intervened. "Joseph, don't do this and surely not here. I refuse to let you mess up my baby's special day more than you already have. Now, what you can do is take your black ass where you have been all of these years and pretend that we are dead to you, as you have all this time." Frances crudely and unemotionally declared with a crinkled forehead.

"Look, Frances, you have nothing to do with this." Joseph shot back furiously. "My daughter is old enough now that I can talk to her and I don't need your input."

"Negro please! Your daughter's been old enough!" Frances shouted, walking closer to Joseph, wanting to slap the hell outta him. "Your daughter just graduated high school. You had plenty of time to talk to her." She was in his face now.

"Frances," Joseph had a warning gaze. "I suggest you get the fuck outta my face."

"Nigga, and if I don't?" She pointed her finger in his face. Henry sat back and observed. He wasn't going to let Joseph disrespect his woman, but he was going to let Frances get whatever she needed to say off her chest.

Henry reached for Frances's arm and gently pulled her close to him. "Yeah, Playboy, get your woman." Joseph threw a fist barely which missed Henry. By this time, people were looking in the direction of the confusion. This was the last thing Sya wanted on her special day. Frances noticed the embarrassed expression on Sya's face and calmed herself a bit.

"Baby," she clutched Sya's arm, slightly. "Go have fun like you were about to do before this nonsense took place. I want you to enjoy your day. This is a very important and special day for you. I refuse to let anyone fuck that up." She looked at Joseph with bullet eyes, while going into her purse and pulling out a one hundred dollar bill.

"Ma, I have enough money. I don't need anymore." She tried to give it back.

"No, baby, take it, you can never have enough money." Sya declined the bill.

"That's right, sweetie, your mom is right." Henry reached in his pocket and gave her two fifty dollar bills. She accepted the money and once again gave them both hugs, looked at Joseph with fire in her eyes and she and Kendra walked to the white Camaro her mom rented for graduation.

"Sya, wait up, baby girl." Joseph jogged behind her with a pink envelope in hand. "Here take this." He held it out to her.

"I don't want anything you have to offer." She turned to leave but before she could make a mad dash, Joseph stuffed the envelope in her occupied arm and walked away.

Frances caught up with him and told him exactly how she felt.

"I knew the time would come for me to ask you all the questions I've been waiting to ask you for so long." She sighed with Henry standing off to the side. He trusted Frances and he was going to let her have this moment so they could move on with their lives. "Why did you leave your family, Joseph?" He looked away before he answered and then took a deep breath.

"You really wanna know, Frances, you really wanna know?" He repeated seriously.

"Naw, I'm just asking to hear myself say something. Of course I want to know." She reacted with calmness.

"I was a coward!" He replied heatedly. "Now, I said it. You were working, bringing in the money, holding down the bills and taking care of me. I felt useless to you after a while. When I couldn't find a job that hurt my pride, seeing my wife doing what I shoulda been doing. Then to add insult to my wounds, I knew you were fucking your boss." He paused waiting to see if Frances would deny the allegations. But to his surprise she let him continue and she didn't say a word. "There were times when I would come to the store and you would be gone with Hassan all day. And then when you came home you would go and shower and go straight to bed. I would see Hassan from time to time and he made it known that you was tipping out on me. So I figured since the muthafucka was taking care of you, I'll move out the way and let you be happy." He concluded.

Frances looked at Joseph and shook her head at him. "That's some bullshit if I ever heard any. What kind of shit is that?" She calmly stated. "I didn't have to fuck to get or keep my job. I did what was expected of me as a loyal employee, nigga. And if you think I had to fuck to get my position, well you are sadly mistaken. I was loyal and did what I had to do for my family, unlike you." Her nostrils flared and she was steaming mad, but she held it together. "I can't believe you didn't talk to me about this. But it goes to show what I said before. I had to do what I had to do to take care of my family. With you being a man and all I would have thought that you would've understood, but I was totally wrong. And just for the record, nigga, I ain't ever had to fuck to get anything I have. I worked for it and it paid off tremendously. I'm now part-owner of the store. My baby and I will never want for anything. I knew this time would come." She walked away grabbing Henry by the arm and strutted to the black Cadillac Escalade, leaving Joseph standing there heated.

10. It's All Good!

Jabari's shift was ending and he wanted to relax and go into chill mode after delivering packages all day. He stopped at The Area Code Sports and Grill bar on Natural Bridge Boulevard by the airport before he went home. Sitting at the bar viewing Sports Center on the flat panel television, waiting to see the LA Lakers and Miami Heat defeat each other, sipping his Corona beer, he observed two females coming through the door. Damn, she's thick. He thought undressing one of the ladies with his welcoming eyes. Admiring the colorful form fitted Rock and Republic jumper, paired with "6" inch stilettos, with colorful bangles dangling both wrist. A pretty scarf drifted around her neck and "18" inches of Brazilian hair draped her face. She barely wore any make-up. One female went straight to the restroom while the other female sat next to him, immediately focusing her attention to the flat panel television mounted above the bar.

"I'm just in time for the playoffs." She said facing the television.

Jabari saw this as an opportunity to address her. "Who are you rooting for?" Jabari asked her taking a sip of his beer.

"Who are you going for?" Sya inquired. She couldn't help thinking to herself: This nigga is fine and thick. I love a man in uniform. She examined his pretty white teeth and gave him a welcoming vibe. She loved a man with perfect teeth. It says something about his hygiene. She then went on to notice his broad shoulders and wide torso, wondering if his chest was hairy and if so, was it silky or nappy? Judging from his appearance, whether nappy or straight, it was well kept. Continuing to undress him with her eyes, she wished she was the brown shorts adoring his muscular thighs. To see his exposed calves and then the construction Timberland boots only turned her on more. Muscles swathed his entire body. She quickly peeked at the soft bump lying to the side of his Dickey shorts. She instantaneously had to get a hold of herself.

"Miami," Jabari went on to say, oblivious to her lust, "Lebron James is an excellent player and he deserves at least one ring before his career is over. With Wade and Bosh he can do that with the Miami Heat." He finished.

"My point exactly." She responded becoming aware of his freshly styled dreads and tidily trimmed salt and pepper goatee. The salt and pepper goatee made him look more distinguish and sexy as hell.

Kendra returned from the restroom noticing Sya's in a deep conversation with the sexy guy at the bar. She made her way to the back where the pool tables were located and boldly called a bet on a game. She was dope with the stick and the guys had underestimated her game. Kendra kicked ass. "I have twenty bones on the table. Every call I make I want one of you niggas to go heads up with me." She ordered.

"I got you, lil' mama." Keith told her, looking at her fat ass. Then the other two guys looked on and laughed.

"I got forty bones you don't make the shot in the side pocket." One threw the money on the table.

"I'ma double that and put eighty on the table." She replied bending over, exposing her round apple bottom in a pair of True Religion ripped jeans. The paws tattooed on her thighs peeped through the holes and a set of white PF Flyers tennis shoes crowned her feet. Her natural mane adorned her entire face, with a white flower on the side to accent the wild Jill Scott look with golden-brown streaks.

Pawww! The balls erupted and spread over the table. Her ball took its time going in the hole, slowly inching its way there, with much hesitation it finally entered. "Let me get that, my brotha." Kendra removed the money from the side table and stored it in her back pocket. "It was nice, y'all." She walked away.

"Hold up, lil' mama." The handsome guy reached for her arm, with her snatching her arm away. "You not gon' let me try to win my loot back?" He licked his lips at a snail pace.

"I play for keeps, homeboy." Kendra told him opening her Christian Dior bag, removing a business card and throwing it on the pool table.

Kendra made her way to the bar as the game was in the first quarter. She sat on the other side of Sya. "Damn, they're only in the first quarter." Kendra shook her head then waved for the waitress.

"Hush." Sya told Kendra putting her finger to her lips.

"Excuse the hell outta me." She rolled her eyes focusing on the game.

"Good shot, James." Jabari hit the bar excitedly. "That's what's up my nig." He replied. Kendra looked at him with arched eyebrows.

"I assume that you are a Lebron James fan?" Kendra asked.

"Pretty much, I know he's getting a ring rolling with Miami." He responded. "Can I buy you ladies a drink?" He offered. The ladies accepted, while Elle Varner voice busted through the jukebox, singing her hot new song. "Can I get a refill, can I get a refill, can I get a reee reee, refill?"

"That's your song, Sya." Kendra snapped her finger to the beat of the song.

"This you know, mama." Sya bobbed her head from side to side. The three of them continued to converse throughout the game. After the game was over, and the ladies where leaving, Kendra left her business card in front of Jabari. The card read. *"Adult Entertainment will fulfill any fantasy."*

****

Sya was sitting in her bedroom admiring all that she had accomplished. Business was good and this was the life she wanted. She had gone into the phone sex operation business for herself while coming up on a lick to purchase a duplex home.

She'd remember when she had to break the news to Frances that she was moving out. It wasn't as bumpy as she thought it would be. Thinking back a smile covered her face.

While Frances was working, Sya had moved her personal belongings. She didn't take any of the furniture with her. She had purchased everything new in her home. Sya was on the phone when Frances walked in. "Kendra, you need to be ready by 7 a.m. You know box braids take all day. I'm gonna charge you only a hundred dollars cause you're my girl. You better not be late or you will pay the full two hundred dollars," she joked.

Frances was sitting on the sofa when Sya came and sat next to her. "What's going on, Hunny Bun?" Frances asked leaning over, kissing her on the forehead.

"Nothing, what's going on with you, Ma?"

"I'm a little tired, but overall, I'm good." She shook her head up and down. "I see you're finally moving out, huh?" Frances threw at her, wasting no time. "Girl, I'm your Mama, you can't hide anything from me."

"Ma, before you disapprove, let me explain." Sya said in her defense.

"You don't have to explain anything. I understand that you want your privacy. Believe it or not I admire you for wanting to be responsible. If I can do anything to help you, just let me know. I'm here to help you and I want you to always feel that you can come to me about any and everything. My feelings are kind of hurt that you didn't share this with me. I could've helped decorate your new place." She smiled letting her daughter know that she wasn't upset with her.

"Ma, thanks for understanding. I think its time I get my own place. I know you're not rushing me out but I want to be grown. Something you have already explained to me, so I want to experience that avenue of life." She explained smiling.

"An experience is what it will be without a doubt, baby. If you need for anything, you better call me and ask for my help. I'm going to always be available for you. I will never leave you stuck in this cold cruel world. That's why I do all that I do because I never know when the good Lord above will call me home. But you will be set for life if I have it my way, and know that things are my way."

"Like Burger King, Ma?" Sya laughed.

"Like the Whopper, baby." Frances reached over and gave her baby girl a tight hug.

"Ma?"

"Yes, baby?"

"I can't breathe." They both laughed.

11. Every day I'm Hustlin'

Sya loved the adult entertainment business and it was paying off. She was also attending college. Her bank account was pretty and she was allowed to live as she wished. Even though the money was good, she was searching for ways to expand her hustle. Looking at the toys she kept around her place, she came up with an idea. This would increase her bank account and make her job easier. She called Kendra to share her idea.

Dialing Kendra's cell phone, she sang along with the call tone. Sya didn't hear Kendra say hello. "Sya, if you don't stop singing, it's gonna be deuces for you bitch." They both laughed as Sya tried to sing Chris Brown's song, Deuces. "What's up though, Sya?" She asked.

"Aye, check this out. I was thinking about having a passion party. I'ma need for you to gather some of your home girls and I'm going to call Bunnee to see if she can get some of the girls to participate. If I get twenty girls to come, I can make a few grand. Then you can have one at your place next month. How does that sound? Money is always the motive with me." Sya informed her elatedly.

"That's what's up, Sya. I can order that stripper pole I want in my bedroom for a much cheaper price than I saw in Dr. John's and Fredrick's." Kendra chimed in loudly and more alert.

"Yeah, I'm sure. But I'm about to get up and make some calls, then I'm headed to the grocery store to get finger foods. Why don't you bring your ass and come go with me? Hang out with your crony for a while."

"Okay, let me make some calls to get this thing rolling and

I'll meet you at your house in two hours." Kendra told her. "And Sya, by the way, I have a lot of fresh sponsors. I guess it's from the night at the sports bar."

"What you mean the *sports bar?*" Sya asked a bit confused.

"I left my business cards behind. I'm tryna expand my business. More sponsors bring more money. Money is the motive." Kendra said matter-of-factly.

"You must know that. Every day I'm hustlin', so I can't knock your hustle or the hustler in you. I'll see you in a minute." Sya finished.

"That's what's up, holla."

Sya dialed Bunnee's number and informed her of the little passion party she was throwing. Bunnee assured her that she would contact some of the girls and invite them. She also asked if there was anything she could do to help. "Bunnee, if you don't mind, I would like for you to meet and greet the girls when they arrive. You are so good at that, only if you don't mind, of course." She reiterated.

"Sure, Sya." I'll see you shortly.

Over the years Bunnee and Sya had become close and Sya really considered Bunnee her friend. She had proven it so many times.

"Thanks girl, you're the best." Sya ended the call. She then called Toodie the owner of Toodie's Hair Salon and asked, if she would coordinate the small event and she gladly accepted. Things were now in process and looking profitable.

****

The Passion Party:

Bunnee greeted the ladies with brochures and order forms at the door. She also issued the tickets. Bunnee admired Sya's place. The energy that surrounded her home was cozy and comfortable. The light brown sectional housed the corner section of the room, directly across from there sat four dark brown chairs accentuated by small tables. The tables also held the tools Bunnee gave out at the door. The four walls were painted different shades of burnt orange, brown, beige and off white, which gave the room an energetic feeling. A small bar sat in the back of the room. It was home to several bottles of wines and champagnes. Next to that stood the table with the refreshments, which consisted of erotic fruit, decorated nicely. The vegetable bowls held a variety of several dressings. The small chicken nibbles had tooth picks poked in the center. She also had cupcakes made by Danielle with small penises from frosting. The place looked nice, perfect for the occasion.

Once the ladies were seated, Sya took the miniature platform that held a small bed and stood against the huge wall. There were two chairs with brochures on the table next to them, with a table displaying the more popular items.

"Ladies, ladies. Thanks for coming." She yelled above the chatter. "Let's get started," she gabbed. "I have a special treat for you all. Please feel free to eat and drink as you wish. The place looks amazing, thanks to my home girl Toodie. Everything looks remarkable." Sya glanced around the room thrilled.

"Now, if you'll open up the small packets and remove the Love Is In The Air booklet, turn to page twenty," she instructed. "There are sample massage lotions inside. Let me be the first to recommend the Slick Stik. It makes the driest place a slip and slide in the playground. The thick lubricant is perfect for long nights. And ladies, it contains vitamin E and Aloe Vera. Also ladies Bedroom Kandi has organic lubrication. You can use it with your vibrator and your man, and for some, your woman." She concluded.

While Sya gave the ladies time to marinate their thoughts, a muscular naked man entered, stepping on the platform and took his place. Following behind him was a young lady carrying the product dressed in a pink slik robe. "Girls, I want y'all to see the effect that this product could have on your sexual relationship, here's a demonstration." Sya pointed her finger to the models. The girl squeezed a small amount into the palm of her hand, grabbed the soft penis and massaged it gently. The expression on the model's face displayed pleasure as well as his penis became hard.

Sya then showed the ladies more lotions to enhance their pleasures. "Here's the Fresh & Frisky wipes for a quickie. It's convenient for when you need to get back to work." They all laughed. "Let's not forget about the Sensual Warming lubricant, this is our best seller. It creates sensual warmth on contact. If you don't believe me just watch and see." The Eve look-a-like appeared, followed by another guy in his birthday suit. The girl had on a short silk pink robe. Each girl had on the same robe with nothing underneath. It hugged her curves magically, exposing her succulent breast. The male model lay down on the twin sized mattress in the middle of the platform. The Eve look-a-like poured a dime-sized amount of lotion in her hand and stroked the man's penis gently. The man then became aroused and grabbed one of the girl's exposed breasts and took it into his mouth softly, sucking her hard nipple. He then flipped her onto the mattress and entered her calmly, massaging her clit from behind, massaging her up and down with the tip of his hard shaft. The girl was moaning and you could tell that she was enjoying the feeling. She wasn't bothered by her live audience. One chick got out of her seat and threw a twenty dollar bill on the miniature stage, making sure to order the lubrication.

Sya observed the amount of money that was being thrown on the platform. She made sure that this money was going to be divided equally. "Ladies, I need your undivided attention for a second." She made sure she had everyone's attention before she continued. "Before we go any further and to ensure that you receive, what you paid for, form a line, and Bunnee over there," she pointed at Bunnee standing in the corner. "Will give you a wrist band, in which this will entitle you to your purchase and pleasures. I have to make sure that I'm paid and that you are a satisfied customer, so get in line and show me the money ladies." Sya ceased.

Sya was hustling by any means necessary. She couldn't complete the introduction of the other products due to an orgy breaking out. The models took their time to display the effects of the product. The male models made several women cream themselves. After the personal tutorials, the women were reminded that the products were for sale and the ladies were buying them. Sya told the ladies. "And just for the record, there are more models in the back just in case you need to test a product; a demonstration is always an option. I almost forgot about the Bedroom Kandi vibrators, one's disguised as a tube of lipstick, it's called Kandi Kisses and the dual stimulator is known as "Happiness and Joy" for those of you that are into pleasing yourselves." The ladies were choosing up, testing the products. Each person wanted something different. Some wanted to be sucked on, others wanted to be long stroked, and

then there were additional individuals that wanted it from behind, back door and all. Sya had no idea that things were going to turn out this way. She was glad they did and she made
a nice piece of change, double on what she'd anticipated. Sya
quietly exited the side door and went to the private area of her
home downstairs, her living quarters. She needed to put her
money away. She'd also retrieved her pistol just in case someone wanted to trip. She had stumbled across another hustle.
She never intended on having orgy parties in her home but if
this was going to make her this type of cash, she was with it.
She would have a passion party once a month. It was all about
the hustle, and every day she was hustlin' hustlin'.

12. Attraction

Sya had everything prepared for the parents-teacher conference. She always kept her parents abreast of their children's progress. She figured if more parents partake in their children's education, the dropout rate would decrease. If Sya didn't believe in nothing else, she took education seriously and she wanted others to feel as she did; becoming an educator was important to her.

After graduating from college, she found a position teaching at Bates Elementary School in the St. Louis city area. This past year had been an experience for Sya, a good one indeed. The staff took a liking to her immediately. With her being the youngest teacher on staff, the others felt that they could give her pointers on how to handle the children. If only they knew she could give them a few helpful tips and they were clearly observing her techniques, taking in her patience with the children, as well as her energy to help them demonstrate their best.

"Ms. Fields," she heard her name called from down the hall. "I'm sorry to show up without an appointment. I didn't get the schedule form until last night looking through Jordan's folder." Jordan's mother apologized.

"That's fine, Mrs. Bright. When I didn't receive Jordan's form, I immediately left several messages for you to return my calls. I have a few seconds before my next appointment, so I can squeeze you in." She went to Jordan's desk and retrieved his folder. Just as she was about to go through the contents, Jordan's father walked in the classroom. Jordan's parents were separated but they both were active in his education and were always cordial to one another. "Hi Mr. Bright, Sya reached out to shake his hand.

"Hi Ms. Fields." He accepted, turning to face his wife. "Hello Deidra." He acknowledged dryly.

"Hi Dejuan." She weakly returned.

"Now that the both of you are here, let's begin." Sya directed them to the table to discuss their child's performance. Sya went on to enlighten them about Jordan's grades.

Sya noticed that her next appointment had arrived; she wrapped things up, trying to stay on schedule as much as possible. Walking the Brights to the door, she welcomed Jabari. The Marc Jacobs cologne was intoxicating and abusing her nostrils. Jabari was pleasing to the naked eye and Sya was wrapped into his eyes. His well-developed biceps fitted his shirt as if they were a layer of skin. His built legs stood strong. Jabari's teeth were white as the football player Terrell Owens's. His long locs were braided to the back, with a dapper lining, and included his salt and pepper goatee. She wanted to feel his muscle bound thighs. Sya had so many thoughts rushing through her head about this man. Her midsection was damp and she knew why. Sya had never been penetrated by a man before, but she was seriously thinking about letting this man bust her cherry. She had to get a hold of herself and deal with the situation at hand.

"We meet again," Jabari shook her hand warmly.

"Yes we do." She didn't reject his hold on her. "I assume you're here for Tory."

"You're correct." He assured her. "Tell me something?" He removed the folder from the desk and moved to the table where the both of them could sit.

"What's that?" She loosened up some.

"How's my nephew doing?" His nature was serious.

"Well, I can't complain. Tory is one of my best students academically. He's always well-behaved. I really can't say that I have any problems with him, only when he gets frustrated with things he doesn't understand." Sya told him thumbing through his folder. "You know we take spelling tests weekly but for some strange reason, week six was the most difficult for Tory. I had never gotten that much attitude from him." Sya shared.

"Did you ask him what his problem was?" Jabari asked letting Sya know that he didn't tolerate attitude.

"Yes I did, and he told me that he'd gotten in trouble at home and he couldn't play his WII Game. But I got him together. He didn't do as well as he had been doing, but he made it up the following week. Still, I do want him to read more and brush up on his comprehension skills. He's a little rusty in that department, However, he has gotten so much better. I want to recommend an after school tutor for him on Mondays, Wednesdays and Thursdays as well. That will help him tremendously." She acknowledged seriously.

"Anything that will help my nephew I'm all for it." He announced willingly.

Sya then went over his report card and Jabari was pleased to know that Tory was doing well. After the main focus was out the way, the conversation went to a more personal level. Jabari appreciated the way her curvy hips filled the dress. He stared at her beautiful, toned legs and arms that were muscular and taut, apparently from regularly exercising. Her flat smooth stomach was so tight and tiny he could wrap his hand around her waist and use the same hand to do it again. Jabari secretly desired to be that lip gloss polishing her full lips. He could see himself taking her lips into his mouth and not releasing them until he was good and ready. His penis instantly stood at attention when the thought of her huge breasts in his mouth entered his head. He thought about how he would suck them all so tenderly. Sya broke the silence and removed herself from the chair, walking over to the desk to put the untouched folders away. "Ms. Fields." He demanded her attention.

"Yes, Jabari?" She turned to face him.

"Are you taken?" He boldly asked.

"Why do you ask?" She inquired.

"I would love to take you out."

"I don't think that would be good." She honestly informed him.

This was not the reaction that Jabari was looking for, but he wasn't going to give up. He wanted Sya and he was going to have her. "Ms. Fields." He continued.

"No, call me Sya." She interrupted him.

"Okay, Sya. What is so wrong with me taking you out once? "He wanted to know.

"I don't date my students' parents." She went on to say disappointedly. "That's never a good thing."

"Well, I won't pressure you, but if you ever change your mind, here's my number." He wrote it down on a tiny sheet of paper. He wasn't enthused at all. "Thanks for your time." He shook her hand again.

"You are so welcomed and thanks for coming." She replied as he walked out the door. Damn I creamed myself, she inwardly thought.

13. Just Let Me Make It.

Sya and Kendra were making decent paper. Sya felt it was time to cut Damon and T-Money lose completely. It wasn't that she was ungrateful, but she wanted to branch out and expand her business. Her main concern at this point is the competition. She knew Damon had a competitive spirit and would do whatever to maintain his status. Sya knew there was enough paper out there for everybody.

She was finding new hustlers in the adult entertainment industry every day. Even when she went into business by herself, she still worked for T-Money and Damon three days a week, and they got a cut of her money. She wanted to do her own thing without the middle man. The time she was investing in their company, she could have been dedicating to her own.

Sya sat around preparing for her finals, she was furthering her education. She wanted to become a principal one day and wanted the knowledge and credentials that was needed. Singer K. Michelle's CD played through the speaker. She sang alone with the CD until she heard the doorbell ringing. This was out of the norm for her. No one came to her home without calling first, including Frances. She knew the cameras she had installed would come in handy, strictly for occasions such as this. Damon and T-Money had made an unexpected visit.

"What the hell do they want?" She asked herself walking to the front door. She swung it open, but stood in the doorway to stop them from entering. "What's up Damon, T-Money?" She found their actions very unacceptable. "What brings y'all by unannounced?" She asked, making it clearly known that she didn't appreciate being intruded upon.

"We needed to talk to you about something." Damon informed her, speaking first.

"Speak to me about what?" She inquired undoubtedly unimpressed.

"Danger, you are the best girl in the company. You bring in hella' money and I thought, well we thought," Damon corrected himself, "that you may want to take this to another level."

"You think you're making money now, on the phone, but you can triple your money with adult films." T-Money chimed in.

"No, I don't think so." Sya tried to stop the conversation before it began.

"No, wait a minute, Danger, before you throw the idea out the door just hear us out. You don't have to do nothing you're not comfortable with." Damon tried to guarantee her.

"I know, because I'm not living raunchy to get by. I'll go wait tables before I stoop to that level." She was visibly upset. Damon and T-Money looked at one another. Damon's patience was running thin with Sya. Little did she know they knew about her working for herself, she was still bringing in the money but it wasn't as plentiful as her past earnings. They also heard about her passion party and the money that it brought in.

"Look, Damon and T-Money, this is a sealed subject for me. I will not be a porno star for everyone to see. That's just something I'm not interested in. When you brought the idea to me a few years back I declined and I'm doing the same thing now."

Damon gave her a mischievous smirk and she paid close

attention to it. On the other hand, it seemed that T-Money understood where she was coming from but she had to watch the both of them. After continuously trying to persuade Sya to investigate the other world and no luck, T-Money closed the subject. But before they exited, Damon told Sya, "Danger, I really wish that you would reconsider your decision. There's so much money to be made and only you can do it."

"I'm sure someone else would be happy to make that money." She informed him.

"Yes they would," Damon told her. "Kandi would do it in a heartbeat. But we think that you would be a better candidate.

"I'm sorry, I think your best candidate is Kandi. I just don't get down like that." She'd uttered while closing the door on them. It was something about the way Damon looked at her. She made a mental note to keep a watchful eye on him. She couldn't disclose her decision that she decided to discontinue working for them all together. This was becoming more of a problem than she had predicted. "Damn, just let me make it. That's all I'm tryna do." She spoke out loud.

Later on that day, Sya called Kendra and told her about the offer Damon and T-Money came at her with. She wasn't pleased one bit, but Kendra was thrilled. Sya didn't mind that Kendra wanted the position and was excited about it, but this wasn't something she wanted to do. The money was coming plentiful as it was and she was living as she wanted, and that was comfortably. She was going to fall back and do her. Sya had to get her mind right. She had to prepare emotionally for the task at hand, getting her master's degree

14. Don't Tell People Your Business!

While studying for her finals, she took a small break from her night life. She wanted to be completely focused and Damon and T-Money allowed her this time. That's how she found time to host the passion parties. She sponsored them twice a month on the weekends. Even though she was juggling a lot, she made it happen, which allowed her education to come first as well as her day job.

A Few weeks later:

She did well on her finals. School was ending and she would be out for good. There was one thing she was positive of, and that was going on vacation to clear her mind. Still, at twenty-four years old she had never been penetrated by a man. She learned how to do her job by watching flicks, listening and practicing with cucumbers, bananas and vibrators. She wanted to know how it felt to get touched by a man. If it felt anything like the vibrator or dildo she'd experiment with then she had been missing out. Frances always told Sya her body is a temple and only give it to the man she truly loves; no causal sex, and respect yourself and others will do the same. Those words always stuck with her.

Bunnee was at the office scheduling appointments for the adult firms. While waiting on the camera crew to get things organized, she dialed Sya. "Hey Lady, what's going on?" She asked.

"Not too much of anything. What's up with you?" She dryly asked.

"I was wondering if we could have lunch together. I wanted to run something by you, which you may find interesting."

Bunnee enlightened her with a little information.

"Will this benefit me or break me?" She tossed at her.

"Well that depends. Tell me you'll meet me at Me'Shon's on Tucker in downtown.

"This is an upscale atmosphere I assume?" Sya asked looking through her oversized closet.

"It is and very nice. What time should I expect you there?

"What time should I be there?" Sya asked suggestively.

"Let's say around five. Will that work for you?" Bunnee inquired.

"Perfectly, see you there, and Bunnee, please don't let people all up in your business." Sya warned seriously. She felt that she could trust Bunnee, but you can never be too sure in her line of business.

"I got you, Sya. See you later, hun." Bunnee finished.

"That's what's up." Sya replied before the call was terminated.

★★*★*★*★*★*★*★*

Sya hadn't seen her mom in a few days and decided to pay her a visit. She never knocked and always used her key, something she told herself that she would stop. Frances didn't have a key to her home, so what gave her the right to use her key unannounced? Frances was in the kitchen fixing a cup of tea when she heard the front door open. "Hey, Hunny Bun." She walked over and kissed Sya on the cheek.

"Hey Ma, what's going on with you?"

"Nothing, baby, just lounging around the house, that's all. What brings you to my neck of the woods?"

"Nothing for real, I just wanted to see you. I haven't talked to you in a couple of days. I've been working hard, and grading papers." Sya sat on the couch with her legs crossed.

"Do you want me to fix you something to eat, Hunny Bun?"

"Naw, I'm good. I'm meeting a friend in a few. I'll grab something then."

"You look well." Frances moved a piece of hair out of Sya's face. "So how did your finals go?"

"I can't complain. Everything is going smoothly. What's going on with the stores?"

"Everything's cool. I have that so under control." Frances informed Sya with them both breaking into laughter.

"Ma, you need to cut it out." Sya tried to contain her laughter. "Where's Mr. Henry?"

"He's at the new store on the north side. When you get time, pay him a visit." Frances gave Sya a personal invitation.

"Where at on the north side? You know the nasty north runs deep." Sya stated sarcastically.

Frances chuckled again, "That's right, Hunny Bun, on the corner of North Grand and Dr. Martin Luther King. You know, across the street from the old London and Sons," she finished.

"The straight hood," Sya yelled and began laughing again.

"Yes indeed, baby, it is. I totally agree, but there's money to be made everywhere."

Frances and Sya sat around talking and before long it was time for Sya to meet Bunnee. They said their goodbyes and promised to meet for lunch the following week.

Sya arrived at Me'Shons rocking an edgy chocolate brown halter jumpsuit, a pair of Jessica Simpson's peep toed claws that styled her feet well, with the matching bag. The huge wooden bangle wrapped around her wrist neatly dangled as did her gold hanging earrings and necklace to match. Bunnee was seated comfortably on the black sofa awaiting Sya's entrance. Once she was seated the waitress immediately approached them and filled their orders.

Sya cut through the preliminary chit chat and got to the point. "Bunnee, why did you want to see me?" Sya had a domineering manner that dared anyone to get in her way, staring her in the eyes while taking a sip from her glass.

"You don't waste any time, do you?" Bunnee asked rhetorically before continuing. "Damon and T-Money have been asking a lot of questions about you lately. And before you even think I'm coming to you on some bullshit, discard the thought. I'm not on that." She informed her. The server quietly approached the table and placed their food in front of them. "You see, I know how grimy Damon can be if he doesn't get his way." Bunnee put a small amount of salad in her mouth.

"So what does that have to do with me?" Sya unenthusiastically asked.

"All I'm saying is watch yourself. With them knowing that we hang out sometimes, they want to be all up in the business." Bunnee gave a sista' girl neck-roll.

"Whose business?" Sya tried to mask her concern. "Your business or mines?" She raised an eye brow. "I would appreciate if you not disclose any of my business to anyone. What we do stay amongst us." Sya kept it real with her miss-me-with-the-bullshit attitude.

"Sya, I have never discussed anything that has to do with you with them. Now on the flip side of things, I can't say the same about your girl Kandi, or Kendra, or whichever one you refer to her as." She wiped her mouth with the napkin.

"What do you mean?" Sya looked confused. "What are you trying to say?" She wanted to know, making sure this wasn't a hater move or maybe even a set up. Sya didn't trust no one and she had good reason not to.

Bunnee went on to say that she'd overheard Kendra in the office a few days ago, informing them that she's having a passion party at her house. "Damon is a greedy, thirsty nigga and he wants a cut from everything. He feels that if it wasn't for him giving you the opportunity he did, you wouldn't be where you are now." Bunnee explained.

Sya knew something wasn't right with him. She soaked the information up like a sponge and Bunnee went on to say: "The day after your passion party, they learned everything that went on. When Damon announced that he wanted to see me in his office, I knew something was up. He more so told me what happened instead of asking me what happened, you know what I mean?" Bunnee said.

"Yeah, pretty much." Sya said shaking her head and picking up her fork while looking sternly at her plate. Bunnee knew that Sya would be disappointed to hear this, but it was something she needed to know. Bunnee respected Sya's hustle, and loved her drive.

"Look, I think you good people, and plus, you're a sister try-ing to get it. I'm not into knocking others." Bunnee sipped her drink. "But don't sleep on your girl Kandi. She doesn't have your back as you do hers. The first stack thrown her way, you are totally sold out. She's living raunchy as hell, and where's the loyalty?" Bunnee went back to eating her salad.

Sya modified her approach before she went in. She was try-ing to distinguish if Bunnee's concern was sincere. "Bunnee, don't take this the wrong way but I don't give a damn about what another bitch or nigga say or think about me. I'm not worried about Damon or T-Money coming at me the wrong way. No one is going to stop me from eating. But tell me something, Bunnee?" Sya paused.

"What's that?" Bunnee answered giving Sya her undivided attention.

"Have they asked you to come at me about the flick?" She fell silent momentarily. "And keep it one hundred, Bunnee."

"Let's just say that I'm giving you a heads up." She arched her eyebrows.

"Thanks," Sya said raising her glass lightly, clinking Bun-nee's, answering her own question. Another hustler came into play. *Money is the motive and Bunnee could get in on it, if she was down.* Sya thought.

Sya explained to Bunnee what she had in mind and Bunnee was down. They sat and ordered more drinks and discussed how to execute their plan. Just in case Bunnee was throwing game, she had insurance and time will tell if she needed to ever reveal it.

15. Watching Closely!

Sya, Kendra and Bunnee were having a girls' night out at Dessert on the Blvd. in the Central West End. Kendra walked around the bar untarnished. The Jessica Simpson yellow v-neck dress swayed with every curve. She had business cards in hand ready to dispense amongst the crowd. Sya sashayed in modeling a white linen spaghetti strapped balloon legged jumpsuit. The red platform booties polished her well-exercised calves. Bunnee donned a pair of Seven jeans with a white tank top and colorful blazer, paired with colorful heels. They occupied the white couch in the corner accompanied by the matching table. The place was packed and the music was on point. The ladies chilled to the sounds of Frank Ocean.

Kendra left Sya and Bunnee at the table hitting the dance floor. Sya sat back observing Kendra's every motion, trying not to be obvious. Bunnee was booed up with a short brother all up in her face. Sya could tell by Bunnee's body language and facial expression that she was falling for the lame game dude was dropping. This could have been a trick for all she knew. Trust no one, she could hear Frances voice in the back of her mind. Her mother's words of wisdom meant everything to her.

Across the room sat a matching couch and love seat with a flat panel mounted on the brick wall. The couch and love seat was occupied with three guys and two females. The ladies seemed to have been enjoying themselves. The one guy kept his eyes glued to the dance floor, while the other two entertained their company. Looking closely, Sya watched Damon stare at Kendra on the dance floor. Kendra's body language told a story of its own, while their eyes connected instantly. Sya was beginning to believe that it was some truth to what

Bunnee revealed. This could have been a trap for all she knows. Trust no one, Sya's mother's words of wisdom repeated.. She informed Bunnee that she would be back. Bunnee looked in Sya's direction and told her okay, but her attention was completely focused on dude in front of her.

Sya strutted to the table across from her unannounced and turned heads. T-Money gave Sya a surprised look and stood up to greet her with a hug. Her scent was absolutely breathtaking and he looked like he wanted to wrap her up in his sheets. "Hey sexy, what are you doing out tonight?" He asked holding her hand in his.

"I'm out having a drink with the girls." She told him. T-Money then introduced her to the others that she didn't know. Damon stood and gave her a hug but it didn't feel as genuine as T-Money's. She previewed Damon's game and she wouldn't be caught up in his mess.

"Why don't you have a drink with us?" T-Money moved over so she could sit next to him. Sya observed the nasty looks on the females' faces and took pleasure in making them more uncomfortable.

T-Money poured Sya a glass of wine and his attention remained on her. "Would you excuse me a minute, Danger?" He asked and then tenderly grabbed the female's arm he was talking with and walked out of ear shot from the others. Sya could tell by the female's body language that she didn't like what she was hearing. It didn't seem to matter that much to T-Money either. He left the girl standing there with her mouth open.

Damon made small talk with Sya while she watched his every action. She felt he was the enemy. "Danger, are you enjoying yourself?" He gathered a fake smile sipping from his glass.

"Actually, I'm having a nice time." She replied, fabricating a much bigger smile.

"I know you don't want to hear about business tonight-"

"Absolutely not." Sya shot him down.

"But I was hoping that you would change your mind about what we talked about." Damon continued after being cut off.

"Absolutely not and as I told you," she cut her eyes at him. "That's not my line of work. I'm good doing what I do." T-Money walked back to the table. He perceived tension in the air and from Sya's facial appearance, he knew something wasn't right. He looked from Sya to Damon and noticed the other female had left the table.

"Here, this is for you." He told Sya, giving her a rose. "Who's that cat over there with Bunnee?"

"Shit, who knows? He seems to have all of her attention." Damon spat as if he was upset about it. Sya came to realize that Damon was just a straight hater. "I'll be right back, I'ma go holla at Ms. B." He left Sya and T-Money at the table.

T-Money and Sya sat and talked. Sya was really enjoying his company but she didn't know if she could trust him. He didn't seem to be as sinister as Damon, but you never can be too sure. Maybe they were playing that good cop/bad cop routine. Whatever it was, she was prepared and wouldn't fall for the dumb shit. "Sya, I want you to know that I understand and respect your decision. This business is not for everyone. Your girl over there," following T-Money eyes to Kendra, "will do anything for some paper; real talk, ma, she out here."

"Really?"

"I kid you not." He gave her a serious look. "Just so you'll know, I'm not trying to get in your business but you need to keep your business a closed matter." T-Money warned her.

"Why do you say that?" She was beyond curious but she knew the real deal. She was not naive by any means.

"It seems that Damon and I know everything that's going on with you. We know about your parties and how they turned into orgies. We know about you working for yourself, we even know that you are trying to get out of your contract with the company." T-Money showed no signs of anger, but Sya needed to know how he felt and what Damon's intentions were.

"Really," she replied. "T-Money, tell me something, and keep it one hundred." She tried to rationalize the situation. "How do you feel about it?" She quizzed.

"Honestly, I don't care. I respect a woman that holds her own. I can't speak for Damon, but it's cool with me." He remarked honestly.

"So what you're telling me is, that you don't care that I'm messing with your paper? That doesn't bother you? I asked you to keep it one hundred." She had a doubtful expression plastered across her face.

"That's exactly what I'm telling you. I had to sit down and think about the matter at hand. How can I get mad at you for not wanting to abuse and sell your body for the world to see? Not only that, there will be a whole crew filming. That's your body and you can do what you please with it." He paused. "Danger, you said keep it one hundred, right?"

"Right." She nodded.

"There it is, flat out, baby." He countered seriously.

Sya didn't know where this conversation was going, but she was listening carefully. T-Money was a clean-cut guy and his appearance was always on point, but tonight he was looking super sexy. Sya never had an outing with T-Money outside of business. She knew that he was smart and a money-making businessman; he'd displayed that so many times in the past. T-Money gets his paper.

He hooked up with an old head by the name of Mr. John from back in the day and he showed the young boy how to get on. Mr. John drove 18-wheelers for a living, from state to state, at lease that was his cover up. He would scout beautiful girls from different states to star in porno flicks. He carried the amenities to accommodate the ladies, such as pricey clothes, expensive jewelry, fancy cars and a cozy place to live. Nevertheless, he did have a down ass chick by the name of Marquita Wright running things. The money became more plentiful when Marquita suggested that they open an adult store together and sell any and everything that has to deal with this business. Mr. John totally agreed with her and purchased his equipment to make his business rewarding. They would accommodate every sexual taste. She ran the store while he was on the road. Mr. John sold DVDs and everything pleasing for all sexual appetites from his truck.

Mr. John would always see T-Money around the hood, and he was always by himself. He saw something in the young cat that he liked. He was reclusive. He needed to bring someone on to help with the filming. He could have gotten many of his partners, but he refrained. He dug young Money's profile. That's when he stepped to T-Money, as he called him. T-Money was wise beyond his years and paid attention to everything surrounding him.

T-Money also noticed Mr. John kept staring at him out of his peripheral view, and he wanted to know why. He would always see Mr. John around with Mrs. Wright, so he figured that he'll get a chance to approach him soon.

Just as he was about to step to Mr. John, Mr. John circled the corner of the store and asked T-Money could he speak with him. "What's up, young money?"

"What's good?" T-Money said.

"I wanna help you make some money." He told him point blank. T-Money looked at him strangely and listened to what he had to offer.

"Shoot, I'm listening, old head." Mr. John ran the proposition down and they have been making money since then, and they are still close to this very day.

16. Getting to Know You!

While Sya prepared for the night ahead of her, T-Money's words replayed in her head. *"Don't tell people your business."* He warned. *"Your girl will do anything for a dollar."* That wasn't a surprise to Sya, she knew how Kendra got down, but she thought what they discussed stayed between the two of them. They both were trying to make it in this business, but Kendra was going about her money differently. Sya didn't knock her hustle; it's just that she saw things in a different light.

Sya was caught more off guard when T-Money revealed that he wanted to take her out. She didn't know if it was good for business, especially after keeping it professional for so long.

Sya had a small talk with herself and decided that she would accept his invitation. He was smart, fine and had a decent bank account. She couldn't judge him; they were in the same line of work. At that moment, she dialed T-Money's number. "May I speak to T?" Sya asked a bit nervous.

"Speaking, who this?" He asked with Jeezy playing in the background.

"Danger, I mean Sya." She corrected herself.

"What's up, babe?" He turned the music down. "What's good?"

"Is that invitation still good?" She loosened up some, letting the words flow from her mouth.

"Of course, whenever you available. I don't renege on nothing." He stated with much confidence.

"What's a good time for you?"

"Right after I drop something off to Damon, I can be on my way." He informed her.

"Naw, not tonight. What about tomorrow night?" She didn't want to work tonight, but she had to remember, money before pleasure. Sya knew that T-Money would understand, and he went along with her program.

"Tomorrow night it is. Where would you like to go?"

"Why don't you surprise me?" She threw at him, catching him off balance.

"Bet that. I'll call you tomorrow around," he paused, "let's say six." He summed it up.

"Talk to you then, T." She closed.

"That's what's up."

Sya lit a blunt and took a drag as she placed her phone down, inhaling the smoke before releasing it in the air. Once her lungs were clear she sang along with Alicia Keys,

"If you ask me I'm ready. I'm ready."

"If you ask me I'm ready."

Feeling the beat, she took her first call sitting on the sofa with a 55-inch flat panel facing her. The man on the screen took his time caressing the woman's body. He softly and gradually sucked the woman's hard nipples, biting them lightly. The woman demonstrated pleasure. He then lightly kissed her washboard stomach until he reached her navel with a diamond ring hanging from it. His tongue then circled the ring. Just when Sya thought he was going down further, he brought his face up and met the female. Their tongues intertwined, with their tongue rings meeting for the first time dancing to their own beat.

The man leaned up enough to display his enormous penis to the lady. She massaged it tenderly, stroking it up and down her wet opening. The man then drove his penis in her juice box. The voices from the television, released pure pleasure. Sya described every action taken place in front of her to her client.

Sya was becoming very aroused, viewing the action taking place on the flat panel. She could hear her sponsor on the other end of the phone releasing to what she was telling him. "Did Sweet Pussy fulfill your fantasy?"

"Yes, baby." The man exhaled, satisfied.

"My job is done. Sweet Pussy will talk to you later, and daddy, don't forget to tip me well, okay?" Sya disconnected the call and went to the restroom. She had to regroup before she continued to her next call. What she really wanted to do was call T-Money and let him put some penis in her. The thought was quickly discarded. She went back to work to fulfill more fantasies. However, she had a client that she absolutely loved to hear his voice and she hoped that he would call. He had a voice that sent chills through her body. The effect his voice had on her made her want to get to know him personally. Feeling some kind of way lately, she would step out of her box tonight and ask him out on a date, if he called. She knew that she would be stepping out of character, but this was a chance she was going to take if the opportunity presented itself.

T-Money was glad that Sya accepted his invitation. He'd secretly wanted to get with her a long time ago, but Damon tried to get on every hot chick that came in the office. This was something he didn't do. He didn't mix business with pleasure, but Sya had a distinct manner about her. She carried herself well. She also asked questions and you couldn't get anything over on her. But what he liked most about her was the hustler in her. She couldn't be compared to the other females that strolled through there. She was more polished. But again, he had to keep it professional. Now that she was working for herself and dismissing the company, it was fair game.

The Next Day:

T-Money called as promised. He informed Sya to meet him at the Boat House in Forest Park. He also informed her to dress comfortably. Sya was excited and did just what he asked. She searched her closet and pulled out a blue Sista' Sista' Original flowered blouse and a pair of balloon leg crops and white Gladiator leather sandals. She pulled her hair back and clipped it with a decorative banana clip, showing off her baby face features.

Sya observed T-Money leaning against the yellow and black two-toned Camaro. She also perceived his gear game. He was rocking a Prada linen outfit, accompanied with Prada sandals, exposing his pedicured toes. Sya parked next to him on the parking lot and they walked hand in hand. Reaching the log cabin, T-Money gave his name and they were escorted through the back of the cabin to the water bay, where there sat a small yacht on the water. They had to walk down a lane, where the captain was waiting for them to board. The boat was absolutely breathtaking.

Sya looked around the yacht astonished. Stopping on the lower level, there was champagne awaiting them, as well as exotic fruit and candles. The white table cloth setting and expensive dishes blessed the table. "Do you like what you see?"

T-Money asked.

"I love what I see." She eagerly responded.

"Well it doesn't stop here, babe. Let me take you on a tour before we begin dinner."

"Sure, but if you want to stay here we can." She gripped his hand tighter.

"Naw, there's more to see, but we can come back." He assured her.

Climbing the cherry wood stairs Sya fell in love with the petite bedroom that housed a full sized bed and armoire. Flat panel televisions graced the walls of the bathroom, bedroom and living room. Beautiful art work also styled the small living quarters. "Does this belong to you?" Sya asked, wanting to know his money status.

"In fact it does. I purchased it a little over a year ago. Do you like it?" He asked, turning her face with his index finger.

"I do," she replied gazing into his eyes. Sya was absolutely taken to another level when T-Money's lips met hers and she didn't reject. She let her tongue dance with the beat of his. Sya pulled away not knowing how to handle this situation at the moment. She wanted to feel this man all up in her, but she was afraid. Noticing her discomfort T-Money pulled away.

"I'm sorry, I'm not trying to make you do anything you don't wanna do, ma." He told her and grabbed her hand.

"I'm cool." She bashfully told him and he led her back to the dining area.

17. Gonna Get that Paper!

T-Money and Sya had been dating well over a month and things were going great. Sya still didn't know what it felt like to have a man inside of her. They had been together on numerous occasions, even staying the night with each other and nothing had transpired with the two of them sexually. Sya would soon bring that to an end. She came to the conclusion that she would not lay in bed with T-Money another night without him making love to her. She needed to know how it felt.

Bunnee was happy when the two of them had hooked up and confided in her about her feelings. Bunnee told him how she could see that Sya was actually happy with him.

Earlier at the office T-Money had informed Bunnee that he wanted to speak with her. What he was about to do would determine Bunnee's loyalty and if he could trust her. He knew the decision he was about to make would cause some friction amongst Damon and him, but he always made moves that would benefit him and expand his pockets. T-Money had Sya to meet him downtown on Washington Boulevard at Ozzie Smith's Sport and Grill Bar.

Waiting on her to arrive, T-Money sipped on a beer. He noticed Sya and highly approved of her appearance. The premium jeans hugged her body as did the purple balloon fitted shirt. The gold hanging ear rings moved side to side with the sway of her hips. The pyramid wooden bracelet with gemstones refined her wrist with a huge purple Chloe bag on her shoulder and purple booties stilettos poised her feet.

"You look fly, babe." T-Money told her kissing her on the

cheek. "You smell even better," pulling the chair out for her. "What is that you wearing? It smells so good, damn girl."

"It's Heat by Beyonce, you like?"

"No doubt, you gone make me do something to you; smelling good enough to eat." He playful stated, but was so serious.

I wish you would. Sya thought silently. "What might I owe to this date?" She asked.

"Take a second to look over the menu and I'll let you know, but first, let's get something to eat. I'm hungry as hell."

Sya couldn't help but to wonder why T-Money wanted to talk to her. She knew with them dating a month or so that he may have wanted to take the relationship to another level, but he could have told her that when they were alone at his house. Just so she didn't have to wonder anymore she asked. "T, what was so important that you had Bunnee to call me?" She asked. "By the way, where is Bunnee?"

"I don't know, but I wanted to talk to you about a business deal. You straight about your paper, ma, and I think we can make some for real paper together." T-Money remarked seriously.

"Come on, T. Don't come at me with that bullshit you and Damon came at me with before. As of matter of fact, if that's what you on, I'm outta this piece. I knew this was too good to be true." Sya was in a rage, removing her body from the table. T-Money didn't stop her, he let her continue. He liked the fire in her. It turned him on fully. "Just to think that I wanted to fuck you, give you my virginity." She concluded walking away. T-Money sat there waiting on her to come back, but was shocked by her statement.

T-Money retrieved his phone from his hip to call Bunnee as Sya walked back in. "I forgot this." She grabbed her purse from the chair.

"I knew you'd be back." He had a smile on his face.

"So you think this shit is funny? I'm just another bitch you wanted to expose to the world?" Her nostrils were flared widely with hurt feelings.

"Come on, Sya, you know that's not the case. I straight dig you, ma. I called you here tonight for another reason. Calm your ass down so I can explain, if you let me." He tried to rationalize with her.

"Who the hell you talking to like that? You absolutely have me fucked up with one of your other bitches. When you think that you're ready to talk to me with respect, give me a call. I'll holla." Sya began to walk away again.

"Sya, come on with all of that. Come sit down so we can discuss what I wanted to talk to you about." He defended himself.

"And if I don't?" She interjected.

"Then you lose out on this paper." He shrugged his shoulders. Sya calmed down and took the seat she'd occupied before.

"Okay, I'm listening, come with it." She growled.

Sya was fuming, while T-Money seemed as if he was laughing on the inside. If she knew nothing else she knew that if you didn't stand for nothing you would fall for anything and Sya stood on hers. He told her that he liked that in her, so she was confused about his true motives.

"What is it, T? I don't have all night to be fucking around with you." She clenched her jaw with hostility and rage in her tone.

"Now Sya, didn't you ask me to give you respect? I'ma need for you to do the same for me, okay babe?" He grinned.

"Yeah, whatever, but you better come on and tell me what you want. I don't have any more time to waste with you or on you." She refused to mask her aggravation.

T-Money didn't want to waste anymore time so he went into detail. "Check this out. I know you about your paper, and I think that we can make more paper together."

"And how can we do that?" Sya interrupted again.

"Would you let me finish?" T-Money checked her. "I heard about your parties and I was thinking that we could schedule them once a week." He paused. "It will be called "By Any Means Necessary," with any and everything taking place of course with a price to pay." He waited on Sya to cut in, but she didn't. However, she did have a look of unconcern displayed across her face. "See, here's the thing. I will provide security and the workers. You will give a class on how to please your mate with all the tools provided. I'm sure you have used them." Sya looked at T-Money with much attitude but let him continue. "I was thinking that I, I mean, we, could hire both males and females."

"Where would this take place?" Sya asked, thinking that she was always up for making money.

"I will handle all the formalities, but to answer your question, I was thinking that we could purchase a nice enormous loft downtown. With many thousand square feet and I need a down ass moneymaker on my team," he broke before proceeding, "And guess what," he looked Sya in the eyes, " I chose you, babe." He concluded. Sya felt beyond foolish. She felt embarrassed for accusing him of not respecting her wishes. She didn't know what to expect since Damon had come at her sideways about making movies. It ran across her mind that they could have been playing good cop bad cop. Damon had demonstrated that he was indeed the bad cop, but T-Money displayed a dissimilar type of character. It really was a pleasure being in his company.

Sya didn't want to keep interrupting, but he illustrated sexiness to the maximum. Not being able to contain how turned on she was by his confidence and mannerisms she detached herself from the chair, walked around to his chair, grabbed his face and long tongue kissed T unabashedly.

Coming up for air Sya told him, "Let's go to your place." She seriously stated.

"Are you sure that's what you wanna do, babe?" T-Money had to double check, making sure there weren't any regrets in the morning.

"If I've never been so sure about anything in my life, I'm absolutely positively certain about this," Sya retrieved her purse and headed for the door. T-Money trailed closely behind, leaving a massive tip on the table.

18. The First Time!

Once they reached T-Money's condo, clothes were flying all over the spacious living room. This was the moment Sya had been waiting for. She never thought in a million years that T-Money would be the man to capture her virginity.

Sya was all over him. He loved the attention and energy she displayed. Nevertheless, he wasn't sure if he'd heard Sya correctly when she yelled that she was a virgin. *Damn, it's not many of those around these days.* He thought to himself.

T-Money gently broke his embrace from Sya. He went to the stereo and the surround sound system dispensed Anthony Hamilton's soulful voice throughout the condo. It captured the night and he took full control of the situation. T-Money reached for Sya's face and looked intently into her eyes and said, "I play for keeps, so I hope you ready to roll with a nigga'. Once we reached this level, ain't no turning back, ya dig?" He held her face softly, discharging his signature smile.

"I can dig it, babe." She slightly smiled, kissing him delicately.

****

Bunnee was struck at the office with Damon searching for his next porno star, something he and T-Money did together. But for some strange reason T-Money wasn't available tonight. He had something very important to handle is what he told Damon. T-Money was a private guy, he didn't disclose his business.

They sat at the conference table with the photos spread around. The bell rang and Bunnee went to open the door for

Kendra/Kandi. She walked in the office/house as if she was the HBIC. "What y'all still doing here?" Kendra unleashed her ghetto mode.

"Trying to find the girl that best qualifies for the upcoming movie." Bunnee said making it known that she was displeased to be there, clearly when she had plans. Also, that was her way of informing Kendra that she didn't mean shit to Damon, he unmistakably passed her clean up.

"Dang, what's wrong with you, Ms. Thang?" Kendra joked. Bunnee didn't answer, but Damon did.

"We wouldn't be here if that bitch Danger woulda took the role." He was angry.

"What you mean?" Kendra gasped. "I told you that I would star in the flick. What, I'm not good enough?" She paused giving much sister girl attitude. "You make it seem that if Danger doesn't star in the film it won't be a hit. You don't even know how she gets down. At least you know my pedigree; you know how I get down, first hand." Kendra was offended.

Bunnee never said a word, she just listened. She knew that Kendra was jealous of Sya, but she didn't know that Kendra would cross her. Bunnee considered Sya her friend and she would warn her once more about Kendra's raunchy ass.

"Danger don't even know how to fuck, she's still a damn virgin." Kendra announced spitefully.

"Kendra, how in the hell do you know all of that?" Damon gave her all of his attention.

"Because I've never heard her talk about anyone she had sex with." She assured him. "Bunnee, I know you woulda known."

She tried to recruit Bunnee.

"I don't be all up in people's business like that. We don't talk about our personal life. We keep it strictly professional." She defended her friendship with Sya.

"Well I really need her and if she thinks that she can quit and branch out on her own, she has another thing coming. She can either break bread with me and we all are happy or I'll take mines." He spoke in a composed menacing tone. Bunnee knew her time was limited with the company. She couldn't take Damon's conniving ways any longer. She had grown to like Sya and she wasn't going to let Damon destroy her as he did so many girls in the past. She wished there was a way she could help Kendra, but she was too money hungry and an attention seeker. What Kendra failed to comprehend is that Sya was working for the long haul and this business had paid for her college tuition. Sya had a degree to fall back on and she had a master's degree. She's a teacher with benefits. Kendra had nothing but sex tapes.

****

T-Money caressed every inch of Sya's body as his head nested between her legs. Sya didn't know another human being could make her body feel so loving. The feeling she felt was unbelievable. She felt tingling in her feet with her toes curling from the sensation of his fat wet tongue flicking in and out of her pussy. She moved her hips in the direction of his tongue. "T, this feels incredible. Mmmm…" She whispered loudly. T-Money's penis was brick hard, exhibiting how badly he wanted to feel the inside of her. He was taking his time with Sya. She knew that he saw her as delicate and he told her how he didn't want to hurt her. "Put your penis in me T." She demanded.

"You sure, babe?" He asked cautiously.

"Give it to me T, stop playing!" She ordered. He climbed on her and began to maneuver his penis into her tight vagina. "Ouch, shit!" Sya yelled.

"I'm sorry, babe; I'm going to ease the head in. Just relax, I'll take my time." He coached, smothering her with soft kisses.

"Okay, take your time." Pain covered her face. T-Money rotated his hips slowly, as he slipped further inside of her wet opening. "Yes, T, that feels gooood." Her eyes rolled to the back of her head.

He slowly gyrated whispering in her ear. "This here," he grinded unhurriedly, "is the best pussy I've ever had in my life. Damn Danger!" He continued to stroke her. "I see where you get the name Danger from. This pussy will make you fall so deep in love." His eyes were closed and he was totally in the moment.

After repeatedly making love, they couldn't release anymore, so they showered together and shortly after they were out for the count.

19. Really!

Sya woke up to the smell of breakfast. Without a doubt she knew the smell of Goody Goody's food anywhere. Goody Goody is the hood café on Natural Bridge, where all the balla's and hood fellas attended on a daily basis. After breakfast Sya rested in T-Money's arms and thanked him. She also got around to asking questions she should have asked before giving him her body.

T-Money also showed how he wanted to know any and everything there was to know about Sya. He wanted to know her favorite perfume, food, color, clothing designer and everything else. She was a mystery to him. She was a challenge and he adored that most about her. She knew what she wanted in life. She was about her hustle. Lifting her face with the tip of his fingers, he sensitively kissed her succulent lips. "Tell me about Danger and introduce me to Sya Fields the school teacher." He kissed her again.

"What is it that you want to know?" She kissed him back.

"Everything," his nose rubbed hers.

Sya took a deep breath and told T-Money her story. "Let's see, where do I begin?"

"At the beginning." T-Money replied seriously.

"Well I'm an only child, raised in a single parent home by a beautiful, black, strong woman. My daddy is a bitch ass ninja that couldn't handle his responsibilities. He left after he lost his job and couldn't find work. My mom became the breadwinner and he jetted from envy. My mom dated one of the stores owners she worked for and we have been fine ever since. Don't get it twisted, things were rough for a minute, but Moms held it down." She paused giving him enduring eye contact, waiting before she continued to see if he had any questions. Seeing that he gave her a look that said carry on, she did. "Entering high school I wanted my own money and had to find a way to earn it. I knew that I would be a teacher one day. That was something that I always wanted to be. But in the meanwhile I needed some cash and I needed it fast. Just know that Sya is caring, loving and passionate about the people she loves. Now on the other hand, Danger is the same person, but she does what she has to do to make that cash. I'm not into doing anything that I'm not comfortable with. I'm not selling my body for no amount of paper but what I will do is use what I have to get what I want in the most professional way I know how. You see, Danger don't have to see these thirsty niggas, she's just using her voice over the phone." She kissed his lips and sat up on her elbows, shaking the hair out of her face. T-Money moved a braid tenderly from her face as well.

T-Money positioned himself to face her. "Really," he responded impressed.

"Really," She answers back. "Now that I've told you about me, why don't you tell a sister a little about you? She waited for him to reveal his upbringing.

"Well I was raised in a two parent home, where my mom drank all the time and my dad kept everything afloat. After the death of my grandmother, my mom's mother, the bottle became her best friend. My dad tried any and everything in his will power to help my mom's addiction. See, it wasn't out of the ordinary for my mom not to come home for days at a time. That was something I was used to."

"Really?" Sya interjected, not believing a mother could leave her child for days at a time like that.

"In that order." He assured her. "One day I came home from school to a ringing telephone. I was only allowed to answer the phone at certain times of the day and if there was an emergency I had a contact number for my dad and if he needed to contact me outside of the hours he set, he would use the secret code we formed. He would call and let the phone ring once, and then hang up. Again it would ring twice, and then he would hang up and finally it would ring three times, and then he would hang up. So that's how I knew it was him and it was okay for me to answer on the fourth call. But on this particular day the phone continued to ring, continuously, nonstop." T-Money reached over on the night stand and lit a rolled blunt. He then proceeded. "I called my dad and asked him if I could answer the phone. With his permission, I did so. Hearing the operator's voice on the other line, it was a collect call from the St. Louis County Correction Center. It was my mom and she had been picked up on shoplifting charges. My dad went to get her out of jail. She stayed home around a week or so and vanished for good. So, you see, our stories are somewhat the same, but different." He explained to her.

"Well at least we had one good parent in our lives." She reached up and kissed his lips again. She smiled, reaching for his hand. Can I ask you a question?"

"Absolutely?

"What is your name?"

"Raheem, Raheem Ivy. Now, have I answered your question?" He kissed her nose.

"Absolutely," She nodded her head in approval. "Raheem, huh? What a nice name for a sexy individual."

"In that order?" T-Money at that instant, positioned himself to his knees to gather leverage. He pushed Sya soothingly on her back, clutched both legs and placed them on his shoulders. His tongue easily slid down the middle of Sya's pussy lips to her clitoris. Her body jerked letting the feeling take over her. T-Money kissed, sucked, rubbed and nibbled all wonderfully on her pussy.

She couldn't believe that she'd waited this long to explore this side of life. She grabbed his head while his tongue navigated through her sweet walls. "Woooow!" was all she could muster up to say, mind-boggled.

20. Are You Kiddin' Me?

Kendra had a long night that carried over to the next morning entertaining her favorite client that paid handsomely a few times a week. She always reserved Friday and Saturday nights for Mr. Clean Cut. Mr. Clean Cut had been Kendra's client for a little over a year, and she pleased him however he asked and wanted her to. She would participate in threesomes, foursomes or whatever he required. He was trouble-free on the eyes and smelled delicious at all times. His golden dark tone and low hair cut made him look ten years younger. He was also financially stable.

Coming up for air Kendra kissed the tip of his penis. He rubbed his hand through her hair, massaging her scalp. "Baby, why did you stop? Your mouth felt so good and warm. Just a while longer please." He begged.

"Okay, baby. You can have whatever you like." Kendra put his penis back in her mouth and sucked it slowly, noticing how in the moment Mr. Clean Cut was. She increased her speed, making the head of his penis swell.

"Suck it, baby," he whispered as his eyes rolled to the back of his head, never releasing her head. He did his business and she swallowed all his droppings.

****

Damon was jealous that T-Money dated Sya and not him. Damon knew on the inside that he would have treated her like garbage. He just wanted to smash and run. But after finding out that Sya was a virgin changed the game. He wanted to break that cherry in. That way he could govern and control her every move. He would have brainwashed her into filming porno flicks. Damon was the type of guy that was always looking for a quick dollar. Whatever and whoever he had to hurt to achieve his goal, oh well. He thought T-Money was trying to persuade Sya, but after hearing what he heard last night confirmed something different.

After calling T-Money several times last night he was disgusted to realize that T-Money kept sending his calls to voicemails. When Damon called this morning, T-Money thought he'd pushed the ignore button, but he didn't. He accepted the call and Damon heard their entire conversation. He'd even heard them making love and jerked his penis off. That's when he became super angry and envious. "Are you fuckin' kidding me?" He shouted about to bust a vain. At that time, his thoughts were if Sya wanted to play with his money and lighten his pockets, her pockets would indeed decrease tremendously, and possibly her life.

****

Bunnee was still upset about staying at the office so late on a Friday night. She did have plans and spending them with Damon, looking at naked ass bitches, was not on her agenda. Some of the women looked like the girls at the Pink Slip strip club on the east side. Some had war wounds, stretch marks, baby fat and cellulite. They didn't have the best bodies up in the Pink Slip; nevertheless, there were some decent applicants.

She didn't give a damn about what Damon had planned in the office that morning, she was doing her. It was the weekend. She needed a pedicure, manicure; eyebrows waxed and eyelashes done. She headed to Tina's Nails on South Broadway to receive the services. After that was done, she took South Grand to Highway 40 and exited at Clayton and went to the spa for an awesome massage. Before leaving home she phoned Sya but got no answer. Sya wasn't dismissing her calls; she didn't have any charge on her phone. It was completely dead. Bunnee then decided to text her.

Sya and Raheem finally showered again, releasing each other once more and promising to hook back up at Sya's house later. Sya decided to stop by the grocery store to pick up a few items before going home. She made sure they had plenty to drink. She also needed to make sure that the house was clean. She didn't know how to act being that she never had male company. And more than likely, he was going to stay the night. She couldn't wait to have that penis inside of her again. She also made sure she'd purchased more condoms. She wasn't on any sort of birth control and babies weren't optional.

"Anybody home," Sya yelled entering her mother's house. "Hello?" She shouted louder picking up some mail she re-trieved from the kitchen counter with her name attached. She shifted through the mail and threw it in her huge bag. With no one home, she left and locked the door. Getting in her car Frances was pulling into the driveway beside her.

"Here, help me get these bags outta the car." She unlocked the trunk. Both women reached the kitchen and Frances looked at her daughter smiling.

"Ma, what's wrong with you?" She turned her head away from her mother.

"Somebody got their coochie popped." She continued to stare.

"Now why would you say that?" Sya became nervous, not wanting to answer any questions; she knew where Frances was going with this.

"Girl, I birthed you. I'm not going to further embarrass you, but how did you like it?"

"Ma, not now." She continued to blush, smiling on the inside. "I really have to get going." She made her way to the door.

"I just bet you do." Her mother retorted, kissing her on the cheek. "Call me later, Hunny Bun."

Sya smiled all the way home thinking about Raheem. In the midst of doing her running around, she charged her phone in the car. It alerted her that she had messages. Sya pulled into her two car garage, sat in the car and retrieved her text messages. "Call Bunnee please. M$. Bunnee." She deleted the message. "Let me know you made it home, waiting to see you. T." Sya felt some kind of way reading T-Money's message. "You will see me sooner than you think, Raheem." She said out loud reaching for the bags she had on the backseat. Getting out the car she deactivated the alarm system from her key ring.

Entering through the side door she rested the bags on the table. Quickly looking around her place, something seemed out of order. Removing the razor from her breast, she gradually walked into the living room not pleased at the sight. Her flat panel television was ripped from the wall, leaving behind a few hanging wires. The glass tables were turned over, with its contents spread across the hard wooden floors.

Sya stepped carefully over the glass and walked in her bedroom. Her panties and bras were spread wildly on her bed with some of them cut into pieces. "Are you fucking kidding me?" She whispered to herself. Her walk-in closet was open and shoes were thrown out their boxes, clothes were split and torn from the hangers. Searching deeper for her pistol, she realize it was gone. Sya felt totally violated. She didn't know if the intruders were still in the house or not. Before she checked the upstairs, known as the Pleasure Pleazer, she phoned Raheem. Waiting on him to answer the phone, she thought to herself: Are you fucking kidding me?

21. Whose Down With Me?

As Sya was about dial T-Money's number, he called her to check on her. "Hello?" Sya's tone was even.

"Babe, why didn't I hear from you when you made it home?" He wanted to know sensing something was wrong.

"I was about to call, but some muthafuckin' loser has broken in my house." Her voice raised a notched, displaying her anger and worry.

"Stay put, I'm on my way." T was already in traffic making a u-turn in the middle of North Jefferson heading downtown. "Are you all right, babe?" He wanted to keep her on the phone until he reached her.

"I'm fine; I'm totally not fuckin' impressed though, not one bit. I feel so violated." She carried on expressing just how upset she is. "Raheem, could you just please hurry up? I need to check upstairs."

"Babe, I'm on my way, just calm down. Are both garages occupied?" He asked while pulling up into the driveway.

"No." She answered back.

"Open the empty one." He pulled the black Suburban in.

Sya met him at the side door. Exiting the car he removed his gun from his waist. He told Sya to stay put.

"Babe, I'm not staying down here. I'm going upstairs with you." She told him grabbing his arm leading him through the side door up the stairs. T and Sya reached her work area. The furniture was not touched but her phone lines were pulled from the walls as well as her credit card machines. The phone jacks were confiscated from the walls. They made their way to the first bedroom where she stored her toys and other supplies. That room was beyond destroyed. The toys were out of the boxes, broken; spray painted and soaked in bleach. The pictures on the walls were spray painted in black. The flat panel television was badly beaten and broken into millions of tiny pieces. T couldn't stand the fumes any longer. "Come on, babe." He pulled Sya away so they could go and check the other rooms. The other rooms were pretty much in the same shape. The bedding and appliances were marinated in bleach as well. Sya couldn't do anything but hold her breath. She opened the windows to let it air out.

"Who's down with me?" Sya sat down on the couch holding her head.

"What the fuck you mean who's down with you? What, I'm just for play? Me being here don't answer your question, ma? Huh?!" It was clear that Raheem was upset.

"I'm not saying that, Raheem. It's just that-" He cut her off.

"It's just that you think I'm on some bullshit like Damon. I know you think that I was with you last night because I want you to get down with the flicks." He looked Sya in her eyes, explaining that he was with her and not against her. "Look, I just don't make love to any woman like I did with you last night. You're special." He grabbed her hand. "Now you can trust me or let me walk outta this situation right damn now. I can't be in a relationship where there's no trust and communication." He clarified.

Moving closer to Raheem on the couch, she embraced herself in his strong arms. "I trust you, Raheem." She whined.

He liked it when she called him by his birth name. She was the only woman besides his mother that called him that. "Don't be mad at me for having my back." She pointed her finger in her direction. "I strongly feel that Damon is behind this." She looked around the room.

"I don't think that he would stoop this low." T-Money countered, but thinking in the back of his mind, I hope Damon isn't behind this. But knowing how he felt about Sya turning the role down, he knew that Damon could be vindictive when he didn't get his way. But he would never talk down on Damon to Sya. They held a tight connection.

T-Money and Sya cleaned as much as they could. Some of her things were salvaged and there just wasn't any help for the others. They returned downstairs to order Imo's Pizza and chill out. Raheem wanted Sya to go back over to his house but she wanted to stay home. She didn't know what was going on but she was certain to uncover the truth, with or without Raheem's help.

22. Living Raunchy!

Frances had a date with Henry and decided to hit up a few boutiques. Her first stop was downtown on Washington Avenue where several shops and cafes were housed. She purchased a few items before continuing to the next store. She then chose to hit the Central West End where Essence's was located, her favorite boutique. "Welcome to Essence's, Mrs. Frances." Shakira greeted her as she always did.

"Thank you, Shakira." Frances smiled at the young lady.

"We carry the latest fashions for any type of event. What are you looking for; evening wear, casual wear or sexy, with-my-man wear?" She chuckled. "Whatever you need, we have it. Give me a holla." She walked away continuing her duties. Searching through the neatly folded racks of designer clothes, Frances found the most sophisticated dress; something that would make Henry appreciate what he has. "Shakira, I need to try this beauty on." Frances uttered, as she followed Shakira to the fitting room.

Frances looked amazingly beautiful in the cream Sista' Sista' Original dress. It cuddled her body flawlessly. Shakira also gave her the cream shoes that matched well, with a dark brown blazer jacket. She went on to purchase accessories too. The reflection that stared back at Frances in the mirror was a better person and she loved it. Frances paid for her items, thanked Sharika, and left the store. Walking to the café, Frances sang an old tune by Marvin Gaye, "Sexual Healing." Reaching the cafe she stood in line, waiting to be seated. Noticing a couple that seemed to be in love, standing in front of her, reminded her of Henry and the relationship they shared. There wasn't anything boring about him.

The waitress came to escort her to the table. She informed the waitress that she wanted to sit on the patio and without delay the lady seated her. "Can I get you anything to drink to start you off this afternoon?" She politely asked.

"A glass of white wine would be nice." Frances answered back.

"I'll be right back. Take your time to order." She walked off to retrieve Frances' request.

Sitting there flipping through the menu, Frances became aware of the happy couple again. She also observed the age difference. The gentleman showered the young lady with kisses and she giggled like the little girl she was. The waitress was at their table taking their order. "What can I get for you folks?" She had pen and paper in hand ready.

"I don't know." the female answered. "Joe, what are you gonna have?" She asked leaving the decision up to him. It was something about this couple that appeared odd to Frances. Just to make sure that her ears and eyes weren't deceiving her, she decided on going to the restroom. She would have to pass their table. In doing so, she stopped in her trail, "You have to be fucking shitting me." She turned her attention to the couple.

Catching them fully off guard, Frances stood there with her hands on her hips. "My, my, my, what do we have here?" She shook her head totally disgusted.

"Hi Frances." Joseph faked a smile.

"Mrs. Fields." Kendra had an even sillier expression on her grill.

"What is this all about?" She had a puckered brow. "Tell me what the fuck are you doing with this baby? And what the hell are you doing with your best friend's dad?" Frances questioned them waiting for a reply.

"With all due respect, Mrs. Fields," Kendra broke her embrace from Joseph. "I don't think that's any of your business. We are grown and owe no one an explanation about our relationship." She pointed from Joseph to herself.

"You're absolutely right, dear, you owe me nothing, but my child, how could you two do this to her. Her father," she looked at Joseph, shaking her head. "And her best friend?" She then looked at Kendra, still shaking her head. "The both of you are sick." Frances was becoming sick to her stomach. "Joseph, what do you have to say for yourself?" Frances directed her attention back to him.

"He doesn't have shit to say. He doesn't have shit to say about your daughter selling sex for a living." Kendra disclosed Sya's business. "Come on Mrs. Fields, you know her teacher's salary is not taking care of her that well."

Frances, never in a million years, thought Joseph would stoop to this level. "Let me tell you something, Kendra dear. Don't think for one second that Joseph gives a damn about you. You both are living raunchy. He's going to leave your stupid tail, that's the type of man he is." She threw some much needed knowledge to the youngster.

"He ain't going nowhere, Mrs. Fields, or should I say Frances." Kendra got real sassy. "I give him this pussy just like he likes it." She kissed his lips, outlining them with her wet tongue.

"You'll learn, young chick, you will learn." She walked back to her table, recovered her belongings and exited the café steaming with rage.

****

Bunnee was chilling, enjoying her day when Damon called her and asked her to come to the office. She tried to decline but he assured her that he only needed an hour or so of her time. On the way over Bunnee came to the conclusion that she's jumping ship with Sya and leaving Damon's company. She planned on informing Sya after she met with Damon. She wanted to know what he was up to this time. She knew he was up to no good from his tone.

Reaching the office, it appeared vacant. She headed to the conference room looking for Damon. Upon her arrival, she heard Damon on the phone.

"Yeah, I know that bitch is shook right about now." He bragged, laughing. Bunnee couldn't hear what the person on the other end of the phone was saying but she went off of Damon's conversation. "Did you smash the phone lines and murder the money machines?" He asked happily.

"That's what's up." He laughed again.

Bunnee knew Damon was unforgiving but she'd hope he didn't go to this measure to destroy Sya. She didn't know for sure if he was talking about Sya, but she was almost certain that he was. She knew how low down Damon could be when he couldn't have his way. She's brought his company major paper, Bunnee thought. She made sure to turn the recorder on her phone on when she entered the office. She would make sure she put Sya up on game, especially if this was pertaining to her and her well-being. After hearing this bit of information she wanted to get this over with. She walked back down the hall as if she'd just entered and started to shout Damon's name. "Damon, where are you?" She shouted walking in his direction.

"I'm in here." He yelled back wrapping up the call.

Bunnee entered the office and took a seat in front of Damon. "What's so important that you needed to see me?" She asked with much attitude.

"I need to talk to you about what's going down, or should I say, what already went down." His devious tone made the hairs on her arms stand up. Damon went into detail about what he did to Sya. He informed her that he'd gotten an old friend to invade Sya's home and destroy her belongings, mainly the Pleasure Pleazers.

His crime buddy, Rocky, was an expert at breaking and entering. He could disable the best state of the art security system. Damon knew that Sya's house was secure with nothing but the best, so he hired the best man for the job. After Rocky completed the job, he armed the system just as he found it and went on about his business.

"She won't make any more dough up in that bitch." He boasted.

"Okay Damon, what does this have to do with me?" She wanted to know.

"I know you two communicate on a regular and it's just more than business." He looked at her sideways, letting her know he didn't believe anything she was about to say. "Kandi told me you are at every function of Danger's." He confirmed.

"I'm not denying that, but it's strictly business." She announced with a straight face.

"Okay, whatever. I want you to keep a close eye on her. Make her think that you're her closest friend. Also, keep me updated on her and T-Money's situation." He concluded.

"Are we done here?" Bunnee seemed uninterested. She couldn't believe him.

"Yeah, we're done." Damon got up from his seat walking around to Bunnee's chair. He lifted her face with force.

"Bunnee, don't fuck with me or I will bury your ass alive. This ain't no game. This is about my paper. I will kill my mama about my money. Do you understand me?" He yanked her face harder.

"Yeah I understand." Her body language changed from, *I don't want to be bothered to I'm afraid.*

23. Hurt!

Frances couldn't believe that Kendra had the nerve to say that her daughter sells sex. She knew that her daughter wasn't a prostitute. She carried way more respect for herself than that. She wondered how Joseph could live with himself for the way he'd treated them. Leaving them didn't seem to be enough, now he was sleeping with their daughter's best friend. "Wow, how raunchy?" Frances thought aloud. Listening to Sade's voice soothed her as she got dressed for her date with her man. Frances was old school and rolled a joint with the Tip Top papers. After taking a few puffs and sipping on her drink, she continued to get dressed. Once finished she looked herself over in the mirror and was pleased at the sight, but her heart was heavy. Henry was waiting for her in the family room. He'd been ready.

Reaching Tucker's Place, a nice restaurant located in the Soulard area of St. Louis, Henry observed that Frances was relatively quiet. "Suga', what's on your mind?" He grabbed her hand and stroked it softly.

She felt there wasn't any need in keeping the information from him.

"Well, honey," she paused looking him back in the eyes. "While shopping yesterday, I stumbled upon something that I wish I hadn't." She rubbed his hand.

"What is it?" He asked with major concern.

"I bumped into Joseph and Kendra, together." She had a shocked gaze on her face.

"Don't fuck with me, Frances." Henry lifted his eyebrows.

"No honey. They were all hugged up together, kissing and shit, like they were teenagers." She took a sip from her glass. "That's not half of it. That little bitch Kendra had the nerve to get slick at the mouth with me. But I shook it off, excusing her, considering that she's a baby and don't know any better." Frances went on to enlighten him on the event.

****

Sya and Raheem got up the following morning to go look at some property for their new project. Sya fell completely in love with the warehouse. She had major plans for the place. They could expand their business beyond. On the way back to Raheem's house, Bunnee phoned Sya.

"Good morning, girlie, what's going on?" Sya asked in her Madea voice, slightly laughing.

"You silly." Bunnee responded not really laughing back. Sya could tell something was wrong.

"What's wrong, Bunnee?" Sya asked, not liking her tone and looking over at Raheem. Bunnee began to cry lightly.

"Sya, I need to talk to you. That dirty son of bitch Damon had someone to break into your house and that bitch ass nigga raped me with his raunchy ass." She cried harder.

"Bunnee, where are you? I'm on my way right now. Do you need to go to the hospital?" She needed to know.

"No, I'm fine, but I need to put you up on some things." She calmed down enough to reveal her whereabouts and Sya and T-Money headed in that direction. Sya brought T-Money up to date about what Bunnee shared with her and knew that she had to do something about Damon, immediately.

Sya and Raheem reached Bunnee's home in record time. Upon their arrival, Sya became furious looking at Bunnee's face. She had a busted lip, black eye and bruises on her body. Raheem was infuriated and expressed it as well. He didn't think that Damon would do this to Bunnee. She had been down since day one. She was a huge part of the adult entertainment business. She was the person that brought the girls in. She was the person that networked on the internet and did the advertisement promotions. She invested enormous hours and time into that company. It caused her to lose the only man she ever loved. Damon and this company has caused her so much hurt over the years, but she stayed, because she was loyal.

After sharing what Damon did to her, Raheem left the ladies and decided to go into the office to see what was up with his partner. He waivered on calling Damon; he wanted to see him face to face. Body language was a dead giveaway. Pulling into the private parking lot, he noticed Damon's new red pickup truck with the temp tags on them. *This nigga' done lost his damn mind. Damn dog, what is your problem?* He thought, walking into the office/house. He wanted to keep everything cool until he found out what was going on.

"Big Dog, what's up?" Damon dapped it up with T-Money.

"Shit nigga, what's up with you." T-Money looked around the place. "Man, why is the place in a mess?" He waited on Damon to respond.

"Man I had some freaks up in this camp. I even videotaped it. Man, they get down."

He pushed the button to activate the flat panel. These girls looked as if they were still in high school. T-Money became disgusted as he looked on. Damon pulled a sucker move and urinated on both girls, including in their mouths.

"Man, I don't think people will enjoy seeing shit like this. This shit is not entertaining or tasteful." He frowned. "This bullshit is horrible and raunchy." He grabbed the remote and turned it off.

****

Frances and Henry had a wonderful time after Frances revealed what was bothering her. Henry explained that she should inform Sya. He also wanted to know if Sya selling sex was true. He'd heard about a phone sex service from one of his buddies and became curious a while ago and called. He was almost sure that the young lady sounded much like Sya but he thought he was tripping. Before he knew it he'd become a frequent customer, spending large sums of cash weekly.

Henry excused himself and Frances took this as an opportunity to call Sya and get to the bottom of this madness. Sya answered on the second ring "Hey Ma, what's going on?" She detected that something was wrong in her mother's tone.

"Baby, I have something to tell you. I've always been honest with you and I've never sugar coated anything. And in return, I do need for you to be completely honest with me, okay Hunny Bun?" She warned Sya.

"Yes ma'am. What is it?" Sya didn't know what to expect. She kept looking in Bunnee's direction. Bunnee knew from the expression on her face that something was wrong. She wanted to know what was going on.

"What?" Bunnee mouthed and Sya gave her the wait-a-minute finger.

Sya carefully listened to what her mom was saying and tears silently rolled down her cheeks. "Mom, you have to be kidding me." Sya finally uttered.

"No, Hunny Bun, I wish I was." Frances interjected. "Hunny Bun, please answer this for me?" Frances went on. "Do you sell sex?" Frances simply asked. "You can be totally honest with me. This is the no judging zone. You know our policies, only God can judge you." She ended. Sya's eyes almost popped out of her head.

"What, Sya?" Bunnee asked again becoming louder. Again, she gave her the finger.

"Ma, I'm not going to lie to you. Know that the decisions I've made in life have nothing to do with you. You have always been a good parent. But to answer your question, yes. I'm in the adult entertainment business." She paused, knowing this was an awkward moment.

"Sya." She heard Frances say in a low disappointing tone.

"No Ma, it's not what you think. I don't commit any sexual acts physically. I'm a phone sex operator. I've never had sex with any of my clients. I don't even know how they look. I'm not living raunchy," she defended her character.

Sya heard Frances breathe a breath of relief. "Ma, I've only been with one man and you called me out on that. I promise that's all I do. Now Kendra's lil' nasty tail will do anything for a buck, and I don't get down like that 'cus my mama taught me better than that." She smiled. "You know Kendra is going to get chin checked for coming at you like that, with her disre-spectful behind. She wouldn't have even graduated if it hadn't been for you encouraging us to do the right thing. She was about to drop out of school when we started hanging together, but I pushed her through it, reminding her that she had come too far to quit. Now she's knocking my sperm donor down? Man, you gotta be fucking kidding me. You always said keep your friends close and enemies closer. Man, my heart hurts after hearing this mess," she confessed seriously with tears rolling down her face non-stop. "Ma, I'll be through there later. Thanks for always keeping it real with me and I love you."

"I love you too, Hunny Bun. I would never lie to you. Do know that only God can judge you. Talk to you soon." Frances assured her baby girl.

After they disconnected Sya informed Bunnee on her conversation with her mom. After she phoned Raheem and didn't get an answer. She decided at that time to head over to the office. Something just didn't feel right. If Kendra turned on her, there's no telling what Damon had in store for Raheem. Sya knew after what Bunnee told her that Damon was, without a doubt, jealous of their relationship.

✶✶✶✶✶✶✶✶✶✶✶✶✶✶✶✶

Damon and T-Money couldn't agree on what was tasteful and what was trashy. "T, man, you need to get your panties outta your ass man and let's make this paper." Damon said in a ruthless tone.

"Man, gone on with that bullshit. Get the fuck outta here. While you're up in here making this distasteful bullshit, I'm out trying to find other avenues to expand this business." He rose from his chair, jumping in Damon's face. Damon didn't show any signs of fear.

"Man, you can sit on back down in that chair. I have a

proposition for you. Since you're so all wrapped up in Danger, you seem like you don't have time for this company any longer. So I've taken it upon myself, as well as Bunnee, and had Brianna, my attorney, to draw up some papers-" Damon stood up with defiance.

"What the fuck you mean? Did you forget that this is not your company? Nigga, I put you on," T-Money was beyond upset. "I gave you a job when no one else in the Lou would fuck with your raunchy ass." He pointed in Damon's face.

"Well, my friend, I have the Lou on lock amongst other states." He unflinchingly boasted.

Damon walked over to his safe, opened it and removed some papers. He then stood face to face with T-Money. I hate it had to come to this," He looked T-Money in the eyes. "You can either sign these," waving the papers in the air. "With no confrontation, or you can get one to the head or maybe two and the entire operation will belong to me. We can do it my way, like Burger King, or your way, casket sharp." He concluded holding a .38 special to T-Money's head.

"Well, my friend, we know it absolutely will not be your way. So do what you have to do, dawg. You will do and hurt anyone to get what you want. First, you get mad at Sya because she wants better for herself and have someone break into her house and destroy her property. Then, you rape Bunnee and she put hella' years into this business, causing her to lose the love of her life. And now you want me to sign over my company to you? Something I started and let you in on? Man, are you fucking kidding me? You're living beyond raunchy." He snickered shaking his head. "Man, how could one cause so much hurt amongst so many people?"

"I did what I had to do, my guy. Now, what will it be; signing papers or meet your maker?" He didn't have a remorseful bone in his body.

"Well, its two things we must do in this world. For starters we must live and without a doubt we gonna die. I guess it's my time." T-Money humbly and confidently told him.

"Have it your way, my dude." Damon pulled the hammer back pointing the gun at T-Money's head.

"That's what's up." T-Money smiled letting Damon know he was not afraid of death. He stood on what he believed in. Pow, pow, pow was all T-Money heard.

"Noooooooooo!" Sya and Bunnee screamed at the top of their lungs standing at the door of the conference room, both firing major shots to Damon's body. His body jerked uncontrollably and blood was flying everywhere. Sya then dropped her pistol and ran over to T-Money, not giving a damn about Damon.

"Are you hurt, babe?" She kissed him on his forehead, tears falling from her eyes.

"Naw, I'm good babe." He told her looking at his now dead friend and holding his woman in his arms.

24. Don't Fuck with Me!

Bunnee couldn't believe the events that took place. She never wanted to see Damon dead but after what he'd done to her, she didn't have a regretful bone in her body for him. *That's what happens when you treat people that care about you like shit,* she thought as she just stood there and looked at his bullet filled body. She still had the empty gun in her hand. "I told him not to fuck with me, Sya." She expressed balling out of control at this point. "I warned him over and over again," She continued to cry. Sya released her grip from T-Money and ran over to Bunnee and hugged her.

"It's all right, mami. We'll get through this." Sya assured her.

"We have to call the police." She became more hysterical, breaking Sya's embrace reaching for the phone on Damon's desk.

"No," Sya and T-Money yelled at the same time.

"Sweetie, listen to me." Sya tried to reason with her. "We can't involve the police. We will have to handle this on our own. Trust, T and I will handle everything. You will be fine and nothing will happen to you, but you have to promise me that what happened today will not leave this room." Sya held both her shoulders, making direct eye contact with her.

T-Money, Sya and Bunnee went back to his place in North County. They had finally gotten Bunnee to calm down and assured her that everything would be fine. Bunnee trusted T-Money without a doubt and she knew if Sya was with him she could trust her as well. Once T-Money had gotten the ladies situated he had to go get the mess cleaned up at the office. He called his street team that handled messy situations as this and had them to do what was needed. T also informed them to take the dead body across the river to old man Tate's farm where he feed dead bodies to his animals. He also informed them to clean the office from top to bottom. He didn't want any evidence of Damon, flat out.

T-Money felt bad about how things went down with Damon, but it was either *him or me*, he thought. He was always warned about doing business with Damon. Niggas from the Lou and surrounding areas didn't get down with him, because he was one of those guys that were known for cutting you at the throat and thought nothing of it once he got what he wanted. T-Money was told that Damon was so sheisty, that he once beat his mama to the point that he put her in the hospital because she stole some money from him. But still knowing that bit of information didn't deter T-Money from fucking with Damon. He was a strong believer of once you cross him, that's when you destroy all ties with him.

****

Several days later they were back at the house and Bunnee and Sya were sipping on some wine while blazing a blunt. The haze had taken Bunnee's mind off of the events and she was relaxed to the point that she was laughing with Sya and listening to music. Listening to J. Cole's cut "Crooked Smile" put her in a zone. "Sya, what do you think would have happened if we hadn't showed up when we did?" Bunnee turned to face her with a serious but frighten stare on her face.

"Bunnee, let's not talk about that right now." She informed her.

"Yes, let's talk about it right now." She demanded. "You know just as well as I do, that Damon would have killed T. We don't have to sugarcoat the situation. Yeah, I know I was a little shaken up after it happened, but I'm cool with it now." She had a look that showed she was good. "I told Damon on many occasions not to fuck with me. I was going to take his ass out the night he raped me but I had other plans for him."

"What were you going to do, Bunnee?" Sya wanted to know.

"Let's just say that I had something for his ass, but I guess it wasn't meant for him to have it." She smirked.

"I guess he got what was coming to him." Sya established.

"Yes he did." Bunnee confirmed. She then jumped from the couch and ran to the phone.

"What are you doing?" Sya asked, confused by her sudden actions.

"We need to contact T-Money and inform him to pull the tape from the back so there will be no evidence on this encounter." She stated.

"I'll text him but I wouldn't disclose that over the phone." Sya then grabbed her phone and texted T-Money and told him she needed to speak with him, but not over the phone. Sya and Bunnee sat on the couch listening to music, both in their own thoughts.

****

Kendra and Joseph were out on the town as if they didn't have a worry in the world. Neither of them seemed to be worried about being seen together. They were walking hand in hand in the Central West End eating ice cream. "Joe, baby, let's go back to my place and do you-know-what." Kendra playfully stated, bringing his hand up to feel her breast.

"You know I would love to do nothing more than to caress your body, but baby, I have an early appointment in the morning. I need to turn in early. I need to get my things together tonight." He concluded.

"Just like an old man." She teased.

"There's nothing old about me, darling, just my age; and don't let that fool you." He announced assuredly.

"You sure we can't get a quickie in? You can leave as soon as you release. I just want to feel you inside of me, daddy." She stated in her childlike voice.

"I guess I don't see why not. One quickie and then I'm out, darling." He informed her in a fatherly tone.

"Sure, baby." She agreed, thinking that once he was there, she would pressure him to stay the night.

Once they reached her house Joseph got comfortable on the queen sized bed and turned on the flat panel television that sat on top of her dresser. Kendra came in the room wearing a black lace bra and panties. Joseph was turned on, but he had his daughter on his mind and he wanted to get close to her, but he knew that she wasn't fucking with him. If there ever was a chance for them to be close, he knew that it would never happen in this lifetime due to Frances seeing Kendra and him together.

Kendra began to kiss all over his body, but he stopped her. "Darling, I want to ask you something." He had a solemn look on his face.

"What is it, Joe?"

"How close are you and my daughter?"

"Well at one point she was my best friend, but I'm almost sure that has come to an end after seeing your ex-wife. I'm more than sure she has informed Sya of the situation with us. But do know I don't give a damn, because I love you, Joe." She pleaded.

"I didn't want her to find out this way. So I'm going to have to make this situation better somehow. She's my daughter and I love her and what we are doing is wrong." Kendra detected hurt in his tone.

"Now you have a conscious?" She became angry. "Where was your conscious when you left her ass years ago?" She yelled. "I don't want to hear this shit. You came here to fuck me and that's what I want you to do." She pushed her tongue down his throat. Joseph pushed Kendra off of him. He pushed her with much force than he intended and she fell off the bed.

"What the fuck is your problem, Joe?" She got off the floor gritting her teeth, steaming mad.

"Don't you ever speak to me that way, little girl. You don't want to fuck with me and you don't want to ever speak to me about my daughter and not in that tone ever. Next time you'll find yourself picking up your teeth off the floor. Do we have an understanding, darling?" His tone was calm and he made no facial expression.

"Sure." She uttered through clenched teeth.

"What was that, darling? I didn't hear you." He put his hand to his ear as if to hear her better.

"Sure," she repeated much louder.

"Good, now come over here and give me some of that sweet

pussy." She looked at him strangely but obliged his request, thinking to herself: *No, you don't want to fuck with me, old man.* She lowered herself on his throbbing member and rotated her hips, making him feel all of her.

25. Missing Person!

Calls had been pouring in the office for Damon. There were even females that came to the office looking for him. He had promised several females jobs and they were ready to get things popping.

Glitter only worked there part time and she was sick of the untamed girls, and she was putting in her two weeks' notice. She couldn't stand the way Damon talked to her. She refused to be his therapy for abusing people. She came in the office to retrieve her things and T-Money asked her if she would reconsider her decision. She informed him that she would have to think about it. She also informed him that if she decided to remain there, she would only work for him. She wanted no dealings with Damon, none whatsoever. He told her he understood. T-Money also knew that Damon would no longer be around so she had nothing to worry about.

The renovation of the warehouse was going great. T-Money had found a temporary spot for business until it was ready. He refused to lose any money, and Sya and Bunnee worked just as hard as him. They were a team and they were loyal to each other. They didn't want to raise any suspicion, so T-Money knew that with Damon being his business partner he would have to make a missing person report, knowing that his body would never be found and no one could be charged for the murder. He wanted to keep everything running smoothly as possible and so far that was happening.

The three of them were at the house when he notified the girls of his decision to make the report and they both agreed. "Babe, I was thinking that the other day." Sya spoke up.

"So you cool with it, Bunnee?" T-Money asked, keeping her involved, since she was part of the shooting.

"Yeah, that's cool. It's not like the dirty bastard is coming back. I don't give a damn one way or the other." She retorted as if she didn't give a fuck, which she really didn't.

"Cool, I think it should be done at the office." Sya told them.

"I agree." T-Money said rubbing her back.

T-Money had so many projects he was trying to accomplish but time was not on his side. Sya was busy with teaching and the business while Bunnee was holding most of everything down as she always has. The money was plentiful and no one was complaining, they just needed more help.

The three of them went to the office to handle business. But before calling the cops they made sure everything was in order. The clean-up crew had done a fabulous job getting the mess cleaned up. T-Money always liked to be safe rather than sorry. The slightest thing could incriminate him. He was one of those thorough niggas, always a step ahead of the game.

They all were sitting in the conference room when the call was made.

"911, what is your emergency?" The operator asked.

"I'm calling to report a missing person." T-Money informed her.

"How long has this person been missing?"

"Like a week now." T-Money was becoming frustrated with all the questions. "Can we just have an officer over here, please?" He finished.

"Sir, I understand your frustration but these are the questions that have to be asked; it's protocol." She recited, sounding a bit irritated as well. "But I will get an officer over there as quickly as possible, sir." She tried to rationalize the situation.

"Thank you." He snapped.

"You're welcome and I hope you find your loved one. Good day." The operator ended and the line was disconnected.

"Now we all know what to say if they ask any questions." T-Money went over the last minute details. Both ladies nodded.

"Cool," he declared, lighting a wine Black and Mild.

"I think I'm going to pour me a glass of wine." Bunnee told them. "Have some, Sya?"

"Shit, why not?" Sya accepted. Just as Bunnee poured the wine, the door bell rang.

"Showtime," T-Money clarified before buzzing the cops in.

26. All Work and No Play!

Things had been going wonderful for business. The Pleasure Pleazers 2 was finally finished and Sya was ready to get things moving. She no longer entertained as a Sex Phone Operator. She was the boss of all bosses. She formed a crew of classy females and trained them how to do the job as if she was doing it herself. She wanted classy and qualified candidates for this position. Her company was upscale and she wanted nothing to discredit her reputation. She was totally business orientated. Her vision expanded way beyond and her next adventure would be to entertain females, something they have talked about on more than one occasion.

T-Money and Sya had been so busy with the opening of the company that they hadn't been spending much time together. He wanted to hook his baby up. She was working so many long hours he could tell that it was getting to her. "Teach you how to love a woman." Beyonce's and Mary J. Blige's voices danced through the speakers of Sya's home as she graded her students' homework. She didn't hear T-Money come in and she was really into the song. He crept up from behind her.

"Teach me how to love my woman." He whispered, kissing her on the neck.

"Raheem, boy, you scared me." She playfully hit him in the chest. "Don't be sneaking up on me like that. Get your ass popped like that." She displayed her gangster girl façade.

"Girl you ain't gon' pop shit." He lightly hit her on her butt.

"Okay, sneak in here again and see what happens." She warned him.

"Yeah whatever." He walked into the kitchen to retrieve a beer.

"Babe, how long you going to be grading papers?"

"I don't know. I have a lot of work to catch up on. I have all night, no school tomorrow." She continued doing her work.

"I wanted to take you out to celebrate. You and Bunnee have been putting in work and I think that we both deserve to get out. You know, have a few drinks and kick back?" He clarified, walking back in the living room kissing her on the cheek.

"Ummmm," She frowned wiping her cheek, loving his lips touching her anywhere. "Boy, gone somewhere with that wet ass kiss."

"You know you like it." He teased.

"Absolutely not," she provocatively stated.

"So are we going out or what?" He wanted to know.

"Raheem, I will have to get dressed and I don't feel like it. I have too much work to do." She complained.

"Just this one time, babe." He stood in front of her, removing her glasses from her face. He then took the pen out of her hand and pulled her up by both hands to her feet. "Look babe," He stared her in her eyes. "All I have been doing is working and you have been working super overtime. All I want to do is take my lady out to enjoy herself. Maybe even give you some of this good dick." He sucked on her neck. Sya's eyes were closed and she enjoyed the pleasure she felt from his wet tongue. "Is," he kissed her lips. "That," he kissed her again. "Too," kissing her again. "Much to ask?" He concluded poking her in the stomach with his hard penis.

"I guess not." She gave in. "Let me get dressed and it's going to take me at least an hour to get ready." She broke his embrace. "You better be glad I love you." She said walking away.

"I love you too, babe." He hit her on her ass as she walked away.

27. The Hookup!

Sya walked in Lola's, a well-known club in downtown St. Louis. Flossing a pair of white tight fitted Bebe jeans, a red and gold Bebe shirt with the words Bebe Bitches imprinted on the front. Serena Williams Signature gold bangles adorned one wrist and a gold and red link bracelet with heart shaped diamonds graced the other. A gold chain with a heart shaped diamond hung from her neck with heart shaped diamond earrings blessing her ears. To complete her fashion statement the gold Michael Kors heels and enormous bag with a pistol inside set her look off wonderfully. Her hair was pulled into a perfect bun to help others witness her flawless face with little to no makeup on, smelling delightful with the scent of "My Life," By Mary J. Blige.

Now her better half wasn't shy one bit. T-Money walked in wearing Gucci, down from head to toe. Even his jewelry was Gucci. He rocked his cap to the side displaying a thuggish demeanor. It was beyond attractive. He also turned a few heads, as did Sya. Taking their reserved position in the VIP area, all the amenities awaited them. Once seated, Sya grooved to Mary J. Blige's single, "Looking for Someone to Love Me." That was one of her favorite entertainers, as well as one of her many favorite songs by her. While singing the chorus she pointed her finger at T-Money. He pulled her close to him, whispering in her ear. "You found him. Here I go." He kissed her on the cheek. She was smiling from ear to ear.

"Babe, is that Glitter walking in." He asked pointing to the girl at the door. Sya looked closely and realized it was her. Sya also noticed that she was not alone. Following closely behind her was a handsome man that she had fantasies about. She wanted this man to touch, kiss and suck her in all the right places. She wanted his muscular arms to pick her up and carry her around her house beating her back out. She had visions of his big penis gyrating in and out of her. She wanted him to position her and hit her in the worst way, but all so good. She also envisioned his sexy wet lips kissing the inside of her juicy thighs and his fat tongue flicking her insides, retrieving all of her juices, without him losing one drop. She wanted him to pull her hair follicles out. That's just how badly this man enticed and turned her on. He would have been her first if he wasn't related to her student. The attraction was so intense that she became moist between the legs looking at him.

T-Money observed Sya licking her lips and perceived a look that she only gives when it's time for him to handle his business. He knew all too well what the look was about. It turned him on and made him do the things he knew she liked. He had to look closely and see if this was for him or someone else. Judging from her eye contact, this feeling was not about him. "Babe, you good?" He asked, bumping her lightly with his elbow, somewhat irritated.

"Yeah babe," She paused. "I'm good." She quickly gathered her composure. "Why you ask?"

"Shit, it seemed that your attention was somewhere else." He replied before getting up to leave the table. "I'll be back. I'm going to let Glitter know where we're seated."

"Okay, babe." She said, kissing him before he exited. She needed to pull herself together. She also wanted to know what type of relationship Glitter held with this fine ass man.

Sya sat and watched the interaction between Glitter, T-Money and this guy. *Damn, St. Louis is a small ass town.*

Everybody knows everybody, what the fuck, she thought disapprovingly. Noticing them walking in her direction, she took a calmer approach, sipping her expensive bottle of wine. I need something much more potent than this. She said with her inside voice. This is going to be a long night. Taking a quick glance at the entrance she saw Bunnee entering. *Damn this was supposed to be just the two of us, at least that's what I thought. That's the impression he had me under.*

Glitter greeted Sya with a hug and introduced her to the sexy man that followed her. Before she could get the introduction out completely Bunnee made her appearance known. "What's up, ladies?" Bunnee spoke loudly over the music, giving Sya and Glitter a hug. Sya noticed Bunnee's unusual actions. That was so not her. She was never the type to bring attention to herself. Jabari was the cause of her actions and Sya was sure of that.

"As I was about to say," Glitter cut Bunnee off. "Sya, this here is my sexy cousin, Jabari." She was smiling as she gave the introduction using hand gestures. "This is my boss Sya, T-Money's wifey, and this is Bunnee who I was telling you about." Sya began to choke for this unknown reason. Fully under the microscope she had to compose herself. Here she is, having feelings for a man she barely even knows. But she was so attracted to him and he's connected to Glitter and she's trying to unite him with Bunnee. This was a hookup she wanted to go entirely wrong. She couldn't be in the company of this beautiful man for a very long time. There had been times when T-Money was making love to her and her thoughts were of Jabari. The few times she was in his presence, he did something to her insides.

"It's nice running into you again. Ms. Fields, right?" He

shook her hand gently.

"It is, Tory's uncle, correct?" She displayed a fake smile. The uncomfortable sensation was visible. Sya really wanted to know how much of Glitter's job description he knew. She didn't want Jabari to get the wrong idea about her or inform the principal of her extra curriculum activities. No one knew what she did with her life outside of teaching and she wanted to keep it that way.

"Well, Big Dog, it's good seeing you again." T-Money gave him another pound. "But I'm about to take my lady on the dance floor. Go ahead and get to know Bunnee a little better. She is a good girl and we gone talk more about that proposition you opened my eyes to real soon. Let's just enjoy the night. I can see this is going to be a major and gainful move for the company." He grabbed Sya's hand and they made their way to the dance floor, dancing to Rhianna and Future's song, "LOVE."

Bunnee was really enjoying Jabari's company. She laughed at all his jokes. Bunnee hadn't been touched by a man in a while and this man made something inside of her warm; real warm and she was ready to do whatever with him, anywhere he wanted her to, she was extremely horny. Looking up from the dance floor Sya noticed that they were real comfortable with each other and it had only been a few minutes.

"Babe, are you having a good time?" T-Money spoke softly in her ear, giving her a wet kiss on the cheek.

"Yes, Raheem, I'm enjoying myself, baby. Thanks for getting me out of the house." She kissed him back.

Back at the table, the five of them talked and drank until it was almost closing time. Sya then excused herself and went to the restroom. Once inside she had to splash water on her face to keep the beautiful vision of Jabari's face from appearing and making her perspire. This man had her thinking things she never did with T-Money or thought of. She finally got it together and applied a fresh coat of lip gloss to her Meagan Goode-esque lips. She made sure her clothes were in place and headed back to the table. Walking into the hallway she got the surprise of her life.

"What are you doing?" She asked Jabari, caught off guard, looking around to make sure no one could see them.

"Relax, no one can see us from this direction. Sya, I'm feeling the hell outta you. I know this is weird but the last time I saw you at the sports bar, I wanted to get to know you better. I also wanted to come to the school every day just to see you and use that 'I'm checking on Tory' excuse, but I didn't want to be that obvious. I've been thinking about you since the first time I met you. Now this is a more difficult situation than I expected. Check this out, T is my man and all, and we go a long way back, but damn." He paused. "I have a thing for you and I can't shake it." He moved in as close as he could and kissed her passionately. She didn't reject or protest. She wanted to jump in his arms and never leave his embrace, something she knew could never happen without someone getting hurt. She didn't want to do anything that would jeopardize her relationship with T-Money or Bunnee. She loved the both of them but her body was whispering other things.

"This is not right, Jabari," she whispered as she pushed him away. "We shouldn't be doing this. I have a man and he's your friend, and my friend is trying to get to know you and see where you all can take this relationship." After she finished

Jabari planted another heated kiss on her lips. She pushed him away from her again and made her way back to the VIP area, mind boggled.

T-Money and Bunnee was at the table laughing. For what Sya could see they were having a good time. Glitter was on the dance floor with some lil' cat with his pants sagging.

"Here comes my baby." T-Money smiled letting Sya in the booth.

"That is one fine man, Sya, and I'm so feeling him." Bunnee licked her finger seductively, rubbing her full breast, winking her eye at Sya, smiling.

"Girl, you's a mess." Sya returned her smile, watching Jabari take his place back at the booth.

"I hope I wasn't gone too long." He touched Bunnee tenderly.

"I was about to come look for you." She playfully rubbed his arm.

"So J," T-Money spoke. "I need you to come by the office tomorrow so we can discuss that business. Another reason to see Bunnee." He finished with Bunnee smiling extra hard.

"I think I like that idea." She responded.

"Well, let's toast to making muthafuckin' money." T-Money yelled and the four of them clinked glasses and drank the remainder of the night.

28. You Are No Longer Needed!

Kendra came to the office looking for Damon in an uproar. "Where the fuck is Damon? I know he's been in the office." She fussed at Glitter who was making important phone calls.

"Hold up, Kandi, don't come in here using that language. I'm trying to conduct business here, with your rude ass." Glitter covered the phone.

"When you finish, the question remains the same, now where is Damon and I want to know right muthafuckin' now." She yelled again. This time T-Money came from the bathroom with a displeased expression on his face.

"Damn, Kandi, what is your problem, coming up in here with that ghetto ass attitude? This is a business. You know, the one that pays your bills," he reminded her.

"Well, I've been trying to get in touch with Damon for a few weeks now and he has not returned any of my calls and I want to know what the hell is going on." She stood with her hand on her hip, standing back on her legs,

T-Money stood there looking at her, thinking, this is the most ghetto fabulous ass female I've ever seen. "Just in case you haven't heard, Damon has been missing." He let the information sink in before he continued. "I filed a missing person report weeks ago. I have not heard from him or seen him. I called all his chicks and even went by his mom's place to see if she heard from him and no one has talked to him. This shit has me puzzled too, ma." He began to rub his temple with both index fingers.

Kendra felt something wasn't right with this whole situation and she planned to get to the bottom of it one way or the other. She knew how money hungry Damon was and he wouldn't miss a dollar if his life depended on it. She remembered the last time she talked to Damon, he informed her that he was trying to buy T-Money's share of the business but he didn't know how it would play out. He also informed her that if T-Money didn't cooperate, he would put a bullet into his head.

What T-Money didn't know was Kendra knew more than he gave her credit for. Damon had promised her the leading lady role in all the flicks. All he wanted her to do was keep a watchful eye on Sya. Then, once he got T-Money out of the picture, he was going to make Sya do the flicks and she would have to answer to Kendra. Just to keep Kendra around, he told her that he would give her a few weeks to think about this task but first T-Money had to be dealt with.

"Well, something sounds really fishy to me. The last time I talk to him he was explaining a business deal that had to do with buying you out and now he's not around." She finished looking at him suspiciously.

"I don't know what you're trying to imply, Kendra. I've been searching for Damon and there is no sign of him. I would really appreciate it if you not let that slick ass talk come outta your mouth and the wrong people get a hold to that bullshit. What you fail to remember, or realize, is that this is my business and I brought Damon on board with me. But do know if I hear anything from the police, you will be the first to know. And oh, by the way, your services will no longer be needed around here. I can't have that type of action and drama in my place of business." He let the news embed in her brain before he continued. "However, I will compensate you until you find another job."

"What you mean, you don't need my services anymore? I brings hella money to your business, unlike Danger, or Sya, now that y'all are on first name bases. At least I thought enough of the company to be loyal and not branch out on my own. I could have made major loot doing my own thing." She yelled, still in hood mood.

Glitter had to disconnect her call due to Kendra being extremely loud.

"That's exactly what you should have done, Kendra. I didn't believe you were burning my name up like this. I really thought you were my friend." Sya told her as she revealed herself from behind the conference room door, looking at her as if she wanted to slap the shit out of her. "How could you do the things you've done to me? First off, I really should beat your ass for disrespecting my mom when she saw you with my sperm donor." Sya moved closer to Kendra. "Then, I'ma beat your ass for fucking with my sperm donor, even though I can't stand his ass or the ground he walks on. But lastly, I'm spanking that ass for putting my business in the streets. All I need to say to you right now is, you need to leave my office before I hurt you really bad." Sya was in her face, poking her in the forehead with her index finger. Kendra's head bounced around. T-Money jumped in between the ladies before a full fledge fight broke loose.

"Bitch, you better be glad your man in between us, because I will beat your ass something terrible." Kendra yelled over T-Money.

"Bitch, you ain't gone do shit. I had to carry you in school because those hoes were always whipping your dirty ass. You already know how I get down, so you know just as well as I do, that this here," Sya said pointing to herself, "is not what you want, trust. I'm gonna see you again, and it's like that for you."

"Bitch, I ain't never scared." Kendra bounced around acting as if she wanted to get to Sya, but in real life, she really didn't. That wasn't what she wanted.

"That's what's up then. Now get your raunchy living ass up outta here before my man can't save you anymore. You rat ass bitch, go back to the alley where you belong." Sya acted as if she was going to hit her and Kendra flinched. "That's what I thought, with your scary ass."

"Bitch, like I said, I ain't scared." Kendra walked backward toward the door to leave. T-Money didn't say anything. He never saw Sya in this rare form and it wasn't a pretty sight, but he liked it and knew that she would get down for her respect, and he needed that type of woman on his team.

29. Business Meeting!

Sya went into T-Money's office to calm down. She didn't want him to witness her hood girl persona, but she couldn't help herself. Kendra had it coming to her and she wanted to give it to her right then and there but she had a better plan. But it took everything in Sya, not to beat the hell out of Kendra. T-Money walked into the office. Sya was sitting at his desk with a mean frown on her face.

"Babe, you good?" He walked over, kissing her on the cheek.

"Yeah, I'm cool. I just let that raunchy ass bitch get under my skin. Babe, you gon' have to forgive me for my foul mouth. You know this is so not me, but I'm mad as hell right now and I'm not gonna be satisfied until I whip that ass, and I put that on everything I love." She hit the desk with her fist.

"Calm down, babe. She is not worth your energy." He told her, kissing her on the tip of her nose.

"Yes she is. When I get through with her, she's gonna wish she never met me." Sya started rubbing her temple to relax. Glitter then buzzed in.

"T-Money, you have a visitor."

"Who is it?"

"My peoples, J-Rock." She did her ghetto impersonation, laughing. So did Sya and T-Money. Glitter was not hood at all.

"Let him know that I will be right out."

"Will do."

After T-Money left his office, Sya became excited just to hear Jabari's name. She felt that feeling that she always felt when he's around. She wanted to go out and make her presence known but her actions were so not together. She decided to take a few moments to compose herself before she made an entrance. She knew he was looking exceptionally handsome.

****

Kendra sat in her car wondering where in the hell had Damon disappeared to. She knew that T-Money was behind his disappearance and she planned to get to the bottom of it. What she didn't know was that Sya had a different agenda for her. Kendra couldn't believe that Sya talked and treated her that way. She really didn't know what to expect from Sya when she saw her. She was absolutely sure that Frances had informed her of the encounter they had. She picked up her phone and dialed a number, turning the speaker phone on.

"Hey, what's up?"

"What's good with it, shorty?" The male voice asked.

"I need a favor from you and I'm sure you will find this interesting." She had a sinister grin on her face.

"What it do, ma?" The voice came to life.

"You know the company I'm working for, right?"

"Yeah." He answered attentively.

"They are trying to play games with my paper. The nigga that was giving me all the jobs have disappeared from the face of the earth. Last time I talked to him, he was buying the other half of the company from his partner, but I haven't heard from him in weeks. I goes into the office today and I no longer have a job and to put the icing on the cake, this bitch Sya done got all up in my face talking trash." She explained in one breath, heated.

"So what is it that you want me to do?" The male voice asked.

"I want you to find out what happen to Damon and rob that bitch Sya and her man T-Money. If they think that they're going to play me, they have another thing coming." Kendra growled angrily.

"I hear all of that, but what's in it for me, ma. I don't work for free. And please don't think that your pussy will get the job done." He told her seriously.

"Name your price and when can you get it done?" She looked at the phone with a frown on her face. "Do know that we split down the middle what you take from them, plus I will give you your paper after the job is done.

"I'm gonna' keep it real with you, ma. T-Money is a hard hitter out here in these streets, so I'm gonna need five stacks. You can give me half now and the rest when the job is finished. Take it or leave it, it's your call." He briefed her in a stern tone.

"Where do you want to meet, so we can get this show poppin'?" She asked aggravated.

"You can meet me at Fritz, in the Loop, in an hour. Is that cool for you?"

"That's what's up. See you in an hour." She told him, disconnecting the call. "I got something for that ass." She spoke out loud, turning the music up, with Chris Brown blaring through the speaker, "Look at me now. Look at me now. I'm getting paper."

****

Sya finally made her way out of the office into the conference room where T-Money and Jabari were discussing business. "Hey, babe," she stuck her head in the door. "Hey Jabari."

"Hey Sya." Jabari replied.

"Babe, I'm going to get something to eat, you guys want anything back?" She asked trying to keep her eyes off of Jabari.

"Where you headed?" T asked feeling his stomach touching his back.

"I was going to Church's Chicken, but if you want something else I can get it."

"Is that cool with you, J-Rock?" He looked over at Jabari.

"Yeah man, that's cool." He glanced at Sya.

"Why don't you ride with Sya and by the time you get back, I can have the projector in progress and you can see what I'm talking about. It seems like it's gonna be a long ass day. So make sure y'all get enough. And babe, don't forget to get me some bombers." He got up from his seat and kissed Sya as he walked out of the room.

"You ready, Jabari?"

"Sure." He told her watching her ass as she walked in front of him to her car. Sya threw her hips and ass extra hard knowing he was checking her out.

30. What are Your Intentions?

Kendra was very angry with Sya, when all Sya tried to do was be a friend to her. Sya didn't need a crowd, she trusted no one but her. After bumping into Kendra at the job, she then welcomed her into her world. She never had much but she was willing to share what she had with Kendra, even throwing knowledge to her about her skills in trying to be a lady. Knowledge is power if used correctly.

Deep inside, Kendra wanted to experience the relationship with her mother that Sya had with Frances. She thought their connection was pure love and authentic. Something she never had.

Kendra's intentions were to never hurt Sya but she wanted to be recognized as doing something better than Sya. She let Damon cloud her judgment of Sya. She didn't know that he had every intention of making the two of them fall out, in which they did. After that was accomplished, he would make Kendra that 'It girl', letting her rake in more paper that the others. In which he thought after the money Kendra brought in it would persuade Sya to participate. Damon had no idea that Sya had other endeavors in life that she already achieved and wanted more in the future. The different between Kendra and Sya was, this was Kendra's career. But Sya's life had expanded beyond this adult world to education. She had already earned a cool million in this business and counting.

****

Jabari and Sya rode in silent listing to "Can you learn," by T.I and R. Kelly. She couldn't keep her eyes off of Jabari. He was outside of attractive, he was sexy and chocolate. That craving a woman has when it's that time of the month, chocolate with a bunch of nuts! It was becoming a bit much for her to focus on the road. At that moment she wished that she could have been the clothes on his back or anything that was attached to his body. He smelled spectacular. His dreads were flawlessly styled, with a neatly trimmed goatee. His well-manicured nails said a lot about him, as well as his fresh pair of white shell toes Adidas.

Jabari sat back and relaxed as Sya drove. He did notice her constantly looking at him. He just wanted to enjoy her presence. Her spirit was tranquil and she was pretty. Sya's also a thick girl, or as the public would say, full figured, and she carries it well. Jabari had a strong desire for Sya. He felt like Lyfe Jennings singing his song, "Stingy." He didn't want her clothes touching her body, nor the lipstick or lip gloss on her lips. He was even jealous of the water that she bathed with. She turned him on further than words. As they continued to ride, Kem's voice rang out through the speakers of the car. His single, "Why Would You Stay," came on. That's when Jabari turn and looked at Sya. "Why would you stay?" Caught completely off guard Sya answered. "What?" She looked in his direction perplexed.

"Why are you with T? You know we had an attraction for each other." He rubbed her leg smoothly, turning back around looking ahead. He wanted his words to marinate.

"Why would you ask me a question like that?" She paused. "I love Raheem and he treats me well." Sya explained to him without thinking about it.

"I can treat you better." He squeezed her leg harder this time, not with force but with sincerity. Sya didn't know what to say, so she didn't say anything all at. However, she did ask herself what were his intentions? She really wanted to know. There is one thing she had to admit, Jabari was fine as hell and any woman could see that.

****

T-Money made a quick run before Sya returned with Jabari. If his memory served him correctly, Jabari smoked that good shit back in the day, but he didn't know if he still got down working at UPS. They could drop him at any time. Even if he didn't smoke anymore, T-Money needed it like yesterday himself. He didn't have a blunt in the office. He was also waiting on a call from the cat he purchases it from.

****

Sya drove to the Church's Chicken on Delmar in Delmar Loop. They delivered her the best service. She was always in and out, even on 99 cent Tuesday, where people ordered four and five special meals at a time. Sya pulled into the lot, killing the ignition. "What will you have?" She politely asked, smiling.

"All of you," He reached over and pulled her close to him. He then lifted her chin with his hand and kissed her overpoweringly. She relaxed and allowed their tongues to dance to the beat of their hearts. The kiss was longer than Sya anticipated it would be, but it was everything she hoped it to be; delightful and memorable.

Jabari took a breath and released his lips from Sya's. She could tell that he didn't want to, but they both needed it.

"I think we better go in and order before-." He cut her off with a kiss more passionate than the first one. "Wait a minute,

Jabari," She pulled back. "We are being real careless right now. I have a man and this is not a good look." She pause to take a deep breathe, holding her chest. "What if someone see us? That's a chance I'm not willing to take." She was still under his spell.

Jabari finally pulled back, and looked intently at her beautiful face. "I understand and I'm sorry for putting you in this situation. I just can't help myself when I'm around you. You're all I think about when I go to bed at night and you are the first thing I think about in the morning. It's just something about you that has me captivated, but the craziest thing is I don't want to find out what it is." He gave her a dazzling smile, the one she loved.

✶✶✶✶✶✶✶✶✶✶✶✶✶✶✶✶

Kendra met her appointment, just as they planned. When she entered Fritz she had to look around to find him. Noticing him sitting upstairs, she made her way. He so enjoyed watching Kendra strut her thing. She walked the steps as if she was on the runway. She was precise with every step. Her short dress that hugged her hips tightly also displayed her define legs and awesome shoe game. Once she reached her party, he stood up and welcomed her with a kiss on the cheek and firm hug.

He looked her over and complimented her. "I like," he informed her.

"Thank you, stranger." She looked him in the eyes. "It's been awhile." She crossed her arms in front of her breasts.

"Yeah, I had some things that needed to be handled. But I'm back now." He wore arrogance like a fitted shirt, but it was harmless.

"That's good; I thought you forgot about me." She flirtatiously stated.

"Never that, but what's up with what we talked about on the phone, ma?" He got straight down to business.

"I think muthafuckas think I'm slow and they trying to play me on my paper. All of a sudden, Damon goes MIA. They have the police involved, but now they tell me that I'm not needed anymore and fire me." She grew angrier.

"When is the last time you heard from Damon?" Her friend asked, listening conscientious.

"It had to be about three weeks ago." She thought about it. "See, here's the thing," she leaned in closer with her hand under her chin as if she was thinking about something. "When I last spoke to Damon, he offered me a leading role in the company and told me to think about it before I accepted. He explained that this would be a lot more than talking on the phone." She broke before she continued to make sure her friend was consuming what she was telling him.

"Okay Kandi, before you go any further, what do you want me to do?" He wanted to know his involvement.

"I'm getting to that, if you let me, dang!" She didn't like his forwardness. He had never acted in this manner with her. She wondered who peed in his Cheerios, but she carried on and got right to the point.

"Damon wanted to expand our career in this adult business, meaning Danger and I. But then Danger went into business for herself and didn't want Damon and T-Money to know about it. So she had sworn me into confidentiality. But they wanted her to do adults films because she brought in good paper on the phone. Damon felt she had the voice and the look to further her career. But since she was doing well, she turned them down." She stopped.

"Well, let me asked you this again, what I'm here for?" His patience was running paper thin.

"I need you to rob both Danger and T-Money." She told him unceremoniously. "Damon told me," she continued pointing to herself. "That he was buying T-Money's share of the business," imitating Damon, using his exacted hands gestures. "And that it would be all about me, but now he's nowhere to be found. I know they had something to do with his disappearance. When I went into the office, T-Money gave me that old fake ass speech; we did a missing persons report bullshit. I also contacted his mother, all that old counterfeit shit." She spat spitefully. "I just want what's owned to me, the leading role, that's what was promised and I want it, no matter how I got to get it, even if you have to knock them. I'm going to need mines." She finished.

King's only concern with this matter was getting his paper, no doubt.

31. You Never Know Who Knows Who!

Bunnee walked in the office looking fierce. Her hair precisely styled, and her dress embraced all her curves flawlessly. "Hey all," She manage to say over her blazing smile.

"Somebody is feeling mighty good today." Glitter teased her.

"Where is everybody?" Bunnee carried on with the questions.

"T-Money made a run and Sya and Jabari went to get something to eat. Oh yeah, Kendra came by and made a donkey of herself, asking about Damon." Glitter delivered the 411 of the day.

Bunnee took a seat across from Glitter at her desk. "Who was here when she acted an ass?"

"T-Money and Sya." Glitter went into hood girl mode again, which caused Bunnee to laugh at her.

"Girl, just tell me the story without the theatrics, please." She laughed more.

"Okay then, I was trying to make it more interesting." Glitter laughed. "But Sya was going to let her have it right here in this office, if T-Money hadn't stopped her. But the conclusion is that they fired Kandi… err.. I mean, Kendra, shoot whatever her name is. But anyways, T-Money told her that she was no longer needed. And before you ask," she raised her finger to stop Bunnee from asking the next question. "It didn't sit well with her at all. She walked out of here making threats and everything." She ended.

Bunnee didn't really want to hear any more of that, she

wanted to know where was Jabari and how long had he been gone. "Okay, Glitter, enough with all of that, how long has your cousin been gone?" The question she'd wanted to ask since she found out he was there.

"They should be on their way back by now. T-Money should be headed back this way too." Just as she finished her statement, T-Money walked in.

"What's good, B? You look jazzy." He gave her a hug.

"Thank you very much." She replied. "You smell even better," she informed him letting him know that she smelled his cologne, weed, and she wanted to smoke with him.

"It's all good, come in my office, we can get it poppin.'" He told her walking to his office.

"What does that reefer do for you?" Glitter asked frowning.

"Why don't you try it for yourself, that way, you can judge for yourself? I can only disclose what it does for me, how it makes me feel." Bunnee explain and headed to T-Money's office.

****

King finally understood what was going on with Kendra. He knew that she was raunchy but he didn't know that she was gutter raunchy. He was all business and no play. He really didn't give a damn why people wanted others robbed, killed or whatever their desire was, as long as the money was right. But this job here was totally out of the question.

King and T-Money came up together. They lived down the street from one another growing up. They were two peas in a pod. They did everything together; from riding their bikes to robbing the Pepsi truck that delivered to the Orange store on Tuesdays, located on the corner of North Prairie and College Avenue. They would put the cases of soda in King's basement, selling them at Williams Middle School for 30 cents a can and 65 cents a bottle. They made a hustle anyway they could, but when King robbed a white man in Clayton and beat him to death, literally, due to the fact that he wouldn't give up his wallet, those white people sent him away for seven years.

Even though he was away, T-Money always looked out for him. His books were always full to the limit. He rocked the latest fashion and he owned a 32 inch flat panel Sony television in his room. Also, his radio was equipped with an I-POD and MP3. He lived well in prison, better than most. Before his prison stay, King served the best weed in the Midwest. Nigga's traveled from state to state to get that "loud," as they called it. After he went and rested for a minute, T-Money made sure he kept his connects. Now that King was back in population he was doing it bigger than ever and T-Money remained his number one customer.

"King, before you leave, I know you have some of that Afghan kush?" She went into her purse to pull out some money.

"I got you lil' mama, and you know I'm not gonna charge you. This is on the house, follow me to the car." He summed up, removing himself from the chair. Kendra followed him. As she tagged along King thought to himself, *you never know, who knows who. This is a small ass world.*

****

Both Jabari and Sya hands were full with bags. They went to Church's Chicken, the liquor store, then to Family Dollar to get paper plates. As soon as Sya pulled up she observed Bunnee's black Impala car. Deep down inside, she was a little disappointed that she had showed up. She wanted all of Jabari's attention, knowing that her man would be in attendance. It was something about this man that she wanted, but couldn't have. She thought about that Eryka Bada song, "Next Lifetime." But she wanted him in *this* lifetime, right now, at this moment.

32. Confused As Hell!

Bunnee and Jabari sat right next to each other in the conference room. T-Money allowed the ladies to attend the meeting. Bunnee had a smile on her face, wider than the Mississippi River. She loved being in Jabari's company. She laughed at every joke Jabari told. Some of them weren't even funny. He had her open and she wanted him to dive deep in her motherland, but for some reason, he would not bite. The times they had been in each other's presence, the chemistry was strong. Bunnee thought that Jabari would give in to her flirtatious ways once he witnessed her in her sexy ensemble, but he acted as if his mind was somewhere else. Bunnee knew any man in their right mind couldn't resist her, but Jabari had her confused as hell. *How can he not want all of this ass?* She thought, knowing she kept it right and tight in all the precise places. Her stomach was flat as a pancake and ass was pump and soft. Her breasts were firm grapefruits and she had a pretty face. True, she was a size 18 but nothing was out of order.

Jabari noticed that Bunnee was in a different place than he and the others. "Are you okay?" He asked bringing her back to current events.

"I'm good." She smiled rubbing his hand that was placed on the table.

"I'm just making sure." He replied truthfully.

****

It had gotten later in the day and T-Money suggested that they go and throw darts and shoot pool at the Midtown Sports and Grill Bar. It was initially the old Bolero's, a bar that had been around a very long time and where the hood hung out.

Now that it was under new management, different hoods came to check it out. The new owners had renovated it nicely. There were 40-inch flat panel televisions throughout the bar. The new owners also had a new seating arrangement; the black and white high back bar stools were accompanied by tall tables that lined the back of the bar, with the kitchen next to them. The full menu served a variety of delicious food. You also had to go outside to smoke and the smokers didn't appreciate that, not one bit. But being a business owner in today's society, that's the only way you could obtain your license and operate your business.

They all agreed to go, except for Sya. But T-Money encouraged her to ride along. She couldn't continue to place herself in an uncomfortable position. But she rode along to satisfy T-Money. Jabari did things to her that she couldn't explain, things that she didn't want to explain. She knew it was wrong to feel this way, when she already had a man that did any and everything for her. She couldn't have asked for a better companion, but it was something about Jabari that stirred something inside her soul. The things she was feeling was beyond confusing as hell. Then this man that she had feelings for was dating her good friend. She couldn't hurt people for her own selfish reasons, especially those she cared about the most, and compromise what she worked so hard for. That's why she wanted to stay clear of the entire situation, but with Jabari talking business with T-Money that would be remotely impossible.

"Are you up for getting your ass spanked in a few games of darts?" Jabari asked Bunnee.

"I only know how to play hi-score. Don't go getting cute on me playing that cricket shit." She playful stated.

"I can show you how to play. It's nothing to it, sweetie." Jabari assured her.

"I'ma hold you to that. And don't act like I'm getting on your nerves when I don't get the concept." She rolled her eyes, laughing.

"I got you." Jabari rubbed her face.

"You better have me, trying to make a fool of me." This time she rolled her eyes harder at him.

"Babe, you haven't said anything. You up for a few drinks and getting your ass spank too?" T-Money asked Sya.

"Not really, you basically made me come, but please don't get it misconstrued, I'm not worry about getting my ass spank, this is what I do, or did you forget?" She boasted, looking him directly in the eyes not blinking.

"Put your money where your mouth is, Ms. Badass." T-Money challenged her.

"Let's get it then and Bunnee you better be a fast leaner." She joked removing herself from the table, trying to keep her eyes off of Jabari, something that seem impossible.

They left the building to go have little fun.

****

They all hopped in T-Money's new black Range Rover and headed to the north side of town. Sya immediately reached for T-Money's CD case to find Ledisi CD, "Pieces of Me," but was surprise to see that it was already in the CD player. "Babe, what you doing listening to this?" She inquired pleased at his choice of music.

"It makes me think of you, when you not rollin' with me." He revealed, kissing her on the lips. She kissed him back.

"Awww, babe, that's sweet. I guess that song rubbed off on you." His words resonated in her head.

"Naw, I like her other song, with Jaheim, We Gone Stay Together." He reason.

"I like the entire CD." Jabari entered the conversation.

"Really?" Sya asked shocked.

"Really, but Kem is my dude." He expressed looking at her through the rearview mirror from the back seat.

"You know good music I see," she paused, then continued. "Unlike somebody I know." She looked over at T-Money moving her head in his direction.

Bunnee didn't want to feel left out. "I love me some Kem too. That man knows how to sing to a woman, with his sexy ass." She got carried away.

"Yeah, he's a good performer. " Jabari declared not wanting Bunnee to feel left out of the conversation. The ride became quiet until "I Miss You" danced through the speakers.

"Now that's my shit right there." Sya looked at T, singing along with Ledisi, melodically quoting the lyrics of the song.

"Why would you be missing me? You have plans of leaving me one day?" He overemphasized his statement, meaning every word.

Sya jumped in. "Baby, you know neither one of us, want to be the first to say goodbye. I have no plans or intentions to ever leave you." She threw it on thick. She then peeked through the rearview mirror from the front seat, at Jabari, noticing a stone expression plastered across his face. She quickly redirected her view and looked out the window.

They were coupled up on teams. Little did the guys know, Sya was coming for their heads in the dart game and Bunnee was poisonous with the pool stick. Both of their games skills were well-polished. Continuously sipping on the Peach Ciroc, Sya was feeling tipsy; she allowed herself to loosen up some. She also found herself bumping into Jabari repeatedly, some bumps more sexual than others. T-Money made a mental memo to ask her about her behavior at a later time; however he did acknowledge her actions and knew that Bunnee didn't allow them to go unnoticed as well. She tended to stand in front of him more and sitting on his lap when he sat down. She refused to let anybody come between her and Jabari. His actions had her so damn confused!

33. Planning!

Kendra wanted to stay in the loop about the situation with King. She wanted to know how things were going and the amount of time that it would take to complete the mission at hand. King was good at what he did and he wasted no time when top dollars were involved. Kendra figured when King completed this assignment, she would have him take care of Joseph for putting his hands on her.

King met with T-Money and gave him the entire run down on Kendra. In which, they came up with a plan to take her out. T-Money refused to let anything or anybody interfere with his paper and made the decision right then and there to have Kendra removed from this earth. It was either him or her, and the way things were going for him, it would have to be Kendra without a doubt.

"What's good with it, fam?" T-Money greeted King.

"Shit, money to be made. Money is the motive, that's my everyday hustle." King responded with a manly hand shake.

"I feel you, man."

T-Money followed King to his kitchen and poured himself a shot of 1738, drinking it straight. T-Money smacked his lips together after the drink when down, hitting his chest. "Damn, that shit tastes wonderful."

"I can't tell, my brotha', you beating the shit outta your chest. Stop playing with the big boys." He playful hit T on the shoulder, headed to the bar to pour him a shot as well. He downed it in 2.2 seconds, reaching for the blunt he already had rolled in the naked-lady-astray resting on the counter.

"This shit right here nigga, is law." He took a long pull.

"Better than what you gave me the last go round?" T became excited. "Good weed always makes it feel good."

The guys sat around watching the baseball game. It was the World Series and everyone was depending on The Cardinals to win this championship.

"Man we're going to all the games of the World Series, home and away games, we there, front and center. Shit, hopefully this shit with Kendra will be over within the next two days," He made sure to let King know this situation had to be handled ASAP. "We can be outta here." T proclaim seriously.

"That's what it is then." They gave each other some dap. "You know, bitches can be something else. This bitch came to me wanting me to off my brother, not knowing she just signed her own death certificate." He took another sip from the glass. "This damn bitch told me to rob you and your girl. She must don't know who she's fuckin' with? She doesn't know your name ring bells across the 50 states?" He passed the blunt.

"Evidently not," T-Money acknowledged, cocky, having the right to be. He is the man, making big moves and his pockets are beyond swollen. He needs nothing holding him down and certainly not a bitch.

"Bruh, what's up with Bunnee? She's acting like she ready to give a nigga some of that poo-thang, but then she be tripping, talking about commitment and shit. I'm not ready for that right now. I thought she had a man, but anyways I'll holla at her when I'm on that."

"That's not what you're on, bruh'?" T-Money asked laughing. He knew how badly Bunnee wanted to have a family one day.

"Naw, not right now. But on the real, Kendra will be taken care of and we will be able to make that trip. Bruh, you taking yo' old lady?" King finished.

"Yep, if she wants to go, if not, we rolling regardless. I know my dude Jabari is rolling too."

"That's cool, let me know. I may take one of my lady friends. Make sure this Jabari cat is on the up and up. I can't get jammed up again, bruh." T understood King's concern.

34. You Can't Handle The Truth!

Frances and Sya were going over the inventory for the new store, located in Wellston. "A Mother's Love" was a clothing/confectionary store. There were two sides and both required its own products. Sya would handle the fashion, and Frances would deal with the food. She wanted to do something different with this opening. Sya gave her a great idea to have Libra and Essence's sing, since they were the first ladies of the Lou. They have been big supporters of St. Louis for some time now and they always participate in events given in their hometown. With all the money they had, St. Louis was still their hometown. Frances had built a good relationship with them over the years. She often shopped at Essence's Boutique, running into Essence and Libra a few times. They were always pleasant. She wanted St. Louis entertainment and reached out to Murphy Lee of the St. Lunatic's and he accepted her engagement. She didn't forget her STL authors: Mary L. Wilson, Teresa Seals, Allysha Hamber, Johhna B and Rose Jackson-Beavers, just to name a few. She planned to have a really nice turn out and she wanted everything in order. They had less than three weeks to have everything organized.

They did an extensive check to make sure nothing was forgotten. Frances went through the list of products and Sya searched through the boxes to make sure they were in fact there.

"Ma, can I tell you something and not be judged?" Sya stopped the count on the Sista' Sista' Original merchandise.

"When have I ever judged you? Only God can do that, Hunny Bun. Sure, you can tell me whatever and as your mother, I'm going to direct you in the correct manner. Now, it's up to you what you do with my advice." Frances sat down the paperwork and gave Sya her direct attention sitting on the counter.

Sya looked at her mother before sharing her secret. She took a deep breath and words escaped her mouth.

"Okay Ma, you know I love Raheem with everything in me, right?" She questioned.

"Right, that's what you tell me." Her mom had a smile on her face.

"No, for real Ma." She pouted like a kid.

"Okay baby, go ahead. I'm just trying to make light of the situation. You look as if this has you stressed, but continue."

"You see, I had a student in my class, that looks a lot like me but anyways his uncle is his guardian. When I say fine, I mean it in every aspect of the word. His shaped chest, toned arms, muscular shoulders and chiseled legs will make any woman release on themselves, literally." She felt a chill shoot through her body and she slightly shook due to it.

"I can imagine." Frances acted as if a chill went through her body and displayed the same action as Sya just had.

"Ma, I see you have jokes today. I'm trying to share something with you, be for real." She continued to pout, this time folding her arms across her chest. Frances felt tickled all over.

"Listen here, little girl. This here is a case of you loving two men," she broke in. "You know, I'm never one to sugarcoat the truth. My question to you is, can you handle the truth? I'm not going to tell you what you want to hear, I must speak the truth." Frances' tone was stern.

"Speak Ma, but before you do, hear me out." She once again took a deep breath. This hunk of a man is dating Bunnee and here's the bummer: he and Raheem are doing business together. Oh and don't let me forget, that he's Glitter's cousin. What a situation?"

Frances reached for her glass of wine and took a deep sip and went for it.

"You want to hear it? Here it goes. You know just as well as I do that this guy is totally off limits. For one, he's a business acquaintance of your man and secondly, he's dating your friend, a definite no-no. There's really nothing else to be said about this situation. Now, you can either risk everything, and what I mean by that is, compromising your relationship with a man that truly loves you and you truly love him; or do you and or lose a friend that has showed you nothing but loyalty. Again I don't recommend it, but you are your own woman." Frances disclosed the best information a mother had to give to her daughter.

"Ma, I understand exactly what you are saying but it's something about this man. I should have been with him instead of Raheem anyways." She wanted the green light from her mother that it was okay to be with this man, knowing in her heart, that it was not the correct way to go.

"This is your life, but think about everything you do; look for the cause and effect. It's just merely lust and it gets you nowhere but in trouble. Most times the truth is so hard to handle. Keep me informed and remember, only God can judge you, Hunny Bun," she smoothly ended.

"Thanks Ma, even though that's not what I wanna hear, but I am listening to you. Now let's get back to business. We have a grand opening to get prepared for. It will be fabulous. And Frances, just for the record, I can handle the truth. I may not like it, but I can handle it." Sya threw her hair back like a super model.

"Watch it, little girl." Frances slightly raised her eyebrows.

35. The Game!

Joe felt bad about the way he treated Kendra. He thought if he took her out and spent the evening with her, he could make things better. One thing he had to admit was that she had the best pussy he's had in a very long time. He called her ongoing and got no answer. He left messages, emails and text messages, nothing. The St. Louis Cardinals were playing at Bush Stadium tonight and he retrieved tickets for the both of them to attend. He even purchased the Cardinal gear, knowing it was going to be nippy outside. St. Louis was sold up tonight. Nelly, City Spud, Ali, Kyquan and Murphy Lee were in the house. Ozzie Smith was in attendance as well as several other celebrities. Downtown was jammed pack with red and white shirts, hats, jerseys and jackets. The Lou represented to the fullest.

Kendra was home lying around trying to make contact with King to see if he completed his mission. She hadn't been able to contact him and that worried her. She heard a knock at the door. Surprised and hoping that it was King, she went to the door, excited. Once she opened it, without researching who was knocking, she displayed attitude.

"What do you want, Joe?" She stood in the doorway not letting him enter.

"Come on, Kandi baby, don't be that way." He pleaded, rubbing her arm. I came over to see if I can take you out tonight. I miss you. Don't do me like that." He touched her the way she liked it and he knew it was working.

"I don't think that I can get past the way you treated me. That's something I will not get used to, so in order for me to not involve that in my life, I have to remove myself from the atmosphere, and that's you." She stood her ground.

"Sweetheart, I'm telling you, if you give me another chance, I can make it up to you. Whatever you want, I got you." He told her kissing her on the neck, smoothly licking his tongue back and forward. Kendra didn't know that he was coming with his LeBron James game. Joe reached inside her super short shorts and fingered her clit until small moans escaped her mouth while her eyes rolled to the back of her head.

Kendra was on all fours, taking it in the ass like the champion she was. Joe rolled her over on her side and stuck his hard penis in her. For Joe to have been 20 years her senior, sticking penis to women was his specialty. He liked Kendra's sex game. She would do anything to please him and there were no limitations when it came to sex with them.

"Sweetie, where's the dog chains?" Joe asked out of breath.

"In the usual place. You feeling freaky tonight, daddy?" Kendra was getting beside herself, so into the moment.

Joe reached over in the nightstand and removed the dog chain from the draw. He then instructed Kendra to stand on her knees. She did as she was told. "Kandi," he said to her in a fatherly tone.

"Yes daddy?" She looked at him wide eyed.

"Lift your head so I can put this chain around your neck." She again did as she was told.

"I want you to get on top of the table so I can get better in that ass." He demanded. She hopped on top of the small table and Joe went to work on her. However there was some discomfort, but Kendra was a pro; she knew how to take dick, anyway it was given to her. She was so into what she was feeling that she didn't hear her cell phone ringing. This escapade went on for way over an hour.

King was sitting outside of Kendra's house watching everything from afar. King had also witness the huge bags in the back seat of Joe's car. He secretly removed the bags from Joe's car and put them into his vehicle. He also confiscated Joe's wallet and tickets to the game from the glove compartment of his car. "They won't need these anymore." He whispered to himself. He made sure not to be seen by any nosey neighbors or moving traffic. He was observing his surroundings thoroughly.

While King sat inside of his car, he phoned T-Money.

"Hi fam, what's up?"

"What's good, my nig?" T-Money asked between coughs, smoking on a blunt.

"It seems that we have company and you know I leave no witnesses."

"Shit, do what you have to do. That's what happens when you fuck with bitches like Kendra. Listen here man, this is your call, get down like you live, and you know how you do. Call me when it's done and over with. Another one bites the dust." T explained, relieved knowing that King was the man for the job.

"Is everything on your end sewed up with old man Tate?" He asked cautiously.

"It's a go. You know I got you, bruh. Now go handle your business so we can make the baseball game, baby. It's going down tonight. One." T laughed while disconnecting the call.

****

Frances and Henry were on their way down to Bush Stadium to watch the game. Henry had tons of money riding on the Cardinals. Frances was also a huge fan and she had a bit of money riding on the Cardinals too. They both wore red and white Cardinals gear from head to toe. Henry showed off his red skully, long sleeve jersey, with a thick St. Louis Cardinals jacket, Levi jeans and red Chuck Taylor tennis shoes. Frances on the other hand, displayed a red and white STL Cardinals baseball cap, a long sleeve jersey, with a thick St. Louis Cardinals jacket, Levis jeans and red and white Air Maxx tennis shoes.

They left early knowing traffic was going to be out of control. Once they arrived, they immediately went to the sky box. Those seats eliminated six stacks from their pockets; in which it didn't hurt them at all.

After they were seated, Frances decided to call Sya to see if she and T-Money were attending. She invited them weeks ago, but Sya never got back with her. Frances knew T-Money was all for it, but with everything going on with their new store, Damon, Kendra and Jabari of course, she wasn't sure if she would attend. To her relief, Sya answered.

"Hi Hunny Bun, what are you doing?" Frances addressed her child in her motherly tone.

"Hi mommy dearest, what you have going on this evening?" She expressed in a cheerful voice.

"The baseball game. I hope you and Raheem are joining us tonight." She told her, taking a sip of Henry's Magen David better known as Mad Dog 20/20 and always known as MD 20/20, peaches and cream flavor.

"Ma, I totally forgot about it. Let me contact Raheem and see where he's at and I will call you right back. Has it started yet?" She inquired, completely forgetting about the game tonight.

"Okay baby, no it hasn't. Call me right back. I'm more than sure we can find someone that wants these expensive tickets." She reminded her.

"Sure Ma, I'ma call you right back." Sya hung up the phone and immediately dialed T-Money's number.

"Hey my babe, what you doing?" Sya asked running her bath water.

"Chillin' babe, what's up?" He released the smoke from his mouth.

"I totally forgot about the baseball game tonight. Ma just called and we have to go, the tickets were three stacks a piece. What you say?"

"Are you dressed?" He wondered, knowing the answer to his question by hearing the water running in the background.

"I'm about to hop in the tub now. It won't take long, I promise." She pleaded her case.

"I'll be there in twenty minutes; and babe, don't go wearing no red bottoms and shit. It's a baseball game, be comfortable. Wear your STL gear." He interrogated her.

"How you know I have any STL gear?" She spat nastily.

"Look in your gigantic closet," He gave details slowly. "Look on the side where all those damn shoe boxes are and you will see the enormous bag from Champs. That's how I know you have some STL gear. I bought it." He laughed.

"Okay, see you when you get here, Mr. Know It All." She laughed back with him. Sya then called her mother back to inform her that they would be there.

36. Death Certificate!

T-Money called and invited Jabari and Bunnee to the baseball game. He also had tickets.

"What's up, my dude? What you have up for the evening?" T asked still smoking on the Loud Loud kush.

"Shit, my dude, just cooling; about to watch the game in the basement." He clarified.

"Naw bruh, I have one better. Why don't you and Bunnee meet Sya and me at Bush Stadium to watch the game up close and personal? It's the World Series, baby." He shouted.

"You better know it. That's cool. I'm headed that way now." Jabari exclaimed.

"I'll meet you out front."

"Thanks fam, that's good looking out, 'preicate it." Jabari anxiously stated.

"It's nothing, bruh. Check you in a minute, one."

****

The game was in full effect and the Cardinals fans were more than disappointed. The other team was letting them have it and if they won, the series would be tied up and they would have to play away from home. Sya and her mom were sipping on the wine when she noticed Jabari and Glitter entering the sky box. Something came over Sya that she couldn't expound and she didn't want to. However, Frances did scrutinize the change in Sya's mood. Frances knew this was the man that had her daughter's mind in a frenzy, and she could understand why. He was everything her daughter described him to be and more. What a hunk of a man, she thought.

Reaching the seats next to Sya and T-Money, Jabari and Glitter made their presences known.

"What's up, bruh? I see you finally made it." They dapped it up. "What happen to Bunnee?" He continued his questions.

"I couldn't get in touch with her, so I invited my cousin." He said.

"That's cool." T told him. "Hey, this is Sya's mother, Frances, and her guy, Henry." T did the introductions.

"It's nice meeting you both." Frances said while shaking their hands and Henry did the same.

****

Joe couldn't keep his hands off of Kendra. This was the type of girl every man wanted in his bedroom. She would do anything to please her lover, even if it meant committing dangerous acts. Joe removed the dog chain from her neck and replaced it with the dog chain covered with spikes. Instead of putting the chain on the proper way, Joe positioned the chain inside out with the spikes pinching her skin, and Kendra didn't interject.

"Tell me something, Kandi." Joe asked as he slid his penis into her mouth. She shook her head up and down.

"Would you do anything to hurt my daughter?" He tightened the chain around her neck. She withdrew his manhood from her mouth.

"Why you say that?" A strange look appeared on her face.

"Even though Sya and I are not on speaking terms, I still love her like a sister. Does this have anything to do with the fight we had?" She felt the spikes grow deeper into her skin.

"Yes, this has everything to do with the fight we had." Joe penetrated his penis deep into her juice box. "If anything happens to my daughter know that I'm coming after you. And believe me, it will not be an appealing scene." He threw himself bottomless inside of her. Kendra let out a scream of pain, that Joe had never heard escape her mouth, the entire time they have been sexing each other.

"I see you get the picture." He kissed her hard and sloppy.

"I get it, daddy." She managed to say in pain. Kendra knew at that instant, that she would have Joe's life terminated. With the pain he'd caused her, he'd signed both he and Sya's death certificate. *How 'bout that,* she thought to herself.

37. What Have We Here?!

Sya was doing her best not to look in Jabari's direction. She couldn't seem to focus on the game. She smelled the scent of his Gucci cologne and became jealous. She wanted to be the scent covering his body. Frances looked at her daughter and shook her head.

"Baby, it's not nice to stare, and close your mouth." Frances whispered in her ear.

"Dang Ma, am I that noticeable?" She smiled.

"Yes, Hunny Bun." She smiled back. "I understand your attraction for him. He's a cutie."

"I know, right." She responded. She paid attention to him looking in her direction from time to time. Glitter wasn't really into the game. She was too busy texting on her phone. Sya wanted to know why Jabari didn't bring Bunnee and took this as an opportunity to inquire.

"Hey Glitter Bug, where's my girl Bunnee?"

"He says she didn't answer the phone and he didn't want the tickets to go to waste." She answered never taking her eyes from her phone.

"Oh I see. Who are you texting?" Sya questioned.

"Aren't we nosy?" She replied without giving her an answer. Sya discontinued her questioning.

T-Money was upset that the Cardinals were losing. He was not paying Sya any attention. He was worried about his money; he betted on this game. It wasn't a small piece of money either.

"I know one fucking thing, Albert Pujols or David Freese needs to do something." He yelled. Sya looked at him and cracked a smile.

"Babe, you really letting this game get to you. Don't do that." She told him rubbing his arm.

"I have too much damn money riding on this game." He fussed. Sya said nothing, however she did note a gentlemen watching T-Money. She made a mental note to bring this situation to his attention.

Jabari and T-Money went to the back of the box. T-Money also became aware of the man Sya noticed. "What the hell?!" He shouted. "Damn, man, it's good to see you." T-Money hugged the man.

"What have we here?" Mr. John shouted back. "I've been looking for you, young man. I hear you are the man around these parts." He gave T-Money another hug.

"I am the man around these parts." He arrogantly declared. "What brings you back around here?" He asked, happy to see his mentor.

"I have some unfinished business and man, I'm so damn happy to see. I know you can help me with my destination and mission." He assured T.

"You know anything you need and I can help, you got it and if I can't, I will do my best trying to help you." He honestly meant it. "Come on over here, I want you to meet my lady and her family."

"Sure," he obliged, walking back over to where they were

seated.

"Hey babe, I want you to meet someone. Remember me telling you about my mentor, Mr. John, Mr. J as I call him? Well this is him, in the flesh." He was beyond thrilled.

"Hi, it's nice meeting you." Sya extended her hand for a shake, but he kissed it instead. "This is my mother, Frances, her guy Henry, and Glitter and Jabari." She finished. Mr. John kissed all of the ladies' hands and shook the men's hand.

"It's nice meeting you all. Hopefully we will meet again, maybe have dinner or something or whatever this knucklehead conjures up." He told them and hugged T again. The game was in the bottom of the seventh and St. Louis was losing. "Looks like we'll be traveling, this is a wrap here." Mr. John summed up. He and T went to the back and caught up on old times. At this time neither tripped off of the game. It was a wrap. Out of town is where they were headed.

38. Game Time!

King grew impatient waiting for the right moment to make his move. "There's no time like the present." He stated to himself and began to gather the tools he needed to handle the manner at hand. He'd been waiting most of the day. Game time.

****

Joe and Kendra were into some dangerous sex acts. Kendra's neck had specks of blood dripping from it. The spikes in the chain drew blood and for some eccentric reason it turned Joe on, and it excited Kendra even more.

Soft jazz played in the background as Joe watched himself in the mirror beside Kendra's bed; softly burying his penis into Kendra's hot pocket. He kept that position going for a few minutes, enough to get her relaxed. He had caused Kendra much pain today and intended to deliver more. He wanted Kendra to understand that if anything happened to his daughter, she would be to blame. If nothing else in this world, he loved Sya and Frances with every breath in his body. He let his pride overrule his love for his family. *When you marry someone, you marry them for good or bad, richer or poor. A wife and husband are considered as one. If one falls the other person is there to pick them up and carry on, that what husbands and wives do, his thoughts haunted him every day.*

"Kandi, turn over," Joe demanded displaying a menacing look. Kendra had become frightened at this point. She didn't have her pistol or anything to protect herself with. Joe roughly jammed his penis up her ass, while blood immediately released itself. Kendra discharged a painful sound, followed by warm tears leaking down her cheeks.

"You don't like this, suga? Where's my little freak bitch at?" He smirked. Kendra was in so much pain she couldn't utter a word.

King climbed through the back window. He knew the layout of Kendra's house. He had knocked her off a few times. He had come to like her as a person, but she made the wrong move this time. She wasn't someone he liked as his lady, just a piece of coochie from time to time. King stood at the entrance of the bedroom, out of view but listened before he made an appearance. He watched as Joe misused and insulted Kendra's backside tremendously. He couldn't take it any longer. The screams were piecing to his ears. Before he realized, he let a shot off and the bullet entered Joe's right thigh.

Kendra was relieved to see King. She was even more relived that Joe wasn't forcing his massive penis in her backside anymore. After King shot Joe, he fell on the floor, beside the bed, holding his thigh.

"What the fuck is wrong with you man?!" Joe screamed in excruciating pain.

"Shut the fuck up, old man, before I blow your dick off with my next shot; and trust, I won't miss."

"I would prefer if you let Kandi give me the blow job. This is not my idea of a threesome. I don't roll like that, young thunder-cat."

Joe had jokes. King didn't find Joe's statement amusing and freed one from the chamber and into Joe's chest. Just to make sure he was dead, he walked up to him and let go of two more in the center of his head. "All right, all right, all right, bitch, you gone learn today." King walked away reciting Kevin Hart's comedy.

Kendra looked on in shock but she was delighted King showed up when he did. "You are my hero, King. I could never repay you for this." She looked down on Joe's body and spat in his face. "He was my next victim anyways, sorry piece of shit." She tried to get up from the bed.

"Here." King grabbed the sheet off the bed and threw it to Kendra to cover her body. Kendra was rubbing her neck, breathing hard.

"What brings you here, King?" She whispered, still gasping for air.

"Look ma, true talk, I'm not here to play with you. The same people you want me to rob, they want me to kill you." King removed the blunt from his Akoo sweatshirt and lit it.

"How much are they offering to pay you? Because I can double that and tell you where he keeps his product, that's worth millions." King took all this in.

"I'm listening," King told her, inhaling the kush.

"It's like this King, true talk. I have two hundred stacks right now, if you walk outta here and leave me alive.

"Show me the paper, ma. Money talks, bullshit walks. You know what it is, money over everything." He puffed the blunt again.

"How do I know you won't kill me when you get the paper?" She inquired, puzzled, and her face confirmed it.

"You will have to take my word. You are in no position to

question me about anything. Now you can either take this chance, or give me the paper or not; either way, you're taking a chance on your life. Kandi, you know a nigga' ain't never hard up for no paper, but I have no problem adding more to what I have." He summed up seriously. "It's your call, what will it be, Kandi-land?

The house was dark except for the light on in the bathroom. King walked over to the cherry oak dresser and lit the candle. He then walked to the bathroom and turned the light off. Kendra was still sitting on the bed in unfathomable thought.

"What you gon' do, ma? I don't have all night. Shit, I wasted most of my fuckin' day."

"I have to go get the money." Kendra confirmed.

"I hope it's in this house." King walked over to Kendra putting the gun to her head. "Don't fuckin' try to play on my intelligence, ma. I'm not the one. You don't have long, so let's get it." Kendra was scared shitless, but she tried to play it calm. "So where is the paper?"

"In my basement." She verified honestly. King pointed the gun at her.

"We can both go down there and get the paper, but if you try anything, that's your ass." King kept the gun pointed at her.

The basement was very well organized. There were two small bedrooms, a bathroom, a lounge area with a bar and a laundry room. King had to admit, Kendra's décor was stunning. "Would you like a drink?" Kendra asked when they were at the bottom of the stairs.

"Not at this moment, maybe later." He kept the gun positioned on her. "What room is the paper in?"

"It's in the laundry room." She began to walk and King followed. When they arrived in the laundry room, Kendra removed the tile and there was a deep hole leading to the floor. She grabbed the gigantic laundry bag. "I need help with this King." Kendra told him, trying to find a way out of this situation.

"Kandi, I'm telling you, if you trip, you dead." He looked her straight in the eyes, cocking the gun.

"Okay, King," Kendra was past frustrated. "Just help me please, so I can get this over with." She rolled her eyes in the air.

"How much is in here?" King wanted to know.

"It two hundred stacks, like I promised."

"Kandi, true talk, ma, you mean to tell me, that you're willing to give me all of your paper." He still had the gun pointed on her.

"I have to do whatever to save my life at this point. I can make more money, but I can't get my life back, King. I know how you get down, so yes it is." She concluded.

King looked at Kendra and made her think that he believed her, but in the back of his mind, he hoped that Kendra didn't take him for a fool. He knew money was this girl's motive and she would do anything to get it. However, he also knew there was more money than she was admitting and before he left her house, he would have it all.

"So Kandi, I'm only gonna ask you this once more. Is there anymore paper in this house?" He questioned, more serious than before.

"No, you have it all."

"That's your word?"

"Yes, that's my word." She validated. King looked at her and instructed her to move in the lounge area of the basement.

"We gon' count this paper and you betta hope it's all there." He demanded.

It seemed to have taken forever to count the money but the task was completed. Kendra relaxed more knowing that she had come through. "So what now?" She wanted to get this over with.

"I'm going to tie you up to this chair while I search the house and then at that time, if nothin' magical appears, I'm outta here and you keep your life. Maybe." He analyzed. Kendra had a funny expression on her face and King noticed. He went on to investigate the mission at hand.

39. Secrets!

The baseball game was over and the Cardinals lost. T-Money, Mr. John, Jabari and Henry decided to go to Mike Shannon's bar downtown for drinks. The ladies declined and called it a night. But before Jabari could join the fellows he had to take Glitter home and since he was playing taxi, he volunteered to drive all the ladies home and meet back up with the guys after.

Frances sat in the backseat with Sya. She informed her daughter before they left the stadium that she didn't mind taking a cab home, and felt that Sya should too. Sya knew this wasn't a good gesture, but she wanted to be in the presence of Jabari. The ride was silent, except for the music playing in the background. Frances and Sya had a quiet conversation where only they could hear each other.

"Baby, don't do anything that you will regret in the morning, or cause you to lose focus of what's important and best for you." She whispered, realizing where this relationship was heading with her daughter and this mystery man. "I know you're grown but I'm telling you what I know." Frances explained to her daughter.

"I know, Ma. I know there are consequences for your actions and I'm preparing for every action I take, depending on the decisions I choose to make. You taught me well and you definitely didn't raise a fool. Do know I appreciate everything you instilled in me." Sya updated her mom before she got out of the vehicle.

"Thanks so much, young man, for driving me home. Here, will you take this gas money for your troubles?" She removed a twenty dollar bill from her wallet.

"No ma'am, I can't accept that. It wasn't a problem at all, but thank you." Jabari was pleasant.

"Very well, and thank you so much. You guys be safe and Hunny Bun, call when you make it home, I love you." Frances told her, Sya knowing what her mother meant. They made sure Frances got in the house before pulling away.

After dropping off Frances, Jabari removed a blunt from the astray and fired it up. "Cousin, when you start smoking that stuff?" Glitter was surprised to see her cousin smoking anything.

"I smoke every now and again, you know, when I'm stressed." He answered puffing harder on the blunt. "Here Sya, you want to hit this?" He passed it.

"Sure, why not," She took the blunt from his hand, singing alone with Tyrese's, "Stay." "That Open Invitation CD is fire," Sya told Glitter feeling the effect of the weed.

"Yes, it is nice," she dryly responded. As she got out of the car, she gave Jabari a look that let him know that she wasn't pleased with his choices, and he knew exactly what they were.

"I'll call you later, cousin." He told her to ease her mind.

"Yeah, all right." She threw at him. "Sya, I'll see you in the morning. You guys have a good night." Before she closed the door, she asked Sya, "Are you coming up front?" Sya didn't say anything, she immediately moved up front wondering why Glitter's attitude was stank.

****

T-Money called King to see had he completed the job. His calls continued to go to voicemail. After several calls, T-Money figured he would get back with him; it was nothing for him to worry about. King was dependable and he constantly came through for him, always. However, T-Money was enjoying himself with Mr. John. He couldn't wait to enlighten him on all the events that had taken places since he hadn't been around; including the incident with Damon. If he couldn't trust anyone, he knew without a doubt or question, that he could trust Mr. John.

Henry was on the other side of the bar mingling with some of his buddies from the store. This left more time for Mr. John and T to catch up on each other's' life.

"T-Money," Mr. John said. "You still carrying that name, and from what I hear, it's working for you." He stated like a proud father.

"You know how I do. I learned from the best. Yes, I took everything you taught me and used it to the best of my ability. Now I'm working with a million dollar plus company, with the help of my lady." T affirmed proudly.

"I knew I wouldn't go wrong, when I handpicked you to jump on ship with me. I'm happy that you are doing well for yourself, young Money. I also heard that Damon was missing. How are you handling that situation?" Mr. John waited for a reply but really knew what happen deep inside. He knew how grimy Damon was.

What a lot of people didn't know is that Damon was Mr. John's son. When Damon was conceived he did everything in his power to help Damon remove his wicked ways. Mr. John witnessed his evil ways and actions as he grew up. Even though he was a child from a one night stand, Mr. John always tried to be a part of his life. He supported him financially, but Damon's mother was a crack whore, so he never got to see the money. His mom did disclose who his father was, when she was in a drinking rage. Mr. John used to always ask himself, *how you could deny your own blood,* but the love he had for Marquita Wright wouldn't allow him to acknowledge his seed. This has been a secret that he's carried for years.

The day Mr. John decided to reveal this revelation, Marquita passed. He couldn't let her leave this world knowing that he'd cheating on her and she had been nothing but good to him. Before she became sick, she lost the two people who were near and dear to her, Linda and Mia, her sisters from another mother. The women did everything together, even raised their daughters, Ressie, Libra and Mya as sisters. Then at that time Mr. John had took on the role of being the girls' father after the hideous murders of their mothers. He and Marquita had invested time and money into a profitable business and he just couldn't risk it all. He knew she would leave him in a heartbeat. She's the reason he's millionaire status now.

"Mr. J, I did everything I could to help Damon. He fucked a lot of people from state to state. I paid hella debt off for him. I had price tags removed from his head, on more than one occasion. My dudes Gemini and Lorenzo wouldn't fuck with him at all. After they found out he was doing business with Caelin, the grimiest nigga in the STL, they totally backed off from the proposition I offered them; and it was healthy and sweet as hell too. We all woulda benefited from it tremendously." T gave Mr. John the rundown on the entire situation.

"Wowser," Mr. John replied before they were interrupted.

Lorenzo, Gemini and KeKe walked over and greeted T-Money. "Man, this is a small ass world, what's good with it, fam?" T asked giving all three fellows some dap and manly hugs. "Long time no see. I haven't seen you niggas in hellas." T was happy to see them. They greeted Mr. John. It had been years, since either of them had seen him as well.

"Man, what about those Cardinals?" Lorenzo asked rocking his Cardinals gear.

"Shit, Texas." KeKe cracked his joke. "Man we gon' have to get together and put some things in motion, like soon." KeKe finished. "Mr. John, you have to come over to the house and see the kids." Keke told him.

"We don't have kids anymore. They are grown folks." Gemini chimed in. "I tell you what, if the Cardinals win, you know we gon' tear this city up, so make sure the both of y'all keep in touch." Gemini informed him.

"Will do," T excitedly expressed. "Damn KeKe, man, I'm glad to see you surfacing around this muthafucka. You were claimed as dead some years back, but then I heard you were more alive than me. I didn't believe it until I saw you at your wife's concert. I'm glad to see you guys doing well." He concluded. Some years back KeKe was presumed dead, he faked his death to protect his family. They all were Still Ghetto.

"Like old times." Mr. John felt elated and the fellows went on about their business.

****

King searched the entire house, beginning with the basement and every room it occupied, to find nothing. He then proceeded upstairs and hit the jackpot. Kendra had a secret compartment hid in her closet. It was a fake shoe box built in the floor of her closet. Kendra was still in the basement tied to a chair. She was sweating bullets. She knew that King was a man of his word and if he felt he was being bamboozled, it was lights out for the perpetrator. Before he went back downstairs to the basement, he turned the music up loudly.

"Kandi, I told you not to fuck with me, didn't I?" He roughly grabbed her by the neck, where the spikes had embedded their marks.

"King, what are you talking about?' She faked the dumb role.

"Look bitch, don't do me. This is not the time to be cute. Your fuckin' life is on the line and you wanna play with me?" He was mad at this point, spitting in her face. "I gave you more than enough time to come clean with me, now you lose your life and your life savings." He pointed the gun at her head.

"Wait a minute," she pleaded. "I know it's something we can do to make this situation not end so ugly." Her eyes were begging for help.

"Speak, and you better say the right thing."

"Well Sya, T-Money's girlfriend, I know where she keeps all her paper at. I know she's millionaire status without a doubt." She revealed.

"What the fuck does that have to do with me, you stupid bitch? You have no loyalty, none what-so-ever." He shot her in the hand.

"Ouch!" she yelled in pain. "What the fuck you do that for?

I was trying to put your dumb ass on."

"Bitch, I know you don't want to keep running your pussy suckers. The next bullet I release will be down yo' fuckin' throat." She saw the sincerity in his face and tone.

"Well, can I tell you this one last thing?" She posed, trying to carefully articulate her next words.

"Make it worthwhile." King lit another blunt and took it to the head.

"Tell T, while he worried about my loyalty, he needs to watch his bitch and his friend Jabari. They are the ones who have the loyalty issues, not me. And King, I know you gonna kill me, but let T know that I know, he had something to do with Damon's disappearance. Oh and by the way, that's was T's girlfriend's father that you killed upstairs. Now suck my pussy bitch." And those were her last words. King released two bullets in her head and just for good measure one in her vagina.

"Bitch, you won't be able to rap about anybody else." He poured the gasoline on and around Kendra's body. He also poured it all over the basement. He then went back upstairs and poured the gas on Joseph's body and around the bed. After, he went to the top of the basement stairs, lit the match, threw it down the steps, lit another one and threw it on the bed and exited the back door, with an undisclosed amount of money.

He shouldn't have been at the wrong place at the wrong time. You see where pussy gets you? He thought on his way to the car.

40. Live, Love and Laugh!

"So, do you think I can taste you tonight?" Jabari looked at Sya in between keeping his eyes on the road. "It's not like we'll be missed. It's just us." He so badly wanted to release his snake and tongue inside of Sya. Sya stared ahead never gave Jabari eye contact. She finally found the words to express what she was feeling.

"Look, Jabari," she took a deep breath. "You know just as well as I do, that I'm attracted to you in more ways than one, it's unbelievable. But right now, I'm torn between what I want and what I need or if I should or if I shouldn't. I'm in a very compromising position right now and I'm not sure if I want to deal with the consequences when and if this shit ever hit the fan." She was being completely honest at this point. "I dig the shit out of you, no doubt, but my loyalty is to my man, Raheem. I'm sorry if I led you on in any way. Only I'm held accountable for my actions and you acted off of my energy." She gave it to him pure from her heart but he ignited a flame in her only he could put out. By this time Jabari was approaching the front of her home. Before she could say another word, he'd leaned over and gave her a passionate kiss, something she couldn't resist.

The kiss became too intense and Sya got beside herself. She welcomed this man without realizing that she was doing exactly what she said she wouldn't do, give in to him. By this time Jabari reached inside her jacket, fondling her breasts. Sya's body was screaming yes but her mind was yelling no! She let her body overrule the right thing to do and released herself to this man. One thing led to another, and she ended with one leg out of her pants and him eating her as if he was at Gladys and Ron's Restaurant, where the food is firah! She was on the edge of losing herself.

Sya was so into what Jabari was doing to her that she hadn't noticed the black on black Challenger parked across the street. However she would rise up from time to time making sure T wasn't anywhere in sight. This could have gotten ugly if that was to happen. Sya reclined the seat and came completely out of her pants. Jabari's penis was harder than the metal made to build the St. Louis Gateway Arch. He was overly excited to enter Sya and did so without a condom. For them to have been in the car, this was the best feeling she had ever felt.

"You like it, baby?" Jabari continued to stroke her slowly but deep.

"Yes, I love everything about it, Bari." Her eyes rolled to the back of her head.

Sya and Jabari made love in the truck for the next twenty five minutes until they were interrupted by a call from T-Money.

"Hi babe, what you doing?" He asked in a good mood.

"Hey babe," she hesitated. "I'm not doing anything, trying to wait on you to come home before I fall asleep."

"Why do you sound like you're out of breath?"

"Oh nothing, just getting my work out on." She laughed slightly, while Jabari continued to eat her out.

"Well babe, you don't have to wait up for me. I'm still waiting on Jabari to come back and plus I just ran into a few old friends of mine. I'll be home shortly and make sure you set the alarm, okay?" He told her.

"Okay babe."

"I love you, babe." T-Money made a kissing sound through the phone.

"I love you back." She whispered while she hung up the phone, as if Jabari couldn't hear her.

Their conversation didn't deter Jabari; he didn't miss a lick. "Jabari, wait a minute. We need a condom, we can't continue like this." She insisted.

"But baby, we already have." He looked saddened.

"No condom, no more ass." She interjected gathering her clothes.

"So you just gonna leave him like this?" Jabari pointed to his rock hard penis.

"Just like that without a hat." She was serious.

"What if I run to the gas station and get some?" He was adamant about making love to her.

"If I get out of this car, it's a wrap." She told him and her phone began to ring again. Looking at the caller ID it was her mom and she knew it was a sign to discontinue her act of disloyalty.

"I have to go, this is my mother," she put her pants back on. Sya got out of the truck, disarming her alarm system from her key ring. Jabari had dissatisfaction written all over his face.

Jabari rolled down the window and told her, "You only live once, so let's live, love and laugh." With that said, he pulled off leaving Sya to her thoughts and she noticed the black on black

Challenger across the street as well as another unfamiliar car parked further down the street. However, she didn't see anyone inside the cars, so she figured it could have been company for her neighbors.

41. We Like to Party!

The Cardinals went out of town, kicked their opponent's ass and came back home to become Champions. The Lou was on lock and major money was ready to be spent. New contracts were in the air to be signed for the players and it was talk around town that Tony La'Russa was thinking about retiring as manager.

T-Money was elated to know that King took care of Kendra, but he didn't know how he would explain to Sya that her father was amongst Kendra when the murders took place. In addition to that, he was the person who requested the order. He knew how she felt about Joseph, but damn, she didn't wish death on him. That was an issue he would deal with when the time was right.

****

T-Money, Sya, Glitter, Bunnee, King and Jabari were partying at Me'Shon's Restaurant and Lounge on Tucker Blvd in downtown St. Louis, getting their party on. Frances and Henry, along with Mr. John came out. Beyonce's song "Party" roared through the speakers, rocking the lounge. Sya had been avoiding Jabari since the episode they encountered and this was the first time they had seen one another since that happen. She didn't want to talk to him, nor be in his presence. She'd already witnessed what could happen when they were alone. The guilt ate away at her and she couldn't perform for Raheem the way she used to because of the thoughts about Jabari that were implanted inside of her body and mind.

Sya was all over T-Money, letting Jabari and every woman in the place know that he belongs to her and only her. Frances noticed her daughter's actions and confronted her about them at once. She knew that Sya wasn't an insecure individual. If she taught her nothing else she rooted self-confidence in her, so she knew this had everything to do with Jabari.

"Hunny Bun, are you feeling okay?" She gave a stern, but concerned look.

"I'm fine Ma, why do you ask?" Sya cut her eyes over at Jabari speaking with a female that was drooling all over him.

"Right there is why I'm asking," Frances cut her eyes in Jabari's direction. "If I can detect this behavior in you, I'm almost sure that your man can. Come on child, you have to pull yourself together or you're going to lose your man. You got it bad for this Jabari character, don't you?"

"Ma, I'm going to get it together. I'm just going to confess to Raheem about what happened the other night between Jabari and me. That way my mind will be clear and free of this nonsense. This shit, I mean, stuff, is eating me up on the inside." She guiltily confessed.

Frances looked at her child and immediately knew she had to step in.

"Child, if I taught you nothing else, I taught you to never tell on yourself. When I said get it together, I didn't mean tell on yourself, I just simply meant get you together. You are all over the place." She had a puzzled expression on her face.

"I know Ma, but-." She tried to expound.

"There are no buts. What he doesn't know won't hurt him; never let him find out. Now, let's have fun." Frances ended.

"You're right." Sya kissed her mom on the cheek.

The night was in full effect and the party was jumping, almost coming to an end. That didn't mean that the night was over for the crew. Bunnee was determined, if nothing else, to have Jabari make love to her. After what she discovered the other night in front of Sya's house, she clearly understood why Sya was acting the way she had, and Jabari not making love to her. Bunnee seductively rubbed her ass against Jabari's penis. She could tell he was enjoying it. He wrapped his hands around her waist and moved his body in the same direction. Usher's single, "Climax," screamed through the speakers and he held her tighter. He entrenched in his brain that he was holding Sya. The fresh scent of Guess perfume raped his nostrils, the same perfume Sya had on the other night.

Bunnee held fixed to his embrace. "Are you going home with me tonight?" Bunnee spoke softly, kissing Jabari on the neck, making small circles with her tongue.

"Without a doubt, lil' mama, if you will have me." He was totally engrossed.

"What are we still doing here? Why don't we just leave?" Bunnee continued to persuade him to leave. Jabari wasn't thinking correctly. He just wanted to release the build-up nut he didn't discharge the other night with Sya.

"Let's bounce." He kissed her on the cheek and escorted her from the dance floor. Sya monitored the activity that was being exchanged between the two and didn't like it, at all. But, she couldn't do anything about it; absolutely nothing.

T-Money held Sya extra tight, whispering in her ear. "Babe, I'm never letting you go. I want you to stay with me the rest of my life." He told her. T-Money released his grip from Sya and turned her around. She read the dark orange neon light. She became absolutely speechless.

"WILL YOU MARRY ME SYA?" Was displayed on the back wall, along with two posters that were separated. One that said yes, and the other that said no for everyone in the lounge to see. He then grabbed her hand and displayed an ornate ten carat diamond ring. She held her hand over her mouth, and her eyes sparkled with falling tears, while she admired the ring he slid it on her finger.

"Babe, you for real? For real, for real?" She asked him again.

"Absolutely for real. I've never been so serious about anything, but this here is the truth. Now what do you say? Yes or no? Go stand in front of your decision on the wall." He pushed Sya to the wall. As she walked to the wall, Jabari took over her thoughts. She swiftly discarded the thought and looked at her ring again. After seeing him and Bunnee together, she knew that they could never be. The other night was a mistake and she had no intentions on ever letting that happen again.

Fuck it, I'm marrying Raheem, he's the best I ever had, shit he's the only thing I ever had, she thought. She heard the crowd yelling, "Say yes, say yes, say yes!"

She played around with the crowd and T-Money by standing in the middle of both answers, then moving closer to no. After teasing a while longer and locking eyes with Jabari, she stood proudly in front of yes.

"She said yes! Babe, that's what's up. I promise I will make you happy." He lifted her in the air, swinging her around, kissing her passionately.

"I know you will, babe, or you better hustle trying." She kissed him letting her tongue slide in between his soft juicy lips.

The best cigars were dispensed amongst the crowd of men and the bottles popped throughout the entire lounge as Wacka Flacka's voice rapping: "it's a party, it's a party, it's a party," echoed throughout the place. The dance floor became overcrowded with bottles popping and champagne splashing everywhere. They were getting congratulations from everyone.

"Sya, I'm happy for you." Bunnee hugged her.

"Make sure this is the right thing to do. You can't go into a marriage with secrets." Glitter whispered in her ear. She knew how Jabari felt about Sya. He and Glitter were close and he'd revealed his true feeling about Sya to her. He trusted her and she didn't want her cousin hurt.

"I understand, Glitter." Sya knew what she was speaking about.

Jabari walked up to both her and T-Money and hugged them both. "Congrats man, congrats Sya. It couldn't happen to a better set of people." Jabari expressed and informed them that he and Bunnee were leaving. They said their goodbyes and the party continued.

King finally made his approach and he gave Sya a look of death. She didn't know what that was about but decided to pay it no mind at this point, but would most definitely keep a watchful eye out for him.

42. Good Old Days!

After the big announcement of Sya and T-Money's engagement, Frances immediately went to planning the wedding of the century. She wanted her baby to have the wedding she'd never forget. She would go all out. Frances remembered the day she and Joseph got married. The only thing they could afford at the time was to go downtown to the Justice of Peace. She also wondered if Sya would have Joseph walk her down the aisle to give her away, but why would she do that? She thought. She would let that be her decision. She didn't want to do anything to ruin her baby's day. Thinking back to how Joseph showed up at her graduation years ago and things didn't pan out well, she definitely wouldn't allow that to happen again. She made a mental note to speak with Sya about that.

****

The grand opening for A Mother's Love was due to open in two days. Everything was perfect and Frances knew it would be a success. Henry walked in the living room, breaking her thoughts.

"What are you doing, dear?" He kissed her on the cheek sitting next to her on the sofa.

"Nothing much, just thinking about all the planning I have to do for my baby's wedding." She rested her leg across his leg.

"This wedding has you excited." He reached over and pulled her closer to him.

"Yes it does. I'm so happy and proud of Sya. She has bumped into a lot of rough times in life, and through it all, she has accomplished so much. She eluded letting anything or anybody hinder her from her goals and dreams in life.

"That's so true baby, but let's not forget, that you are a vast part of her success. If it wasn't for you pushing her and trying to make a better life for the both of you, where do you think she would have found the strength and courage to go on? Especially after her father walked out of her life." He massaged Frances's legs.

"Thank you, baby. You always have the right words to say. I love you and don't you forget that." She hugged him tightly.

Sya was on the phone wrapping up the last minute arrangements for the grand opening when T-Money walked in. He positioned himself beside her and began nibbling on her ear. "Raheem, cut it out. You know I have to finish taking care of this." She moved away from him. He didn't pay her any attention and continued.

"Boy, you play too much." She smiled covering up the phone with her hand.

"You can't tell me what to do to you. You belong to me." He grabbed her, situated her on his lap where his penis stood at attention.

"Let me get done with this first, okay?" She went back to speaking on the phone. He paid her no mind and lifted her gown, rubbing her naked ass, then fingering her. She couldn't concentrate at this point. "Can I please call you back, Mimi?" Sya asked the event planner on the other end of the phone, then hung up before she could respond. Raheem then carefully laid her down on the plush carpet and cautiously inserted himself inside her heated opening. "Babe," she gasps deeply. "I love everything you're doing to me." Her eyes closed tightly.

"I love doing everything to you." He pushed his tongue with awareness inside of her waiting mouth.

"Don't you ever stop." She told him sucking his tongue passionately.

"I don't plan to." Their bodies sang a melody together. This is the one time she didn't think about Jabari. She wanted the good times she and T-Money shared back. The best sex she ever had; really the only sex she ever had.

Bunnee was in route to meet a friend of hers. She hadn't spoken with her friend in years until the saw each other recently. Coincidently, she ran into her friend a few months back and they kept in touch, meeting for lunch and dinner on a regular. She hadn't realized how much she'd miss her friend until they started hanging out again, like the good old days. Back in the day, they were like Bonnie and Clyde and nothing or no one could deter them from one another. They shared mostly everything together until one day, her friend disappeared and her mother moved her to Springfield, Missouri with her grandmother. She hadn't heard or saw her friend in years. Now that they were back united she would never lose contact again.

"Hey Antonio," Bunnee greeted her friend with a hug.

"What it do, ma?" He hugged her tighter, checking her out from head to toe, admiring the H&M fitted top shirt with flared sleeves and skinny jeans. He also loved a woman in heels. "And by the way, stop calling me by my government name." He took a seat.

"Boy, I've been calling you by your real name from day one and now you want me to stop? I refuse to call you King. You are not my King and where in the hell did you get that crazy ass name from anyways?" They both laughed.

"You know the streets have a way of linking you with things that are good and not so good. But anyways, how you?"

"Fabulous, as you can see, and I can do better with a glass of wine." They smiled at each other.

"Wine it is," King humbly stated, waving the waitress over to the table. The waitress walked over with pen and paper in hand.

"Can I start you off with something to drink?" The dingy, blue eyed white girl asked.

"A glass of wine for the lady and a shot of peach Ciroc for me. Straight, no chaser." He concluded.

"Coming right up." She said walking away. Bunnee and King sat there for hours talking about old times and enjoying each other's company like they used to do when they were younger.

The few months that King and Bunnee had been back in contact, he shared things with her that could deter some friendships as well as tear some homes apart. He knew without a doubt that he could trust her and their conversation wouldn't go any further. Bunnee even knew about the murders of Kendra and Joseph, as well as Sya and Jabari's secret relationship. She wondered how Sya could do this to her, knowing how much she valued their friendship; not to mention T-Money and the love he had for her. In Bunnee's own little way, she wanted what Sya and T-Money had and figured she could find that in Jabari, but Sya had to have him too.

"B, remember the time when we use to go to the Orange store on the corner of College and Prairie Street and you would be my lookout and I would steal us all candy and the next day we would sell it at school and make a huge profit?" He laughed, knowing she didn't want to do it but she couldn't and wouldn't tell him no.

"How can I forget? You always had me doing things I didn't want to do." She laughed. Bunnee then removed the smile from her face and became serious. "Antonio, I can never forget what you did for me that day. I guess that's why I love you so much and I'm forever grateful to you." A tear trickled down her cheek.

"B, don't do that. I woulda did that for anybody in your predicament that night. I would not have done a muthafuckin' thing differently. I'm just glad it was you, because you have never betrayed me from that day, up until now. That's why I love you. You see, muthafuckas don't know the meaning of loyalty this day and age, but we still have some riders." He reached across the table and wiped the tear from her cheek. Bunnee's mind wondered back to that dreadful night.

Bunnee was walking home from the store. It was raining and thundering something terrible. She took the short cut through the alley to get to her house faster. There weren't any lights in the alley but she knew her way perfectly. She had taken this route many times before. There were always drunks and dope fiends parading up and down the alley way, but Bunnee felt safe enough to venture through. Bunnee was about four houses down from her home when a man came out of nowhere and snatched her from the back. She screamed, kicked and scratched, but she wasn't a match for the two hundred-plus pound man.

He pulled at her blouse and ripped it to pieces. He then reached for her skirt and tried to remove it. Bunnee was fighting for her young life. She spat in the man's face and that angered him. He slapped her in the face forcefully and held a knife to her neck.

"Bitch, if you move again, I will slice your fuckin' throat," the man threatened. Bunnee was so frightened she peed herself. He then pushed her down to the ground, slashed her panties and moved them to the side forcing her legs open. She couldn't do anything but pray and ask God to save her. The man released his manhood from his pants and roughly entered her young cookie. Bunnee screamed at the top of her lungs as the man pressed harder into her. The pain was horrendous and tears raced down her cheeks. The man tried to go deeper inside of her but fell flat on his face. Bunnee had specks of red blood on her face. The rain washed the red to pink and she moved as quickly as possible to get from underneath him. She saw the knife sticking out the back of the man's neck and ran.

King quickly took off after her. She was totally frightened by King and she threw a few punches at him. "Wait a minute; I'm not gonna hurt you. I'm tryin' make sure you're okay" He grabbed both her wrists.

"Leave me alone!" She yelled still trying to fight him.

"Hey," King yelled shaking her. "Here, take this and cover yourself up." He gave her his jacket, wrapping it around her waist. Once Bunnee noticed that King had saved her, she calmed down some. "Where do you live?" He asked walking down the dark alley with her. She pointed forward. "I'm gonna make sure you get home safely, okay?"

"Okay," was all she said? When they reached her back door

Bunnee told King, "Thank you," barely above a whisper.

"I'll see you around, okay? And don't be walking through dark alleys anymore by yourself." He told her, chastising her as if she was his kid.

Bunnee snapped out of the thought when King put his hand in front of her face, bringing her back to the future. "You all right, ma?"

"I'm good." She came back. "What you having?" She asked with both of them revisiting the menu.

"B, I've been meaning to ask you, whatever happened to that gun you took from me that night?" He looked her straight in the eyes.

"Let's just say, it's long gone. I took it to Springfield with me and did away with it." She smiled. "You saved my life so I had to return the favor." She threw back at him, looking over the menu.

"I'm really not a bad person; I had to do what I had to do to survive." He gripped her hand.

"I know you're not. You saved me and I saved you. That's how we do and I would do it again if I had to." She meant every word.

"I will never put you in a situation like that ever again. I love you and you play a very important part in my life. Now that you know Jabari don't mean you any good, will you give me a chance?" King snickered uneasily.

"Let's not go there. I wouldn't do anything to fuck up our friendship." Bunnee was serious. "Let's talk about something else, now what do you want to eat?" She waved for the waitress.

"You." King answered with a straight face letting Bunnee know he was dead serious. While Bunnee took in King's look, the waitress appeared.

43. Grand Opening!

Today is the grand opening of A Mother's Love and the place was packed. The food was delicious, the champagne fountain was flowing and the music was off the chain. The entertainment was even better. Libra and Essence was in the house, gracing the place with their beautiful voices, as well as Chance, Shakira, Ty, Miracle and Denise modeling the clothing line of Sista' Sista' and Brotha' Brotha' Original. They invited a few of St. Louis authors to promote their novels. The author of "Ghetto Luv," and the sequel "Still Ghetto" was endorsing her books, including the anthology Tales from the Lou, she participated in with other authors from St. Louis.

"Sya, you did a fantastic job putting this together." Frances hugged her daughter. "I could not have done any of this without your help. I want you to know that I appreciate you so much." Frances eyes became shiny from tears.

"Awww, Ma, don't cry. Everything that you have done for me, this is the least I could do to help you. What do you mean; you could not have done this without me. Where do you think I've learned all that I have?" She hugged her mother. "You, my darling, and by the way, you look amazing."

"Why thank you, Hunny Bun." Frances answered back looking like a black Marilyn Monroe, wearing a long black dress, with a plunging neckline, displaying much cleavage. "Now go ahead and mingle with the guests, we will have plenty of time to talk. We have a huge wedding to plan." She kissed her again.

"You're the parent." She told her walking away, smiling.

T-Money walked up from behind Sya kissing her on the neck. "Hey, Mrs. Ivy, you look nice." He admired the short dark blue fitted mini dress, and two-toned stilettos with silver studs on the buckle. The thick silver necklace graced her neckline, while the ten carat engagement ring blessed her finger. The bone-straight hairdo complimented her face well, with little makeup, she had unblemished skin.

"Why thank you, Mr. Ivy. You look and smell fabulous also." She kissed him on the lips. They were walking over to the champagne fountain when Henry's voice blurred through the microphone.

"Excuse me, everyone. On behalf of my lady, daughter and I, we want to thank everyone for coming out and celebrating the opening of our new store. I hope we can continue to serve our community as we have in the past. Please enjoy yourself and don't forget to purchase something." He wrapped up and the room erupted in laughter.

Libra and Essence gave a stunning performance rocking Essence's clothing line Sista' Sista' Original. Before they left the stage they sang a song to Frances from Henry. Their voices tied in unison,

"Frances, will you marry Henry?" Frances didn't know what to say. She thought her ears were playing tricks on her. Frances gave the same expression as her daughter on the night T-Money proposed to her. She put one hand over her mouth in total shock.

"He's waiting on your answer." Libra sang to Frances. All the attention was on Frances at this point. She looked around the room, tears falling from her eyes, shaking her head up and down.

"Is that a yes?" Essence sang.

"Yes!" she yelled across the room. Everyone begin to clap. Champagne was given out to the partygoers to help celebrate this special moment. Sya ran over to her mother and hugged her and Henry extra tight, more elated than Frances was.

"Henry, why didn't you tell me about this?" She lightly punched him on the arm.

"I didn't think you could keep a secret, but I did share this with Raheem." He responded calmly.

"Ain't that something, and I'm your daughter." She pouted playful.

"You are my daughter, but I wanted to see the reaction from you as well. Raheem, helped me plan this." He confessed.

"Is that supposed to make me feel any better?" She rolled her eyes at both Raheem and Henry.

"I wanted to surprise both you ladies, because I had this grand idea that we could have a double wedding. How does that sound?" He spoke in a composed but happy tone.

"I love the idea." She hugged them again and then hugged T-Money. "You sly dog, you." She kissed him overpoweringly.

Jabari and Bunnee were there hand-in-hand, putting on a façade like they were in love. Bunnee noticed the look Sya gave Jabari when they entered. Sya grew moist between the legs, approving the black tuxedo Jabari had on. He looked elegant. His dreads were in order and he was lined up perfectly. Bunnee, on the other hand, wore a matching dress with a wild "22" inch ponytail. Both of their gear game was on point. Bunnee and Sya air kissed each other and hugged.

"You look absolutely gorgeous, hun." Sya admitted truthfully.

"You look even better, mami." Bunnee replied. "This store is nice." She looked around taking note of what she would purchase.

"Thank you, now come on and let's get you something to drink with some kick to it. We have a lot of celebrating to do." Sya chuckled trying to avoid Jabari and the embrace she knew that he would give her if he caught her alone. She didn't know if she could handle it at this time. The peach Ciroc was all the kick Sya needed.

Jabari waited on the proper time to approach Sya. He waited until T-Money was occupied with Mr. John and his buddies from way back then. Glitter couldn't have come at a better time. She kept Bunnee busy while he gave Sya the third degree.

"You look mouthwatering." He whispered in her ear, catching her off guard.

"You look handsome too, fellow." She laughed nervously, looking around.

"Why haven't I heard from you? I know you been getting my text messages." He seemed visible upset.

"Just in case you haven't noticed, I am engaged." She displayed her ring, shaking it in his face.

"I don't give a damn about that ring. All I know is that I have fallen in love with you and you're all I think about. What am I supposed to do?" He was emotional.

"I don't know what you gonna do but I'm getting married and that's that." She unemotionally expressed walking away.

What they didn't know was that King was watching them from afar. He wasn't going to allow Sya to play his boy. T-Money and him had been through it all and by any means necessary if he thought anybody was out to hurt him, he would react. In time he would reveal Jabari's and Sya's disloyalty to T-Money and they would decide how they would handle it at that time with the help of Bunnee.

The grand opening was profitable. The cash registers were ringing and the clothes were flying off the racks. The cause had served its purpose and that was to make money, in which they did. They all partied until the break of dawn.

44. Confessions

Sya and Frances were thrilled about the turn out of the grand opening. This was one of the best business moves they could have made. "Hunny Bun, do you know I had to put in another order for the Sista' Sista' and Brotha' Brotha' Originals already? Those clothes are disappearing off the racks." Her voice sounded pleased over the telephone.

"Ma, that's what's up. I knew we were going to do well. That's why I worked so hard to get Libra and Essence there, so they could represent their merchandise. And they did it well." Her voice was filled with pleasure.

"Indeed, Hunny, they did. Sya, I would like to get together sometime this week so we can go over some things. We have a double wedding to plan and there is nothing easy about this, but I have something that needs my attention immediately." She paused.

"What's that, Ma?" Sya had uneasiness in her tone.

"Hunny Bun, did you know your father and I are still married?

"Yes ma'am, I knew that and I wanted to talk to you about that. I know a well-known attorney that will handle this diligently. She is the best. It would be over with before you know it."

"Can we make an appointment really soon, like tomorrow?" Frances grew excited.

"I will contact her as soon as we get off the phone. Rhonda is the best and she gets the job done."

"Great baby, call me back and let me know what she says. That's been bothering me for quite some time now." Frances felt relieved. "Love you." Frances told her daughter.

"I love you too, Ma. Talk to you later."

****

T-Money and Mr. John scheduled a meeting at the office to go over some things. Mr. John wanted T-Money to handle some things for him while he was out of town. Also he wanted to share something with him. They were sitting at the round table looking at the flat panel, when breaking news interrupted the program.

The reporter, April Simpson, was poised, as she began the tragic news. "Here I stand in front of a burned down house. It was reported weeks ago that a fire was started but at that time no one was inside. Well there was an investigation and two bodies were found. One is believed to be a male and the other a female. At this time names have not been revealed but we will keep you posted." April Simpson signed off.

"That's Kendra's crib," T-Money enlightened Mr. John.

"Young Money, I don't mean to sound insensitive or anything, but I need to tell you something that has been bothering me for a long while now." He injected cautiously, not caring what was going on, on the television screen.

"What's up, Mr. J?" T showed great concern giving him his undivided attention.

"I know you have an idea about who took Damon out." Mr. John raised an eyebrow.

"Why do you say that?" T remained calm.

"I know that Damon was a manipulative little piece of shit and he didn't give a damn about anybody but himself, not even his own mother, but he was my son." Mr. John finally released the secret he'd been holding in for so many years. He let it marinate before he went on. He felt relieved.

T-Money had a surprised look on his face. He didn't know what to say. He didn't want to lie to Mr. John about Damon's death, but how could he tell Mr. John that Bunnee and Sya killed his kid; and to make matters worse, he will never get to see the body. Damn, this was bad news in T-Money's eyes.

"Wow," was T's reply. "Mr. J, I have never lied to you about anything for as long as I have known you and I'm not about to start now. You my dude." T communicated with a pain expression.

"I appreciate that more than you know, son." He replied.

"As you stated more than once, you know that Damon was grimy. He was trying to take control over things he had no right to. He had this big idea that he could put a gun to my head and make me sign over my business to him." T watched Mr. John's reaction then continued. "I told him fuck no, flat out. He would have to do what he had to do. I'm not afraid of death, Mr. J., I know I have to leave this earth one day and if standing up for what I believe in has to be the way, then so be it." He reasoned.

"I can understand that." Mr. John articulated. T-Money continued talking.

"But anyways, before he could pull the trigger Sya and Bunnee released several bullets into his body. He had just raped Bunnee the night before and he had someone break into Sya's house that same night and destroy everything she worked hard for just because she went into business for herself and she didn't want to expose her body for the world to see. Sya has dreams beyond this entertainment business. Mr. J, I'll be damned if I let a nigga or anybody take what I worked so hard for and I'm sure you would have reacted the same way. So, Mr. J, however you want to handle this, we can. I just hope we can settle this like grown men." T-Money summed up.

"Young Money, I do understand the position you were put in. I can't hold that against you. But I will be honest with you. Raheem -," Mr. John said, embarrassed T cut him off.

"How do you know my real name?" T recited irritated, looking at him strangely.

"I'm going to answer all of your questions and I'm also going to be totally honest with you." Mr. John declared, but T-Money wasn't enthused at all.

"I would appreciate that," affirmed T-Money.

"I know your real name because I'm your biological father and Damon was your brother." Mr. John released not knowing how to feel but he felt a load dropped after his confession. T-Money sat there with tears rolling down his face in disbelief.

45. Bad News?

Later that night:

Sya cleaned the house to perfection. She had candles burning and the sounds of Mary J. Blige's CD flowed through the surround sounds throughout the house. She fell deeply in love with the song "Don't Mind." She wanted this to be an intimate night with her man. She grilled the T-Bone steaks on the George Foreman grill, steamed the mixed vegetables, baked the potatoes, warmed the Hawaiian rolls and the banana pudding was in the refrigerator. The table was set, wine was on chill and two blunts rolled to get their heads together. Sya decided to call her mom; she wanted to share some news with her. She didn't know how Frances was going to handle this news, but she had made up her mind.

"Old lady, what are you doing?" Sya asked her mom when she answered the phone.

"Nothing, Hunny Bun, looking through some magazines to get some ideas for our wedding." Frances was overly excited.

"That's what I called to talk to you about. I wanted to share something with you. I don't want to make anyone feel uncomfortable, especially you, but I have decided to get in contact with Joseph and ask him to walk me down the aisle. How do you feel about that?" She shivered, not sure of her mother's reaction.

"Well, Sya, that's your decision and the thought, crossed my mind more than once. I was going to run it by you, I just didn't know when." Frances sadly admitted.

"Ma, you sound as if that would be a problem," disappointment was evident in her tone.

"No, sweetie, this has nothing to do with me. I'm cool with it if you are." She assured Sya.

"You sure, Ma?" Sya's voice faded.

"Sya, is everything okay, baby?" Frances asked concerned. Sya reached for the remote control and put the music on mute and turned the volume up on the television.

"Ma, turn your TV on Fox two news. Kendra's house has burned down." They both listened to April Simpson as she gave details about the events. Neither said anything until the news reporter was finished.

"Ma, I wonder who else was in that house with her?" Sya had sadness in her tone.

"Baby, you knew how loose Kendra was. There's no telling who she had in there. It's sad though." Frances understood her daughter's feeling about her once close friend.

"Ma, I hope-"

Frances interrupted her. "Don't you even say that. I'm sure Joseph stopped fooling around with her after you found out about them. We are going to concentrate on our weddings and find your father. Nevertheless, we will pay our respects to Kendra." She said half-heartedly. "By the way, where is your soon to be husband?"

"He should be home shortly. I'm going to call him when I'm done with you. Also I'm going down to City Hall tomorrow to speak with Joseph. I heard that's where he's working." Sya enlightened her mother.

"Okay, Hunny Bun, keep me posted. I love you."

"I will and I love you too. Enjoy your night." Sya ended the call. She sat on the couch not believing what she'd heard on the news. "You see, when you do wrong, it catches up to you one way or another." She mumbled.

****

Other side of town:

T-Money and King were sitting in T's Range Rover talking and smoking a blunt.

"Bruh, I don't know how I'm gonna tell Sya about her father. Now that the shit is on the news, she will find out." He laughed nervously.

"You act as if this is your fault. You did what you had to do to save everybody that was involved. She should understand and if she doesn't then that's on her." King spat crudely.

"Wait one minute, man. What's up with all of that?" T-Money noticed every time Sya's name came up in a conversation, King became upset. This was not the first time.

"T-Money, you know I love you like a brotha, right?"

"Right." T-Money shook his head.

"I wouldn't do anything to hurt you, right?"

"Right." T-Money shook his head again. "Bruh, what is it?" He grew impatient.

"That bitch is cheating on you." King said angrily.

"Why do you say that? Have you seen her out or something?" T-Money wanted facts. King spoke in a composed tone.

"Yes, I have seen her with a lame and he's right in your circle." King's eyes were low from the weed, but it was no secret that he was mad as hell.

"Who is this lame you're talking about?" He asked King.

"How many niggas you run with?" He inquired.

"Not many." He took a pull from the blunt.

"You do the subtraction nigga. You know I would never step on your toes." He informed T-Money. T-Money seemed to be in deep thought, trying to suppress his anger.

"Jabari's bitch ass!" He yelled.

"Money, now what you wanna do about this nigga? He crossed the line, violated and broke the code. We don't get down like that." King was down for whatever.

"I'll let you know in a few days, but right now, let me go handle my household. This situation here," he paused. "It's detrimental for those involved. See that's that shit I don't like." He told King.

"I'll hit you up and good lookin' out, bruh."

46. If I Could Turn Back The Hands of Time?

Bunnee and Jabari were chilling at his loft in the Central West End looking at movies. Bunnee knew that she increasingly didn't want to kick it with Jabari after finding out about him and Sya, which left a bad taste in her mouth. Bunnee had come to the conclusion that she would give Antonio a try. She knew that he genuinely loved her and he would do anything for her, something that he'd proven.

"Bunnee, can I feel the inside of you?" Jabari asked kissing and licking on her neck.

"Jabari, I don't think that that will be a good idea. I wish you just would come clean with me and tell me the truth," anger filled her voice.

"What are you talking about, Bunnee?" Jabari asked still trying to seduce her sexually.

"Look, Jabari," she broke his embrace, stood and faced him. "I'm not hard up for a man. I can have any man I choose but I want something that's meaningful. I want someone that's into me just as much as I'm into them. But for some reason, I don't get that from you." She looked at him differently.

"Okay, I see where this is going. Bunnee, I must admit, at first I wasn't searching for a serious relationship, but now that you have showed me your dedication, I'm more than willing to give this thing here, with you and me, a try." He reached for her to sit down. She pulled her arm back and continued to stand. "If I could turn back the hands of time, I woulda did things differently."

"I'm sure you would have at this point. Now that Sya's not

available anymore. Not that she was available before, but now she will be a married woman. What do I come off as, some lonely chick that can't get a man? Sorry, that's not the case here." Jabari tried to speak but Bunnee held her hand up to stop him. "You don't have to worry; your little secret is safe with me. I would never hurt T-Money, I love him too much." Bunnee finished, reached for her purse and headed to the door.

"Wait a minute, Bunnee. It's not like that." He tried to explain and she kept walking and he chased after her, grabbing her arm to stop her.

"Then how is it? No, don't worry about it. I don't want to know." She turned to face him. "At first, I couldn't understand why you didn't want to have sex with me. You had me questioning myself, like something was wrong with me. I never had self-esteem issues before and I refuse to have them now. I figured that it was another woman but I didn't expect it to be Sya, my supposed to be friend." She grabbed the knob to exit.

"Don't be mad at Sya." Jabari told her. "Sya didn't want to hurt you or T. She loves both of you."

"When did she realize her love for us, before or after you fucked her in your truck?" Bunnee snapped, slapping Jabari in the face, and left him standing with the door wide open holding his face.

Over at Frances's house:

Frances and Henry were sitting down looking through magazines, when they heard a knock at the door. Henry looked outside the window and saw several marked and unmarked police cars in their driveway.

"What the hell?" He looked at Frances for answers. Frances opened the door.

"Good evening, officers, how can I help you?"

"I'm looking for Frances Fields." The handsome officer looked over his note pad while his partner didn't say anything. The other officers never left their cars.

"I'm Frances Fields. What can I do for you?" She was nervous.

"Can I come in? I'm sure you don't want to do this outside." He assured her. Frances and Henry moved out of the way and let the officers enter.

"This is my fiancé, Henry." Frances said. "Now, what can I do for you?"

"It seems your husband Joseph Fields was the guy in the burning house with Kendra Turner. Their bodies were burned beyond recognition and they could only be identified through their dental records." Frances's hand flew to her mouth to hide the shock. "You were next of kin as his wife. If you can come with us, we can get the paper work completed. I'm sorry, I hate to bother you with this, but it's my job." The officer finished. Frances held one hand over her mouth, with silent tears falling from her eyes.

"Sure, Officer Brown," Henry looked at his name tag. "We will meet you down there. Let her get herself together. Thanks officers." Henry closed the door behind them as they left.

"I'm sorry to hear that, Hunny." He held her in his arms. "I will be there every step of the way." He kissed her forehead.

"How am I going to tell Sya? We were looking at the news

earlier and she said she'd hoped Joseph wasn't there with that child and I told her he wasn't. Damn!" Frances shook her head.

"Are you ready to take care of this?" Henry asked.

"Ready as I'm gonna be. I think after we leave the precinct we should stop by Sya's." She whispered, interlocking her fingers with Henry's while they walked to the car.

47. Real Life?

T-Money was consumed with so much hurt; he didn't know what to do next. With all the information he came across today, he didn't know how to handle it. He never thought Sya would cheat on him, and with his friend. That's what hurt the most. Then to know that she would find out about her dad and Kendra added fuel to the fire, along with him ordering the hit on Kendra. Sya had to know that it was either her, T-Money or Kendra, and it had to be Kendra. Everything he did, he did it for them. He didn't judge her. He loved her like he loved no other woman.

He loved her more than he loved his own mother. With him finding out the news of Mr. John being his father and Damon his brother, weighed heavily on his mind. Maybe if he knew this earlier, he could have done things differently with Damon. He was really mad at his mom for the abandonment she did in his upbringing and if he ever saw her again, which he couldn't give two fucks if he did or didn't, he would let her have it. *What type of woman was she?* He was upset with Mr. John for stringing him along all these years; thinking that he liked him as a person, but it was for his own selfish reasons. He helped produce two sons, but couldn't be a part of their lives and he couldn't let it be known, all because of a woman. *Who does that in real life?* T-Money thought to himself. But, he already knew the answer. Mr. John does.

T-Money felt like he had been played like a fool his whole life. To find out the man that raised him wasn't his real father hurt like hell. But in his eyes Mr. Ivy would always be his father, even though he moved to California years ago. T-Money visited most birthdays and Father's days. As he rode around deep in thought, he let Tupac's words resonate in his head, "keep your head up." He didn't want to have to wonder any longer why Sya cheated on him. He was going home to get clarity on the situation. *It's best to know and be disappointed than to never know and wonder,* he thought as he headed home.

He entered the house to the sounds of Jill Scott and Anthony Hamilton's, "So in Love with You." "Really?" He thought out loud.

"Hey babe." Sya greeted him, giving him a passionate kiss. He kissed her back, hugging her securely. He loved this woman. She showed him how to love. She listened to him. They shared dreams and goals and helped each other to accomplish them. They had each other's' backs. He trusted her, realizing that she knew the most important things about him.

She observed the sorrow behind his smile, love behind his anger and meaning behind his silence.

He knew that love was about taking risks, but he wasn't ready for heartbreak and he refused to give fake love or receive it. He'd gotten his share of fake love from his mother. *This couldn't be real life, but it was,* he tried to reason with himself.

"Hey babe." He greeted her back. "You have it smelling good in here." He walked to the kitchen trying to remain calm and cool, but his disposition stood alone and he couldn't hide his feelings any longer.

"Raheem, what's the matter, babe?" Sya sensed his uneasiness.

"Sya, I'm going to be totally honest with you about everything and I want the same in return. I need to know that you will not lie to me, no matter how much you may think it will hurt me. Right now, all I need is honesty." His eyes pleaded with her.

"Babe, come over her and sit down. What's the matter?" She grew more concerned by the minute. She reached for his hand and led him to the couch.

"Sya," he took a deep breath. "Just hear me out before you say anything."

"Babe, you scaring me, come on now and tell me what's going on." She still held his hand, tightly at this point. She knew something was wrong. She felt it deep down in her gut.

"Today I found out something that will change my life forever." He noticed that Sya was about to say something, but he put his hand up to stop her. "Talking to Mr. John, I learned that he's my biological father." Sya eyes grew big. "There's more," he informed her. "He's also Damon's father and if this is all true, then Damon was my brotha." He paused, waiting on a response from Sya. To his surprise he didn't get one, but her mouth was wide open at this point.

"This shit here is crazy as fuck. To know that I had something to do with my brotha's murder is driving me stupid crazy, man." He removed himself from the couch and stood in front of the fireplace. Before he realized it tears dropped from his eyes. Sya came from behind him and wrapped her arms around his waist. Now the tears were flowing non-stop.

"There's more." He broke, wiping his tears. "I had to turn right around and hear that my wife-to-be is fucking my friend. How true is that?" He yelled, removing her arms from around him, looking at Sya like he wanted to do something really bad to her. "Real life, Sya, is that true? And don't fuckin' lie to me. I can't take it." His face was stained with tears. Sya now had tears rolling down her face.

"Raheem, I'm sorry, babe." She tried to explain.

"It's either yes or no. Did you fuck Jabari, Sya?" The tears rolled swiftly down his smooth face.

"Yes, Raheem, I did. But-" She was cut short.

"But what, Sya?" He sneered. "His dick just landed in your pussy? Why Sya, why my friend?" He pushed her away from him.

"Babe, let me explain. It only happened once and we didn't finish. I promised, it never happened again and it never will. Babe, I love you and only you. I'm ready for the new chapter in our lives that we are about to begin. We had accomplished so much together and I refuse to give that up for anyone. You have to believe me, Raheem." She was balling her eyes out.

"I went against my brotha' for you. I gave you my heart, something I've never done. I love you more than I love my own mother. The worst feeling in the world is to doubt something or someone you thought was unquestionable." He shouted hitting the wall. Sya jumped fearing for her safety.

"Babe, I did make a mistake but if you give me another chance, I will be the best wife a man could ever have."

"Sya, I can't trust you anymore. I'm almost afraid to bring my friends around you, fearful that you will fuck them too." He said out of hurt. His whole world seemed to be crashing down on him. Just when he thought he had it all, he realized he had nothing but lies and deceit.

"Raheem, don't say that. Let me ask you something? Have you ever cheated on me?" Sya asked and her cell phone rang. "Well?"

"Well what? This is not about me, and answer your phone." T-Money wanted to know who kept calling.

"They will call back, now answer the question."

"No," he replied giving her direct eye contact. "I'll never hurt you because I love you more than life. I couldn't take the chance of losing you and you walking out of my life forever. I just couldn't chance that. Now answer your phone." He turned away. Sya retrieved her phone from the table.

"Yeah Ma," her voice was breaking as she answered.

"Hunny Bun, what's wrong." Frances sensed some tension in her daughter's tone.

"Nothing Ma, talking to Raheem. Can I call you back?" she wanted to end this call.

"Sya, I'm on my way over there. I need to speak with you about something very important, and no it can't wait." Frances was persistent.

"Ma, now is not a good time."

"I'm almost there, see you in three minutes," Frances terminated the call.

"What was that about?" T-Money asked.

"That was Ma, saying she had something important to talk to me about." Sya walked close to T-Money. T-Money knew what this was about. He wanted to leave before Frances got there but he really wanted to be there for Sya, knowing that he was the cause of her father's death.

"Maybe I should leave and come back after you're done with your mom." He grabbed his keys.

"Babe," she gripped his arm. "Please don't leave. I'm terrified, if I let you leave, you're not coming back. Please stay so we can finish and try to work this out. I love you." She told him as the doorbell rang. He kissed her on the forehead and put his keys back down on the table, sitting on the couch. This was going to be a long night and he couldn't just walk out on her. They had too much invested in each other. But most importantly, he loved her without any question.

48. Bittersweet?

Jabari had been ringing Bunnee's phone hysterically after she cut him short. She had been thinking about King often and wanted to give him a chance, but she didn't want their friendship to end. It was always said, you must be friends before you become lovers and they were really close friends. They've known each other from way back. He's always respected her, and she the same. Her only problem with King is she wanted him to find another occupation.

Bunnee was watching Tyler Perry's play "A Madea Christmas," sipping on some wine when she heard a knock at her door. She looked out of her window to find Jabari's truck parked in her driveway. She wasn't impressed all at. She opened the door slightly.

"What can I do for you, Jabari?" She asked in a displeased tone.

"I want to talk to you." He tried to enter.

"You fine right where you are."

"I can't come in?" He asked surprise.

"No, and you need to hurry up because the cold air is coming in here and I'm watching TV." Her attitude was in rare form.

"Okay, Bunnee. I want to try to work this out with you. I admit, I fucked up, but I know better now. Give me another try, please." He begged, looked exceedingly handsome standing there in his brown bomber jacket, dreads neatly hanging under a STL brown skully.

"That's something I want no part of. Are you done?" She quickly shot him down at the same time King was pulling up in her driveway. Bunnee was wondering why King would just pull up in her driveway unannounced. A small smile appeared on her face and Jabari perceived it. He turned to see King getting out of his truck, walking to the door.

"He wouldn't have anything to do with your decision, does he?" Jabari tossed, clearly upset.

"What's that, partna'? King asked, boldly kissing Bunnee on the lips.

"Nothing," Bunnee retorted. "He was just leaving. King pushed his way in and Bunnee closed the door in Jabari's face.

"What is that nigga doing here?" King sipped from Bunnee's glass.

"Nothing." He took her glass and filled it with more wine.

"I know he's not trying to push up on my woman." He turned his attention to the TV.

"Your woman, when that happen and where was I when this decision was made?" She countered.

"Right here." King took the glass out of Bunnee's hand. He slowly and gently pushed her down on the couch. He climbed on top of her and kissed her delicately.

"This is what I do to my woman." He nibbled her earlobes, sending her into a frenzy. She was enjoying the feeling but she didn't want to go there with King. They were much too close for this.

"Antonio, we can't do this." She tried to escape.

"Why can't we?" He lifted her shirt, releasing her round grapefruit breasts, sucking them effortless. Bunnee hadn't realized the moans that escaped her mouth. King's mouth felt amazing on her breasts.

"I can't hear you, mama." He rose up and took her shirt off. His chiseled torso enticed Bunnee to the upmost. Her coochie soaked through her panties.

"Antonio, don't do this. I just don't want to have causal sex. I need stability in my life." She rubbed and kissed his muscles in between speaking with her eyes closed.

"I can give you that." He removed her bottoms.

"How can I be sure?" She unbuckled his belt. His penis was so hard, it could have burst through his jeans.

"Let me show you." The tip of his penis felt the smooth skin of the Brazilian wax she'd gotten the day before. She had the tip of his penis wet and ready. "B, I love you, like in love with you and I want to be in your life forever; just let me have that." He inserted his penis inside of her.

"Antonio, there's no bare backing. You must use a condom." Bunnee was on the verge of losing a built up nut. Before King got the condom on he released all over Bunnee's stomach.

"Boy, I hope you have penis control if you talking about being my man." She had disappointment written all over her face.

"You don't know the power of your own pussy. That shit is fire, but before I put this dick to you, we need to talk about this relationship." He sat up on the couch, pulling Bunnee up with him.

"Antonio, you know I can't deal with cheating and I will not cheat on you. However, I do need you to change your lifestyle." She carefully articulated her words.

"Yes, I can do all the above. But you need to get rid of your niggas. All of them. Including that busta that was here. I don't want to have to body nobody." He laughed, but was serious.

"So, I'm your woman and you're my man?" Bunnee positioned herself on top of King sitting up on the couch. He shook his head yes.

"Can I have some of your Mr. Feel Good?" He shook his head again up and down. "Then give it to me." He cautiously pulled her off his lap, laid her on the fluffy carpet, carefully pulled her legs apart and introduced his fat juicy tongue to her pussy. She slipped into a sex induced seizer, loving every touch. Jabari stood on the porch watching through the window. King knew he was there so that gave him the motivation to fuck her brains out, and he did. Jabari jumped in his ride furiously with Fantasia's "Bittersweet," beating though the speakers.

49. I Should Have?

Frances walked in Sya's house with a distraught look on her face. T-Money knew what the look was about. Henry greeted T-Money with a dap and a manly hug. He then hugged Sya and kissed her on the cheek. As T-Money did the same to Frances. Sya grabbed her mother's hand and led her to the couch.

"Ma, what's wrong?" Sya asked as she held Frances's hand tightly, looking at Henry and T-Money confused.

"Hunny Bun, I have something to tell you." Frances broke down.

"Ma, what is it?" She wiped the fallen tears from her mother eyes, really concerned at this point.

"Well Baby, I was contacted earlier by the St. Louis Police Department and," Frances took a deep breath before she continued. Sya mom called her Sy, Sya, Hunny Bun and other loving names.

"Just say it, Ma." Sya was becoming impatient and afraid.

"Sya, your father is dead; he was the other person found in Kendra's house when it burned down." Frances knew at this point she had to be strong for her daughter. She wasn't crying because of Joseph's death; it was the hurt that her baby would consume. Not that she wanted him dead or anything, but Joseph had to pay for the hurt and deception that he put them through. Yes, it was a horrible death, but you have to watch how you treat people. Karma is a bad bitch.

T-Money walked over and sat on the couch next to Sya,

hugging her tightly. Sya didn't say anything; she just laid her head on T-Money's chest and cried silently.

Frances knew that she was in good hands with T-Money, so she decided to give Sya her space. She had more than enough on her mind.

"Baby, I'm going to let you be alone right now but I wanted to be the one to deliver you the news. If you need anything, or just want to talk, you know Mommy is just a phone call away." She kissed her on her cheek, as did Henry.

"Raheem, take care of my baby." Frances gave him a stern look. She knew something was going on when she called but she knew Sya would share it with her when she was ready.

"Yes ma'am." T-Money replied letting them out.

After Frances and Henry left T-Money and Sya collapsed on the couch in silence. Sya finally settled on speaking.

"Raheem, if you're going to leave me, I suggest you go ahead and do it now. Don't stay because you pity me. While I'm hurting I'd rather go through it all at once, than to wake up and find that you're leaving a month or two from now." She looked him in the eyes.

"Babe, I got you. I'm willing to try to make this work. I'm not saying that it's going to be easy, but I'm willing. I need to be able to trust you again, that I will have to gain again." He held her face up with both hands.

"I can understand that, and I'm willing to rehab our relationship. I just wish I could have spoken with my dad before this happened. I had plans on asking him to give me away to you. That's what happens when you put off what you can do today instead of tomorrow. I should have been on it more, trying to make amends.

"Babe, don't go beating yourself up over this. Shoulda, coulda, woulda. But know that I'm here for you 'til the end. You are going to be my wife, and if you hurt, I hurt. I love you." He confessed seriously kissing her on the lips.

"I love you too, Raheem." Sya confirmed kissing him back, thinking in the back of her mind, I should have. They chilled the rest of the night.

50. Putting It All Out on the Table?

The news traveled quickly about Joseph's death. The next day everyone came over to T-Money's and Sya's to give their condolences. King and Bunnee came together, raising eyebrows. No one knew that they were a couple. Bunnee knew that her supposed-to-be friend was hurting, but she wanted to enlighten her on a few things. Frances and Henry was there all snuggled up.

"Sya, can I speak with you in private, please?" Bunnee asked, looking around the room.

"Sure, Bunnee, follow me." Sya guided, taking the bottle of wine with them, escorting her to her office and closing the door behind them.

"What's wrong, Bunnee?" Sya inquired, refreshing their drinks.

"First off I want you to know that I'm so sorry for your loss, regardless of the relationship you and your dad carried. It's never easy losing a loved one." She was beyond sincere.

"I so appreciate that, and thanks for being here. You have truly proven your friendship." Sya expressed sipping from her glass, trying not to get emotional.

"That's what I wanted to speak with you about, our friendship. I want to put it all out on the table. That way, there won't be any misunderstandings. You see Sya, I haven't been anything but a friend to you. I came to you and told you about the horrible things Damon did to you and wanted to do to you. I watched how your best friend Kendra tried to play you with Damon and told all your business. I'm even keeping a secret about a murder we did together. You see, with that said, Sya, my loyalty has been proven. Which brings me to this, how could you betray me and fuck Jabari behind my back?" Bunnee had tears in her eyes. "You knew I really liked him."

"Bunnee, I'm so sorry, but I never intended to hurt you in anyway. Yes, you have displayed loyalty on numerous occasions, but you have to believe me." Sya became misty eyed and really emotional.

"What was so important that you had to have this man? You have a man that loves you and would do anything for you. You two have a bright future ahead, something every lonely woman want. I just don't understand." Her voice raised an octave.

"I don't know how to make you understand, but what I can tell you is that I'm sorry beyond words. I know that it will never happen again. I just want my friend back. Bunnee, believe it or not, I need you in my life. You are the sister I never had." She ended with tears rolling down her face at a fast pace.

"Sya, this is going to take some time, but I'm willing to try. I don't want to lose you as a friend either but I need to be able to trust my friends, and for some strange reason, I do believe you when you say that you will never do anything to hurt me again." Bunnee wiped the tears from her eyes. She walked closer to Sya and reached out and gave her a hug. "I'm sorry about your dad and if you need me for anything, I'm just a phone call away, friend." She hugged her again.

"Thanks sister that means so much to me. Now you can help me plan my wedding," Sya recited excitedly. The ladies broke their embrace when they heard a loud commotion going on in the other room. "What the hell?" Sya said once she entered the living room. "Babe don't do this. This is neither the place nor time." She tried to calm T-Money down.

"You bitch ass nigga, if you don't get the fuck outta my house right now I will blow your fuckin' brains out," he yelled while hitting Jabari upside the head with the butt of his pistol. He was heated.

"Babe, not now, please, let him go." Sya whispered in T-Money's ear.

"Sya, get off of me." He yelled pushing her with his elbow. Sya noticed the amount of blood leaking from Jabari's head.

"Fam, what's this all about?" Jabari pleaded, weakly disoriented.

"Bitch ass nigga, you know what this is about." He announced stoned faced with murder in his eyes. Frances asked everyone to leave, holding the door as they exited. King, Bunnee, Frances and Henry remained.

"You know this is all because of you," King spat at Sya.

"Fuck you." She said walking away. By this time Jabari had gotten up, walking to the door, just before he exited, King punched him in the stomach and he doubled over. Both Sya and Bunnee felt sorry for him, but there was nothing they could do.

"Punk ass bitch, I betta' not see you on the streets and if I do-" T-Money gritted his teeth.

"Babe, I need you to stop this at once." Sya shouted angrily, crying hysterically. T-Money snapped out of his fuming state and humbly apologized to Sya and everyone remaining. He then excused himself and went to their bedroom. Frances and Bunnee stayed to comfort Sya.

51. Can't Wait, Won't Wait?

T-Money knew Sya was upset with him and he was going to do any and everything to make her understand. He loved Sya to pieces and he couldn't wait until she became his wife, that's why he wanted to marry her right now. She peacefully rested in his arms. He endlessly kissed her on the forehead until she woke up.

"Morning babe, how do you feel?" He kissed her on the lips.

"I feel fine." She pulled the covers off of her to go to the bathroom.

"Wait a second, babe." He protectively reached for her arm. "I have something to ask you." He cautiously voiced.

"What is it, Raheem?" She broke.

"I know you're mad at me for the way I handled things last night, but you have to understand-," he said in his defense.

"I have to understand that it could have been handled better than that." Sya snapped, clearly irritated, jerking away.

"Look babe, this is not all my fault. I'm not going to take all the blame for this situation. Where do you hold some responsibility in the matter?" T-Money sighed.

"I take full responsibility for the entire situation but it's not going to change what happened. If I could take it back, yes I would. If we're going to make this work, you have to let go of the past and move on with the future. Babe, we have a great future ahead of us and yes we are going to stumble across some difficult times but it's how we handle them that will determine how we get through them. You understand what I'm saying to you?" Sya sounded exhausted dealing with the entire matter.

"I totally understand what you're saying to me. That's why I want to get married right away. We can go down to the Justice of the Peace." He beamed with pride.

"What about my big wedding? My mother and I have big plans and a double wedding at that." She released with a frown on her face.

"Babe, we can still have the big wedding you want. We're just going to be married already, that's it." He gave her his dazzling smile. She smiled back at him.

"Boy, you better be glad I love you. But on the real, I would marry you anytime and anywhere. So when is this going to take place?" She barked stirred up.

"We can do it on Wednesday." He reasoned.

"Are you sure?" She coaxed.

"Absolutely!" T-Money agreed hopping on top of her, kissing her passionately.

52. Baggage Left Behind?

Rhonda met Frances and Sya at Starbucks in the Central West End to discuss how they would handle Joseph's finances. Frances wanted to get this done and over with as quickly as possible. She wanted to go on with her new life and close the past.

"Mrs. Fields, when Sya contacted me and told me that you wanted me to assist you with your divorce before this happen I was more than delighted." She confirmed.

"Why thank you, Rhonda. I appreciate all that you can do for me."

"I know you do." Rhonda told her, removing some papers from her briefcase. "At that time, I went ahead and started my process so I could be prepared when we would meet. The information I came across stunned me because I never witnessed anything like this before." Rhonda slid some papers in front of Frances and Sya.

"What are these?" Frances asked, looking over the papers then at Rhonda.

"Well, Mrs. Fields, it seems that Joseph had filed for a divorce year ago and it was actually granted, due to neglect."

"Due to neglect? Are these legal?" Frances looked from Rhonda to Sya.

"Yes, I'm afraid they are. You see, it seems that you were served on many occasions but you never responded. Therefore he got you on neglect." Rhonda explained sipping on her latte. But look at it this way; I hear that you're getting married so you won't have to wait until the divorce is final. You are a widow. You can go on with your wedding plans as scheduled." She pled the case.

"Yeah, that man lived raunchy," she shook her head back and forth, not knowing whether to be angry or happy. Sya spoke for the first time.

"So Rhonda, this is legal and nothing will come up later?" Sya wanted to make sure.

"It's so legal and nothing will come about later. Now that Joseph is deceased nothing can come about, but this money he left you two." A big smile appeared across her face.

"What money?" Sya asked, whispering across the table.

"I contacted the attorney that represented Joseph and he informed me of the large estate Joseph had. He not only left you guys' property, but he also left behind a ten year old son, that lives in an upscale neighbor in Chesterfield with his grandparents." Both Sya's and Frances's mouths were wide open.

"Where's the mother?" Sya wanted to know.

"She's a crack head and a prostitute, so her parents take care of the little fellow. Joseph provided well for the child and he will be taken care of for life. He divided everything up evenly between the three of you."

"I don't want anything from that man. You can give everything to my daughter. He owes me nothing, but her everything." She summed up disappointedly. "Muthafuckas know they can leave baggage behind." Frances wasn't enthused at all.

"Ma, you sure you want to do that? You deserve everything you get from Joseph. He did some mean things to us and you took care of the family, so I think you're making a big mistake." She tried to suppress her anger toward her father.

"I'm more than sure." Frances informed her, removing herself from the chair. "Rhonda, thanks for your time. I'll be talking to you later."

"You are more than welcome and I will be in touch so we can sign the paperwork." She stood to shake her hand.

"I'll call you later, Ma. Love you." Sya rose and kissed her mother on the cheek and Frances left thinking, this bitch ass nigga been living raunchy all this time. A child? Wowser.

Sya stayed and talked to Rhonda a while longer. "Rhonda, can you get me all the information on this kid and his mother? I would like to reach out and establish a relationship. It's not his fault." She confessed.

"I can do that for you, but are you sure you want to do that?" Rhonda asked out of concern.

"I'm positive," Sya confirmed.

"Give me a week and I will have everything you asked for." Rhonda assured her.

"Thanks girlie. This is such a surprise to me, but it is what it is.

"Indeed it is." Rhonda agreed.

53. This Here Ain't What You Want?

"Jabari, I'm so fuckin' mad about what T-Money did to you. You can't just let this go." Glitter was fuming. "You have seventeen fucking stitches in your head, fracture ribs and two black eyes, hell-muthafuckin'-no he will not get away with this. If you don't do anything about it, then I will." Her temper was on high.

"And how will you do that, Glitter? I know what I have to do and I don't want you involved. Somebody's gonna lose their life or freedom. I know shit about T that can put him away for a very long time. So just let me handle this. You have to be here for Tory. I will take care of everything." Jabari clarified in agonizing pain.

"That's his fault if he can't control his woman. What about when he tried to get at me? Niggas kill me, they can dish it out but they can't take it. All I know is this here ain't what they want." Glitter sneered.

"Like I said before, you worry about Tory and his well-being. Grandma and grandpa are getting old so you're gonna have to take responsibility and get your child. I think it's time now." Jabari looked stricken.

"Yeah, I know. I don't know what I would have done without you all these years helping me out. The only thing his father was good for was providing, with his old ass." Glitter yelled infuriated. "I will let you handle things but if you need my help, let me know." She calmed down some.

"I most certainly will. I wanted to go see Tory today but I can't go in this condition and you know Grandma worries too much. So I'll go when I heal a little better." He acknowledged level headedly.

"That's cool, but do you need anything, are you in pain?" Glitter was concerned.

"I'm good."

Sya and T-Money went to the Justice of the Peace and got married. Sya was swagged out in a black YSL dress with a pair of Giuseppe Zanotti stilettos. T-Money graced a black Brotha' Brotha' Original suit with matching shoes, looking like a Don. King was their witness and he wore black as well. They didn't want anyone to know about this, so King was sworn to secrecy not to tell Bunnee or anyone else. Through it all T-Money knew that he could trust King without a doubt. After the ceremony took place, King pulled Sya to the side.

"I know with everything that went on in the past and that you don't care for me, and I'm the same flavor here. But as long as you don't hurt my guy again, we cool. I know how much he loves you so I'm gonna let that be the reason, I don't take your head off." He chuckled, but was serious as hell.

"Well thanks for sparing my life." Sya was being sarcastic. "But I'm going to do any and everything in my power to make my husband happy. I love him more than life, so you don't and won't have to worry about me hurting him ever again. We're only human and we are entitled to make mistakes. I'm sure you have made more than your share." She threw at him. "Thanks for coming," and Sya walked away thinking: this here ain't what you want. She didn't care for King and she couldn't hide it.

54. The Results are In?

A week later:

Rhonda phoned Sya and updated her that she had the information she requested. They agreed to meet at Desert on the Boulevard in the Central West End to have cocktails. Rhonda knew after the information she was about to disclose, Sya would need plenty of cocktails.

"Hey sweetie, you look fabulous in those skinny jeans." Sya acknowledged Rhonda, air kissing her on both cheeks.

"You as well, darling," Rhonda complimented back taking her seat. "Shall we get down to business?" Rhonda got straight to the point.

"We shall." Sya agreed.

"Okay, here's what I came across." Rhonda took a deep breath. "The little guy's name is Tory Allan and his mother's name is Glitter Allan. She worked at Bottoms Up Strip Club and she's thirty two years old." As Rhonda gave Sya the information, she also produced photos and slid them in front of Sya.

"OMG, this young fellow was in my class a few years back. He was the sweetest kid and I took to him for some strange reason... because he's my little brother." She timidly stated as tears welled up in her eyes. "And Glitter, she works for our company as the secretary, OMG, this shit is unbelievable." The tears escaped her eyes.

"Sya, I have an address and telephone number where you can contact him." She then removed another sheet of paper containing the information. "I'm sorry you had to find out this way but I'm glad I could shed some light on this situation for you." Rhonda was sincere. "I do think it's best that you contact him because in a few weeks we all will have to meet regarding your father's last will and testament." Sya never said anything else, she just listened. "Go ahead and establish a relationship with your brother, it's not his fault. Remember, you said that."

"Yeah, I think that's what I'll do. But now that I think about it, Jabari used to come and check up on Tory often when he was in my class. He said Tory was his nephew, and when Glitter brought him around she said that Jabari was her cousin. Wow, this is a small world. That bitch knew that I was upset that Kendra was dating my father and all this time she had a whole baby by him, fuckin' slut bag." Sya became noticeably disconcerted.

"Sya, if you want me to go with you I will. This is a situation that needs to be handled. That kid knows nothing about this matter and you owe it to him as his big sister to get to know him; regardless of the circumstances and people involved. That way you will find closure in the issue." Rhonda logically reasoned.

"That's why she was always friendly with me because she was fuckin' my father. This shit's crazy." Sya acknowledged with hostility.

"I know, right. But as your attorney I have to direct you correctly. At the end of the day, there's a ten year old child involved and he needs to know what's going on. You need to know what's going on, for you as well as him. Now do you want me to go with you or not?" Rhonda closed her argument.

"I would like it if you would accompany me. I do need a

voice of reason around, so yes, please." Sya lightened the situation with a chuckle.

"When?"

"Tomorrow afternoon." She summed up.

"I'll see you then."

"Rhonda, thank you so much. I don't know what I'll do without you." Sya got up to hug her.

"You'll see when you get my bill." She hugged her back, both of them laughing.

Later that evening:

Frances was still upset about Joseph leaving behind a ten year old son. Her hatred was enormous for Joseph, even in his death. Deep down inside she loved Joseph, he was her first love. He was the father of her only child. When they were together he treated her wonderfully. And until he lost his job, he was an amazing provider. This was years of resentment toward him. She called Sya.

"Hunny Bun, how you?" Frances asked sounding drained.

"I'm good, Ma. What's the matter?" Sya detected distress in her mother's tone.

"I can't get over this child your father had. I would really like to meet him. I would like to see him for myself." She commanded. Sya didn't want to disclose the information she'd found out but she didn't want to keep it from her mother either. She'd already gotten married without her knowledge. So she broke down and told her mother what she discovered and Frances agreed to go with her the following day.

55. Man Down?

T-Money knew something was on Sya's mind. He lay next to her in bed resting his head on her breasts. She rubbed his head gently as he massaged her thighs tenderly.

"Babe, we're a team and when you're down I'm down. What's on your mind?" He softly kissed her breast, arousing her.

"Babe, I know." She kissed the top of his head again. "It's just this entire situation with my dad." She hadn't revealed the information Rhonda shared with her.

"Just know that I'm here for you, but right now I need you to be here for me and give me some loving." He tickled her, wanting to see her glittering smile. He slid down to her prized position and encased his tongue in her waterfall. He released her mind of the events she had ahead of her.

The following morning:

Frances was up early preparing herself mentally and physically for the task at hand. She was glad Henry had left already. She didn't know why she'd let this bother her as much as it did, but the thoughts were embedded in her head. Sya had explained to her that Tory could very well be her brother and she wanted to be a part of his life, despite the consequences of the situation. Once again, it wasn't Tory's fault. At some degree Frances understood and thought that was big of her daughter. She made herself a cup of coffee and sat on the couch watching The View talk show. She loved that Whoopi expressed herself freely. Frances's thoughts drifted back to when she and Joseph tried very hard to produce a son. That's all she ever wanted to give him was a son, but when she miscarried twice, they decided that she wouldn't put that wear and tear on her body anymore. Then out of nowhere came Sya and they were truly blessed to have her. Sadness over came her and she broke down in tears. "Damn you, Joseph Fields." She shouted throwing the cup of coffee against the wall.

****

Bunnee was lying in bed not feeling well when King came into the room with breakfast from Goody Goody Diner. She loved the sampler platter but in the last few days she couldn't keep anything down. King had had the 24 hour bug a few days ago and she thought it had coasted to her, but in reality Bunnee knew she was expecting. The only problem was that she didn't know who the father was, Jabari or King. She was almost certain that it was Jabari's kid.

At this point in her life when everything was going well, there were always some obstacles. She didn't know how King would handle the matter if Jabari was the father, but she would have to tell him the possibilities. She also knew the love he had for her would conquer all understanding because she didn't cheat on him, this was before his time.

"Open up wide, mama." He had a fork full of eggs, feeding Bunnee.

"Boy, I can feed myself." She opened her mouth laughing. Once the eggs went down, they immediately wanted to come back up. Bunnee jumped up and ran to the bathroom to release them.

"Damn B, you okay?" King looked concerned and was right behind her, pulling her hair away from the toilet. It took her a minute to pull herself together before she spoke.

"Antonio," she paused tears begging to be released. He pulled her closer to him.

"Mama, what's wrong," he inquired, kissing her forehead.

"I don't think this is a 24 hour bug. I think I'm expecting." Her eyes displayed sorrow. He hugged her tightly, overjoyed.

"There's more," she hesitated, but carried on. "I don't know how far along I am, so I don't know if you are the father."

"What are you trying to say, that that punk ass nigga could be the father?" King tried to suppress his anger and take inventory of the situation.

"It's possible," pain washed over her face.

"Why don't I run down to the Walgreen's and buy a pregnancy test?" He suggested trying his best to control his emotions.

"That's fine, but that won't determine how far along I am." She tried to rationalize the matter.

"Then make an appointment with your doctor." He suggested again, lowering his tone.

"I have but it's not until next week." She was a step ahead of him.

"Then we'll just have to wait." He walked out of the bathroom. She followed behind him.

"Antonio, please understand my position. I didn't cheat on you. If this is Jabari's child," she carefully articulated her words. "This was before we got together. I can't do anything about that."

"A condom would have been nice." It came out of his mouth before he realized it, regretting it instantly. "I'm sorry, B." He looked at her.

"We'll just have to wait." She crawled back into bed, pulling the covers up on her.

"I'm sorry B, whatever the results are, I'm with you. I love you, mama." He crawled next to her on top of the covers, holding her.

"That's all I wanted to hear, Antonio." She kissed him and relaxed in his arms.

56. Yes He Is?

Later that evening:

The ride to Chesterfield was silent, except for Mary J. Blige's voice escaping through the speakers of Rhonda's Jetta. Frances and Sya were in their own thoughts. Rhonda drove bobbing her head. She knew the ladies were dealing with a lot so she kept the conversation limited, only asking necessary questions.

They were impressed when they pulled up in front of the house. The grass was neatly manicured with trimmed bushes shaped nicely. The front door was open and they could see through the Windex cleaned glass. Approaching the porch, no one was in the living room. Rhonda rang the doorbell and it chimed throughout the house.

A bald, dark skin older man, with a salt and pepper goatee answered the door, which they presumed to be Glitter's and Jabari's grandfather; in which Jabari favored tremendously.

"Good evening, ladies," he addressed them. "How may I help you?" He was pleasant. Rhonda spoke first

"Good evening, Mr. Allan," Rhonda greeted him by name and he wondered how she knew his name. "I was wondering if we could get a moment of your time? We," she looked from Frances and Sya, "need to speak with you and your wife about a very important matter." He gave the women a look of, what's this about and invited them in.

"Hi, I'm Sya and this is my mother, Frances Fields." They both extended their hands to shake his. The bells immediately went off in his head.

"Ladies, I don't mean to be rude but could you all tell me what this is about. I have to finish dinner. They could smell the aroma in the air. "Let's go in my office where we can speak in private." They followed him, admiring the house. The structure of the house was fabulous.

Frances was heated inside. *That piece of shit left them pretty well off,* she thought and Sya could tell what her mom was thinking.

"Please have a seat." He offered. Rhonda began to speak but Sya interceded.

"Mr. Allan, we're sorry to intrude on you and your family without calling but-" Rhonda was cut off by Sya.

"My father Joseph was killed in a house fire," Mr. Allan's eyes grew wide.

"I didn't know that." He was in total shock. "I'm sorry to hear that. He was a fine man."

"I'm sure, taking care of you and your family the way he has been." Frances piped out, visibly upset. Sya and Rhonda gave Frances a look as to say: "Was that necessary?" Mr. Allan said nothing but his facial expression displayed his dislike for the comment.

"Mr. Allan, the reason we're here is because, I just learned that my dad, fathered your ten year old grandson and I would like to establish a relationship with him. He also left a will behind and it clearly states that in order for him to receive his inheritance, we will have to institute some sort of relationship, Tory and I." Sya finished, lying through her teeth. Rhonda looked at her but didn't interject. She thought it was an excellent approach.

"In my opinion," Mr. Allan clarified. "I don't think that that's a good idea. Tory knows nothing of you and I don't want to confuse him. He already has a sister." The ladies looked baffled at this point. What Mr. Allan wasn't aware of, is that Rhonda did a background check on Glitter, and Tory is her only child and Joseph didn't have any more children that they know of.

"How many siblings does he have?" Rhonda's attorney's instincts kicked in.

"Glitter is his sister." Mr. Allan revealed.

"No, she is not," Sya yelled but Rhonda put her hand up to stop her. At that point Tory busted into the office.

"Papa, I'm ready to eat." He glazed around the room. "Ms. Fields!" he yelled running over to give Sya a hug. Frances, without doubt, knew that he belong to Joseph. He carried the same natural curly hair, flat nose and tall frame.

"Hi Tory, how are you?" Sya couldn't deny the resemblance, reaching down to hug him, feeling some sort of connection. "How are you doing in school?" She released him.

"Good, are you coming back to my school?" He was excited to see her.

"I'm not sure, but in any case, I want you to continue to do your best, okay?" She tried to hold back her tears.

"Okay." He replied.

"Tory, go wash up for dinner." Mr. Allan insisted, faced with the inevitable.

At Jabari's house:

Glitter was over at Jabari's nursing his wounds. She was outside of upset about the way King and T-Money had treated him. She was going to find a way to get back at them. They had to, one way or the other.

"Bari, I know you're not going to let them dirty sons of bitches get away with this?" She was angered by the sight of Jabari's face and bandages.

"In due time, cuzzin'. They will be dealt with." He stared off into space. "Have you told grandma and grandpa about Joseph's death? Now that he's gone we have to grind harder to take care of Tory. As long as I'm living and breathing, he will never want for anything." He was sincere and Glitter could see it through his swollen black eyes.

"I'm going to break the news today when I take Tory his new Jordans. He's been bugging me for the longest about those shoes."

"Do you want me to go with you?"

"Hell naw! Not with your face looking like that. You know Tory gonna have all sorts of questions for you. Stay your ass here and heal." She smirked some.

"If they ask about me, tell them I had to go out of town for a couple of weeks for my job." He implied distractedly.

"Do you want me to do anything else before I get out of here?" Glitter took the food she brought to the kitchen.

"Naw, I'm good. Call me and let me know how it goes. Joseph was very active in Tory's life so I'm sure he will not take it well." He continued to stare off.

"It's Sya, isn't it? She has you buggin', cuz. You really like her don't you?" She whispered.

"It's Sya and Bunnee. I could have been with either one of them. They both are good girls, but it is what it is." He tried to reassure himself.

"Yeah cuzzin, it is. I'll call you later on to check on you." She kissed him on the forehead, observing the pistol under his pillow, which made her feel more at ease. Then Glitter went out the door, dreading her task at hand.

"Man I can't believe this shit." King shrieked at T-Money. "Just when I think my life is coming together, this bullshit comes about."

"Man, shit happens, but you need to be honest with B and yourself. What if the baby turns out to be Jabari's? Can you deal with that?" He logically tried to reason with his friend.

"Know, my friend, that the truth doesn't cost you anything but a lie will cost you everything," King said pacing around the room. He finally stopped and sat opposite T-Money.

"T man, I've been asking myself that question all day. What I do know is that I love B, without question. I'm just hoping that's my seed she's carrying." This had King mentally drained.

"The moment of truth will present itself soon enough." T-Money's suspicion increased. "But check this out. I can't allow that pussy ass nigga Jabari to walk the same streets as me. The STL is not big enough; you know what I'm saying?" T-Money finished rolling the cigar filled blunt.

"So what you wanna do? I don't have a problem knocking that nigga's head off. That's right up my alley." King assured T-Money that he was down for whatever.

"I know that nigga is probably laying low. He can't do too much right about now. We fucked him around good." T-Money lit the blunt and took a pull. "I bet you any amount of money, he at the crib chillin." T passed the blunt to King.

"You know what I'm thinking. You wanna move on that nigga'?" King pulled super hard on the blunt, feeling the effect, coughing uncontrollably.

"Let's get it, nigga." T-Money rocked his Jeezy voice.

At The Allan's home:

"So Mr. Allan, are you saying that Sya will not have a relationship with her brother? It's something their dad requested and I think that you all should allow that to happen." Frances wanted to be reasonable even though she didn't like the situation one bit.

"I will have to discuss this with my wife. I don't want to do anything that's going to hurt him. He's too young to understand all of this." Mr. Allan was not pleased with this situation either.

Glitter pulled into the driveway wondering whose car was parked in front. As she approached the front door, she used her key to the unlocked the screen door. The aroma of the baked chicken hit her in the face. She headed to the kitchen to find it empty. She then went to the family room to find the same results. She knew where she could find her Papi and strutted to his office. Before she knocked on the door, she held her ear to the door due to her hearing voices. She knew immediately who the voices belonged to. She knocked but didn't wait for an answer before she entered.

"Papi, what's going on in here?" Glitter asked looking around the room. She didn't know Rhonda and mugged her up and down from head to toe. Rhonda extended her hand.

"I'm Rhonda Williams, Sya's and Frances's attorney." She professionally spoke with a smirk on her face.

"Well what is this about?" Glitter wasn't pleased to see them here.

"Girl, you know what this is about. Glitter, don't play dumb with me." Sya walked closer to her, getting in her face.

"Ladies, ladies," Rhonda chimed in getting in between them. "Let's handle this professionally. That is not why we're here.

"Fuck that," Sya shouted. "All this time you've been working for the company you were fucking my father? Now you have an innocent kid involved in this foolishness." Sya was all in Glitter's face now. She could feel the spit flying from her mouth.

"I didn't do all of this by myself. It takes two to tango." Glitter implied.

"That's true, but did you have to do it with my father? Damn, I thought Kendra was raunchy. You're no better than she was. You probably had her killed so you could have my dad to yourself, you raunchy living bitch." Sya pushed her in the forehead.

"Bitch, I'm far from a bitch. Go ask your husband who had Kendra killed. Maybe he can enlighten you better than I can. It's funny that your father just happened to be there. Did he tell you that, since you're walking around here like you on top of the world? Your muthafuckin' man is responsible for their murders." She pushed Sya back. Sya swung around and hit Glitter with all of her might and she fell against the cherry oak desk.

"You dirty slut! As long as you live, don't you ever let my husband's or my name ever leave your lips. Our names better taste like shit to you." Sya kicked her in the side.

"Sya Fields-Ivy!" Frances yelled. "Cut this out, we're here for one reason and one reason only and that's Tory. Frances also gave Sya a look that said she will have to explain her being married.

"Over my dead body." Glitter snapped. "He will not have anything to do with you."

"Now Glitter." Her granddad tried to intervene, helping her off the floor. "I'm gonna have to ask you all to leave my home." He walked to the door.

"Not until we have this matter resolved, Mr. Allan. I don't mean any form of disrespect, but this has to be handled right here and now." Frances reasoned.

"I agree." Rhonda blurted in wishing that Sya would knock the hell out of Glitter again. But knowing that she's an attorney she couldn't condone violence.

"Frances, while you're over there thinking that no one knows that you were still in love with Joseph, he told me everything. He even had me to seduce Henry. Ask Henry how the cookie tastes?" Glitter displayed a sinister smile. Frances swiftly pulled a pistol from her purse and ran up on Glitter with it cocked.

"Let me explain something to you, little girl. I'm not my daughter; I will beat your ass in front of your grandmother and grandfather." She knocked her upside the head with the gun.

"Next time, only disclose information when you're asked. Or next time I'ma knock all of your fuckin' teeth out of your mouth, you raunchy bitch." Frances stood holding her pistol tightly.

"Frances, you will have to leave my home at once with this nonsense. We can go to court if we have to." Mr. Allan tried to apply pressure to the small cut on the side of Glitter's head.

"Mr. Allan," Rhonda cut in. "Are you sure that's what you want do? Joseph's wishes are written in stone and the court is going to abide by them. Now we can do it the hard way, or we can do it the easy way. It's your choice, truth or dare, which one?" She demanded to know.

"We don't have to stay here. I prefer that we do take it to court." Sya was calling bluff at this point. "The only person suffering in this situation is Tory. The courts will see that he was a student in my class and that we had a great relationship and they will grant me my wishes as well as my father's. See you in court, Mr. Allan." Sya coaxed, walking to the door with Rhonda and her mama in tow.

58. More Secrets and Lies!

Frances was furious when she returned home. Mr. Henry wasn't home and she wasn't going to call him either. She needed to calm down before she confronted him with the allegations she was tackled with. She was also disappointed to know that her precious daughter didn't share her news of her marriage with her. The way things were going she didn't know if she and Henry would take that walk down the aisle.

Frances sat on the couch sipping on a glass of Seagram's gin and puffing on a joint to relax her mind. Her cell phone continued to ring as well as the house phone but she ignored them both. She had her Pandora radio set to the Patti LaBelle station. So many thoughts congested her mind at once. Sitting on the couch she decided to open the mail that lay on the coffee table. "I've been waiting on this." She spoke out loud rocking to the beat, letting the music relax her.

She carefully revised the credit card statement, noticing the same transaction. "What the hell is this?" She wondered. She immediately retrieved her cell phone from her purse and called her bank. Frances was clearly upset with the news that she received from the representative. *This shit can't be happening?* She thought.

At Sya's house:

Sya called her mom nonstop only to get no answer. She then decided on calling T only to get his voicemail. Knowing that she had cheated on him, she didn't want to jump to any conclusions, but with him not answering his phone it didn't sit well with her. She so badly wanted to reach out to Jabari to make sure that he was okay but he wasn't her concern and it was because of her that he was in his predicament.

She decided on looking at television and she began to surf the channels. Breaking news interrupted the scheduled program concerning a shootout on highway 70 eastbound. *"This is April Simpson coming to you live from the Fox helicopter. There has been a shootout with the STPD and a black male in a black Charger. It's not known at this time how many people are in the car but there was a shooting in south St. Louis, execution style, and the authorities believe that this person is connected. Neighbors heard a loud commotion and several gun shots fired and notified the authorities. The black Charger was identified leaving the scene. When police tried to pull the vehicle over gun shots were fired. It's reported that one officer is in critical condition and his name is not being reveal for safety reasons. We will keep you informed as this story develops. I'm April Simpson reporting from Fox 2 News."*

Sya sat on the couch hoping her eyes were deceiving her. She then picked up the phone to dial T again. Only this time he came walking through the door with blood on him. "Babe, what have you done? Are you okay? Where is this blood coming from?!" Sya asked questions nonstop fearing for the worst.

"Babe, I'm okay." T held his shoulder standing at the door. "Go get some towels so this blood won't drip on the carpet and hurry up." He ordered reaching for his ringing cell phone. "What's good, fam?" Sya knew that was King on the other line. She was secretly hoping that he got caught. "I'll be there as soon as I get my shoulder wrapped up." He disconnected the line.

"You're not going anywhere, until you are seen by a doctor." Sya fussed, applying pressure to his wound.

"Babe, I'll be back. I have to meet King. I can't let him go down by himself." He explained while she helped him change shirts.

"If you leave then I'm leaving with you. I need my husband to come back home to me. I didn't marry you to lose you." She gathered her purse and keys while heading for the door.

"Wait a minute, babe. I see you will have it no other way. Just in case things get turned up, this is what I need you to do." He began to explain, thinking, I got a soldier on my team. And they headed out the door.

59. Hurt!

The news had traveled quickly about the shootout with the police. Bunnee was in tears not knowing if her unborn child would have a father. King was going to jail for shooting a police officer and she didn't know if Jabari was alive or dead. The news station continued to flash his home on the news. She was losing her mind not know what was going on. She tried dialing both King's and Jabari's numbers but got no answer from neither. The tears came full blasting when she read the caption at the bottom of the television, *"Police officer dies from shootout."* She threw the phone across the room. "Damn you King!"

★★★★★★★★★★★★★★★★

Frances was boiling with rage at this point. She didn't want to believe her discovery but the truth was stirring her directly in her face. Her cell phone rang pulling her from her thoughts. Looking at the caller ID displayed she answered. "Yes?" She answered clearly upset.

"Ma, why haven't you been answering the phone?" Sya displayed more attitude.

"I was thinking."

"Are you still upset with me because I didn't tell you I was married? If so, let that go. Just be happy for me, Ma.

"I am happy for you, Hunny Bun. I just want to be a part of your happiness. Don't shut me out."

"I would never do that. I just wanted us to continue to plan our wedding together. Knowing that T and I had gotten marry would have taken the excitement out of everything, that's all nothing more or nothing less. I wanted this wedding to be the happiest day of your life, besides giving birth to me." Sya's sincerity was evident in her tone.

"You are the only thing that makes me truly happy. Your happiness is my happiness." Frances confirmed.

"Ma, what are you saying? Mr. Henry doesn't make you happy?" Sya was confused with her mother's confession.

"I'm not saying that but he was a substitute for you father. I have not been truly happy since Joseph. Since learning of his death I have been really depressed, and then to find out about a kid he had with this young bitch is mind boggling. I tried to give him a son for years. Hunny Bun, I have to go but I will call you back later." She heard Mr. Henry's keys coming in through the garage door.

"But Ma-."

"Later baby." And she disconnected the line.

60. The Final Confrontation!

Bunnee was lost and she didn't want to be without King. Even if the baby wasn't his, she still wanted to be with him, but under better circumstances, but, unfortunately, shit happens. She dialed his number numerous of times only to go to voicemail. Not knowing what else to do she sent him a text message.

"King, I love you and I need you. Even if that means I have to be on the run with you, I will. I don't want to do this alone. You promised me that you would never leave me again and I am holding you to that promise. Whatever you need me to do it's done. Please contact me, I need to know you're okay, we miss you, rubbing my belly in tears."

Mr. Henry walked in to the sounds of Frankie Beverly and Maze, throwing his keys on the table. "Hey Dear." He leaned in to kiss Frances.

"Hey." She dryly responded rolling her eyes.

"Sweets, turn on the news, an officer has been shot and killed." He reached for the remote.

"What the hell are these charges about?" She could no longer hold in her anger, displaying a deadpan glaze in her eyes, holding the bank statement in his face.

"Dear, I can explain." He was caught off guard, slightly stuttering.

"Dear, I can explain my ass. You and I both know what this is about. Your perverted ass knew all along about Sya's phone sex service." She yelled throwing the statement in his face.

"Frances, listen to me." He yelled back.

"So I can hear more lies? I'm beginning to think that you like young girls. Can you explain to me about Glitter as well?" She reached back and slapped the shit out of him.

"Now Frances, we can talk, but what you're not going to do is put your hands on me." He rubbed his face.

"I do what the fuck I want to do." She walked closely in his face.

"Not to me you're not. I can understand that you're upset and all but I'm still a man and you will respect me as such. Now again we can talk about the situation if you like." His voice was firm.

"I don't want to hear anything you have to say. What you can do is pack your shit and leave." She sat on the couch, crossed her legs and lit a joint.

"Is that what you want, Frances?"

"Exactly."

"So are you saying that the wedding is off?" He needed clarification.

"Exactly," shaking her head up and down. "I can't deal with lies and deceit. I will not deal with it." She concluded.

"And you will not have to." He walked off. That made Frances extremely upset and at this point she decided that he would not leave so easy and free.

****

Bunnee was shocked when Sya knocked on her door.

"Look, we don't have a lot of time, so I'ma need you to get a few things and let's roll." Bunnee did as she was told. Sya gently grab Bunnee's arm. "I know that things have been crazy with us but I, in fact, adore you and you are the sister that I never had. We have to put the past behind if we're going to move forward. King really loves you and so do I, even though I fucked up. So with that being said I don't know what's going to happen with everything that's going on, but we're going to ride with our niggas no matter what." She hugged her tightly.

"I'm so beyond that, Sya. I just want to move on and live life; even though we had issues, I'm ready to move ahead. I love King with all my heart and you are the sister I never had. The past is gone. I'm living for a better me. I love you girl." Both girls were misty eyed. Sya's phone began to ring. She knew it was T. "We better get going." She told Bunnee as they headed for the door. As Bunnee activated her alarm and locked her door, she thought to herself, *Things are going to be so different now, but he kept his promise and didn't leave me. That's my nigga.*

61. You Played the Wrong Person.

Frances sat on the couch tapping her fingers on the table waiting for Mr. Henry to appear, thinking to herself. *This nigga thinks he's getting away with deceiving me, but I have something for him,* demonstrating a mischievous grin.

Mr. Henry took longer than Frances had expected. She was headed to the bedroom to see what was going on. Reaching the door she heard him whispering to someone. She didn't want to react before, she gathered information. As she listened to his conversation she grew angrier by the second. After she couldn't take anymore of his dishonesty, she made herself known. She walked from behind him with the gun pointed at his head. "Hang up the fuckin' phone, now." He disconnected the call and then slowly lowered the phone and flinched as he heard the clicking on the gun. Frances let the tears race down her cheeks, hurt was fully demonstrated on her face.

"I didn't want to believe what that young bitch was saying earlier, but deep down in my gut I knew she wasn't lying. Glitter was right about everything she said about you paying her for sex. She also said you knew about Sya and you were one of her high paying customers. And you and I both know that from the fuckin' bank statements." She hit him over the head with the butt of the gun. He dipped over in pain, blood pouring from his wound. "I loved you, Henry. I trusted you with my daughter; hell, I trusted you with my life. You know the shit I went thought with Joseph and this is how you do me?" Mr. Henry tried to speak. "Shut the fuck up! You said enough on the phone. You never thought I would find out about your secret affairs, huh?!" She hit him again but this time in the forehead, leaving a nice gash with blood everywhere.

"Frances, you have to let me explain." He pleaded through his pain, with blood blinding him.

"I don't want to hear anything you have to say. But I do want to say thanks for making me a rich woman." And with that said she blew his brains out. "You played the wrong bitch this time muthafucka." Frances then walked out the room in search of her cell phone.

****

Glitter and her grandfather rushed over to Jabari's house only to get the run around from the cops. They would not release any information. No matter what they said, it was tight lips. The cops were in hunt of the black Charger. Glitter somehow slipped into the house only to find a dead body lying there with a white sheet covering it. As she grew closer tears welled up in her eyes and she was stopped in her tracks by an officer. "What are you doing in here in the crime scene?" The officer frightened her.

"Officer, this is my cousin's house and I saw it on the news and I wanted to make sure that he was okay. If you would please let me view the body to see if it's him, we would appreciate it. My grandfather and I, who is outside, we so need to know." She pleaded through tears, wiping the snot with the back of her hand.

"I can't do that. I have to get permission from my sergeant."

"Well some-damn-body needs to do something." Glitter grew more annoyed with the cop.

"Wait here, young lady, and I will see what I can do." He headed in the opposite direction. As soon as the cop was out of sight Glitter rushed over to the bloody sheet. There laid

Jabari with several shots to his head with his penis hanging out of his mouth. Glitter yelled from the top of her lungs from the horrible sight. Not able to hold her anxiousness inside any longer, she regurgitated on the floor. Several cops ran in from the other room to see what the commotion was.

"Ma'am, I informed you to stay put until I came back." He seemed upset with Glitter. Glitter didn't say anything, she rolled her eyes and tears continued to pour down her face. Mr. Allan heard Glitter yelling and ran inside with the cops right behind. Once inside he stopped and held his chest breathing hard.

"Oh my God." He whispered shaking his head. *How do I tell Tory and my wife about this hideous act?* He asked himself walking over to comfort Glitter. Both of their hearts were heavy from the loss as he hugged her on their way out the door.

T-Money sat in the back seat of the white Impala while Sya drove and Bunnee rode shot gun. Bunnee's mind was consumed way beyond, but she sang along with Bridget Kelly's joint. She loved this song.

"Hurry hurry, please Mr. Mailman, overnight it if you can, I need you to feel me, this is a special delivery."

She looked over at Sya and she was nodding along also. "I rocks with this joint." Sya kept her eyes on the road.

"Yeah, this is a nice song. Too bad all this shit popped off. She's going to be at the Loft tomorrow night and I had plans on taking you. But Babe, shit happens." T shook his head.

"Yeah, too bad." Bunnee rubbed her stomach. "This shit just got real."

"No this shit's been real, it just gone to another level. I'm sorry it came to this, but it is what it is, y'all." T explained, half giving a damn.

"What if he is the father of my child?" Bunnee faced the back looking at T, waiting on an answer.

"What if you have a man that loves you and willing to do anything he has to make you happy and he will be a damn good father to y'all baby?" T rubbed her shoulder to lighten the mood. "I know things are stressful right now but I need you ladies on point. Bunnee, your hormones are all over the place right about now but I know you can do this." He looked at her through the rearview mirror. She said nothing but nodded her head for him to continue. Y'all know them helicopters were on his ass tough, but he got around that and my guy Aubrey had one of his goons to meet King and that's where we're on our way to now. Then we're headed to Chicago and will lay there for a minute. Y'all have nothing to worry about. Everything is taken care of. Can you handle that?" T asked firmly.

"I can, what choice do I have?" Bunnee asked, as she looked down at her stomach while simultaneously still rubbing it.

"You have several, this is your life and you have to do what's best for you. Now once again, can you handle it if the pressure gets thick?" T wanted true clarity.

"I can and I will." Bunnee assured him again. *Yeah, this shit is real,* she thought.

"Cool." T finished as Sya pulled up in front of the house to retrieve King. He'd enlighten Sya of the agenda before they picked Bunnee up.

Frances stood over Mr. Henry's body with tears dripping from her eyes. "Look at what you made me do. I told you I couldn't take another heartbreak and you do that just. I loved you, but you betrayed me and got just what you deserved." She kicked his dead body and stepped over him to answer the door.

"Thank you for coming," she kissed her guest.

"Anything for you, Frances." Her guest held her tightly in his arms. "I'm going to get this mess cleaned up for you. You have nothing to worry about." He released her and then began walking into the bedroom with her following behind him. "Damn." He retrieved his phone from his back pocket. Frances stood off to the side while he talked on the phone.

Once her guest was off the phone they headed back into the living room. "So what's my next move?" She laid her head on her guest shoulder.

"You can pack up and take a small vacation with me if you like. I can use the company and I'm sure you can use the peace to clear your mind with everything that has happen." He kissed her forehead.

"Yes I can." She replied as her guest read a text message and went to open her garage door allowing three men to enter. Frances took this time to call Sya but got no answer. She then headed to her walk-in closet and gathered a few things. By the time she was finish packing the men had cleaned up and disposed of the body.

"So I take that as a yes that you will be leaving with me?" He kissed her again.

"You're absolutely right, it just got real John."

"Real as can be, but I got you. We just have to break the news to the kids about our relationship." "How do you feel about that?" He made direct eye contact.

"It's cool, let's do this." She kissed his lips.

"It's done." He kissed her back and they left the house heading to Chicago.

COMING SOON: "YOU DON'T KNOW MY STORY!"